SINDI IN SILK

'No!' Sindi cried. 'Please, my lord, don't mark him. He is so beautiful.'

The Rubberlord glowered.

'What's this? Love among slaves?' he drawled. 'That will never do.'

He sniffed perfume from his *vinaigrette*.

'*I'll* take his punishment, my lord. Just please don't scar those lovely buttocks,' Sindi pleaded. 'I admit it . . . they were *my* stockings.'

'You are a liar, like all slaves,' he snapped. 'You'll both take punishment! Monsieur Loleelo! Have your girlslaves string them both, then whip them soundly.'

Sindi grimaced as Pan and her girls seized her, bound her wrists and ankles with rubber cords, and hoisted her to dangle helplessly from the gibbet. The Mauritian boyslave beside her suffered the same treatment. Sindi's quim could not help moistening as she looked at his massive penis, again tantalisingly half-erect. She shuddered as she saw Pan lift a nine-tongued rubber quirt, then screamed, as – vap! – the thongs lashed her buttocks. Yet there was something thrilling about being whipped in stockings. She wriggled helplessly in her bonds as the strokes fell, while beside her the Mauritian writhed under a similar quirt wielded by Fafni. He groaned in agony, yet his penis still trembled, semi-stiff.

SINDI IN SILK

Yolanda Celbridge

This book is a work of fiction.
In real life, make sure you practise safe, sane and
consensual sex.

First published in 2007 by
Nexus
Thames Wharf Studios
Rainville Rd
London W6 9HA

www.nexus-books.com

A catalogue record for this book is available from the
British Library.

Typeset by TW Typsetting, Plymouth, Devon

ISBN 978 0 352 34102 0

Penguin Random House is committed to a sustainable future for
our business, our readers and our planet. This book is made from
Forest Stewardship Council® certified paper.

MIX
Paper | Supporting
responsible forestry
FSC® C018179

Printed and bound in Great Britain by Clays Ltd, St Ives plc

Contents

1

Honte d'Esclave

Nude, Sindi shivered with fear and pleasure as she held the sacrificial stockings before her young, tender green eyes in the glare of the sunrays. Her wide pink lips brushed the soft wormsilk of the stockings: white, glistening stockings, permitted only to a high-born noble lady of one of the monopolistic *grandes familles* of Madagascar – the clans of vanilla, clove, pepper, lobster, cucumbers, coffee, tobacco, all of them prized by the merchants of the great ocean. Grandest of all was the *famille* of foppish Prince Een of Toleara, supreme overlord of all Madagascar, the most powerful country in the world, who had the monopoly of the sacred wormsilk stockings and panties – of which a girlslave like Sindi could only dream, except when chosen to be whipped on the bare buttocks as a punishment, in sacrifice to the sacred sun, which nourished the wormsilk. A girl's gleaming buttocks were called her suns.

A girlslave was always nude, whether toiling in the vanilla or coffee fields, the tobacco plantations or the silk farms, or diving to the lobster pots, and thus in naked *honte d'esclave* – slaveshame – except when ritually flogged in sacrifice. For that sacred moment she wore silk stockings. Sindi had worked at all of a slave's tasks but was especially prized as a lobster-diver, her lithe young body adept at deep diving and extracting the crustaceans

1

from their traps, soon to be served, in a peppered sauce of real cow butter, to the *dames de noblesse* for their dinner. There were oysters, too, and succulent *bêches-de-mer* sea-cucumbers, often with the prize of a tiny pearlfish, which burrowed into the sea cucumber and dined on it from within; just as barnacles invaded the body of a crab and ate its insides, obliging the crustacean to change sex. Oysters were awkward, for they were often the prey of starfish or driller snails, the starfish in turn gobbling up the driller snails.

Sindi loved life under the sea, where she felt free amid all this abundance and struggle for food. She had learned to swim in her birthplace, Kerguelen, a sunny isle at the edge of the world, and in the icy waters of cool, forested Antarctique, far to the south, where her family were merchant princes, owning salt mines and stocks of penguin and krill. They divided their time between both places. They had plenty of girlslaves, kept nude even in the cold or a snow-blizzard, for it made them work harder, especially when, as supervisor, Sindi whipped them.

In Antarctique they had a big house of rock – her noble Kerguelen mother's wedding portion – heated by a thermal spring, at the port of Dumont D'Urville, in Adélie Land, where Madagascar ships would call, selling cigars, vanilla, cloves and silk stockings, of which Sindi had treasured her collection. She would spend whole evenings by the fire, rolling Madagascar silk stockings and panties up and down her bare-shaven thighs, as the cool breeze whispered outside. Sometimes she was permitted to smoke a Madagascar cigar. She masturbated at these sensuous pleasures.

But some of those ships were slavers, too, both selling slaves and kidnapping them. One day Sindi was swimming nude, save for her necklace, with its amulet – a bead of amber containing a lizard, which the priests said was a hundred million years old – and had caught herself a fish, a lovely big coelacanth, when she and her fish were

2

hoisted out of the water in a net by an embarking slaver, which had just sold a shipload of cigars and silk stockings to her family, and taken to the slave markets of Socotra, where blonde girls were especially prized. The world was coasts and islands: few ventured far from the coast into the interior, where there were dark things and monsters.

She was not molested by the slavers, for any auctioned girlslave must be virgin, but she had to service the sailors by fellating them and swallowing their sperm, a task she quickly came to enjoy, not least because she was rewarded with a cigar. She had fellated boys before, in Kerguelen and Antarctique. It was important for a noble girl to keep her virginity, but acceptable that she should pleasure boys in this way. Sometimes, a boy would wish to put his penis in her anus and spurt his sperm in her rectum, and this too she welcomed, enjoying the boy's stiff tool inside her as she masturbated to a delicious orgasm. When no boy was available, she masturbated every day, sometimes three or four times.

Fellating the sailors, she frigged, which made her a popular slave acquisition. The sailors liked to watch girls masturbating, and she liked to be watched. Since coming of age, Sindi had always frigged copiously. She would sit nude in the scrubby forests of Adélie Land and finger her clito to orgasm as she listened to the bears roar. She was a copious juicer and could fill a sealbone pot with her come. She found she could make plentiful silver dinars by selling pots of her frozen come to visiting merchants, who found girl come the most exquisite of condiments. She also discovered that if she shaved off her lush pubic fleece, she could sell the golden hairs for a high price. Noble ladies of Madagascar, whose hillocks were shaved, liked to make themselves enormous pubic wigs, merkins, for amusement, dangling them over the silk stockings which it was an aristocrat's privilege to wear, while the most powerful lords in Madagascar sometimes wore only skirtlets of girls' pubic hair.

3

Often bought at auction on Socotra, for ever higher prices, in the thousands of silver dinars, she at last went to Madagascar, as property of the *Grande Dame* Tamrod Gazee, a voluptuous creole who perpetually carried a pet lemur, clutching her shoulder, and would feed it grubs and morsels of fruit, for the *aye-aye* lemur's long fingers were designed to invade tree bark, where grubs lived, and scoop the food. Tamrod was not much older than Sindi and went bare-breasted and nipple-ringed, clad in sumptuous wormsilk stockings, with frilly garter belt and straps. Her *noblesse* privileged her to have two names, a rarity. Tamrod took Sindi's lizard brooch for herself.

After labouring in the vanilla fields and herding cattle, Sindi was put to work as a lobster-diver, which she liked, for the cool of the ocean got her away from the scorching heat of the sun. She could hold her breath for a long time, which pleased her owner, and she loved swimming amid the darting many-coloured fish, like one of them herself. She was careful when removing the trapped lobsters from their pots, for they would fasten their claws on a careless girl's nipples. In the evening she had to cook and clean, then slept on straw in the slave dormitory with the other slaves, chained to posts. All the slaves knew that their turn would come for a ritual sun-flogging.

Now Sindi kissed the lovely white stockings from toe to top, her nose breathing in the sweet smell of wormsilk, delicately scented with a noblewoman's odour. Although she had been kidnapped only a year before, when she had just celebrated her twentieth birthday, it seemed an age. An orange-robed priest of Madagascar had once told her that her name was perhaps *sine die*, from some old language that only the priests knew.

Well, the virgin priests knew everything, for they had the old books: all, it was rumoured (but only among priests and nobles, lest the common folk question their authority), except one, lost for ever – the key to all knowledge, which told the story of both the past and the

4

future. It was supposedly called *The New Centuries* and had been written by a seer about whom nothing was known save that he called himself 'Notredame'. When the priests observed a girlslave's punishment, it was customary for them to masturbate under their robes, and, maddened by so much wisdom, spill their seed on the hot red earth. She wanted to know, before her beating, what high lady – what *dame noble* of Madagascar – had worn those stockings before? Some of her essence would enter Sindi's skin and bring her good luck.

That was why stockings, according to the priests interpreting the ancient lore, were sacred, and panties too. Stockings were worshipped for they contained a woman's essence, and the essence of the sun. A woman's panties, a Madagascar lady's *slip de noblesse*, worn for several days and permeated with the odour of her fluids, brought good luck and could be sold for many dinars in the distant markets of Africa, Arabia and India. Ships went to Mokka and Mumbai and Durban, Trincomalee and Jaffa, laden with cloves and salted beef and vanilla and a large stock of the soiled, fragrant panties of the Madagascar female *noblesse* – and their worn, foot-perfumed stockings, too, for which the greedy ladies, or merchant priests as middlemen, demanded cash in advance from the sea captains.

Soon, Sindi's pink panties would be perfumed with her own sweat and fear and torment, as her naked buttocks squirmed, reddening, under the whipman's fearful lash of crocodile hide. Pink panties and white stockings: light and dark. She rubbed her buttocks, pressing her finger into her cleft, as she had often done, while tweaking her stiff pink clito to bring herself to orgasm under the sun. She knew her buttocks, their skin like silk, were the biggest, smoothest and finest amongst all the girlslaves, and that the girls were jealous. She had heard the other slaves whisper that her golden skin and her perfect French – a language from the past, and a mark of

5

nobility – made her a spy, their enemy. The slaves mostly spoke Austronesian dialects or English, tongues from some strange place beyond the seas, and Sindi was skilled in those languages.

In the Madagascar heat, noble ladies wore wormsilk stockings, and nothing else, except suspenders and garters, and perhaps the skimpy silk panties called *ficelles*, or strings, which showed more of the shaven mound than they concealed. They had golden waist chains and earhoops, and breasts pierced with nipple rings. Some *dames nobles* even had their buttocks pierced with tiny golden rings or thimbles. Sindi's Kerguelen mother had been one such – she had had both hoops and thimbles dangling seductively from her bare bottom, from her breasts and from her headdress of sharks' teeth. It was *très parisien*, she said. Though not knowing what that meant, Sindi too had holes pierced in her nipples and quim lips, to sport bright silver rings.

Priests said that long before the great war, in the distant past, Madagascar and Adélie Land and other islands like Réunion and Nouvelle Amsterdam and Kerguelen had been ruled by a place called France, and that was why speaking French was a mark of nobility, although most people could, or preferred to, speak the *lingua franca* known as English. France had been destroyed, along with a mysterious country called Amerik, which started the war. Most of the world had been turned to wastelands of glowing embers, where only the hot winds howled, by dreadful bombs, which made pretty mushroom clouds. But some places had survived, French islands like Kerguelen and Réunion, parts of Africa and India, and the continent of Antarctique – the southern world. Few people now knew of any other. But those were distant, uncertain memories from the dim dreamtime. Now Madagascar controlled large territories like Congo and Kenya in Africa, where they recruited their medicine men and whipmen.

Sindi's nose was of perfect straightness, her hair platinum blonde and her supple, muscled young body ravishingly slender, yet blessed with ripely jutting breasts and buttocks. She had a pet long-tailed lemur, her only friend, which she would cuddle at night in the fetid dungeon where the naked slaves were crammed together. Yet she was not sure she regretted her enslavement. It was the wheel of fate, and was not enslavement a natural state for a girl? Especially in the rich empire of Madagascar. A slavegirl could always dream of becoming an *odalisque*, a pleasure slave of the prince.

As well as fieldwork, all slaves had pleasure duties. Her sex duties were a relief from the dungeon. She loved the touch of the cadets of the Prince's Guard that she had to service, as they stroked her or pressed their lips to her fesse cheeks and anus bud. A boy's hot wet tongue licking her anus made her belly quiver and her sex juice. In Antarctique she had always masturbated while dreaming of a hot dark boy's penis in her mouth.

But in a short time her pure golden fesses would be quaking, whipped and darkening with bruises. A black whipman, a slave himself, was always nude, and his penis always stiff, as he flogged a girl's bare buttocks; Sindi supposed that the sight of a girl's lovely naked globes squirming in agony must excite a cruel male. The erection of the penis was a fascinating and horrifying mystery, which she feared she must one day experience in her virgin pouch. With whom?

Sindi knew which lady's panties she had. They were a gorgeous pink and of the same luscious wormsilk: the unwashed garment had been the property of her owner, the *dame noble* Tamrod Gazee, she who had sentenced Sindi to whipping – '*fouette la petite chienne!*' – and it smelled of that lady's sweetly acrid aristocratic loins. She knew the taste of Tamrod's sex, for often Tamrod would order her to attend her in her bath and tongue her sex to orgasm. If her climax was in any way unsatisfactory,

Sindi would be caned on her bare. She supposed that explained her current plight.

A girlslave was forbidden to wear panties, or any garment at all save for a white hat of Zanzibar cotton and cowhide boots, as she toiled in the fields of cloves and vanilla or tended the cattle under the burning sun. She lived in permanent nude slaveshame, like the boys kept as pleasure slaves by noble ladies like Tamrod. Such a lady would command a boy to place his male organ in her slit, and thrust until he cried out in spasm and the penis spurted its enchanting white fluid. Sometimes a noble lady liked a male to be dressed as a girl while he performed this task, because it did not seem a sin against the sun.

Panties and stockings were smuggled from Zanzibar, and illicit gatherings of girls would wear them together, risking fearful penalties, while they masturbated. Some boys liked to wear stockings and girl-panties too. It was rumoured that Prince Een's twin brother Loro, exiled in Zanzibar, had a factory producing the illegal stockings and underthings.

Sindi had grown to love the taste of penis-cream as, on her sex duty, she pleasured the cadets of the Prince's Guard, ten or more of them, one after the other, by sucking their stiff organs and swallowing their fluid. Her skill at this task, serving officers, earned her the jealousy of other girlslaves who serviced the common soldiers. That too was *honte d'esclave*. She did not envy a boyslave's lot, for if his penis rose in erection (when he saw girls who would maliciously waggle their breasts, and rub their clitos, to get him stiff), it was considered an insult to his noble mistress and he was mercilessly flogged. If his penis even stirred, unbidden, at the sight of a noble lady like Tamrod, then she would beat the boy's croup with her wooden cane until he fainted from pain. In Antarctique Sindi had had slaves strung up by their wrists, naked, and had flogged them with a sealskin whip for various misdemeanours, but not to the point where they fainted. Things in Madagascar were more passionate and brutal.

Sindi loved the taste of a penis, the feeling of the tender, hard tissue, and the fluid that cascaded into her throat as she sucked the male to come. Sometimes, for the pleasure and relief of younger officer cadets, Sindi would masturbate them with her fingers, rubbing the glans and peehole, loving her power as the male groaned in helpless ecstasy. For that task she sometimes removed one of her boots, so that one foot was bare, the other shod, which seemed to excite males.

Yet Sindi burned with curiosity to feel a penis penetrate her vulva, the stiff organ giving its cream to her girl's body, for she knew that a man's seed was something a girl must have in her belly. By the law, like all girlslaves, Sindi was quim-virgin, but she knew that a girl was one day fated to take a man's sperm at her wombneck, however odd it might seem compared to the joy of an enculed rectum.

She had trembled as Tamrod, after pronouncing the sentence of twenty whipstrokes on Sindi's croup – '*vingt coups, sale petite chienne*' – had taken a last puff of smoke from her cigar, then casually lifted her doveskin skirtlet, showing her pink stockings and garter belt, and rolled the panties down her alabaster thighs, to throw them at Sindi with her lips curled in disdain. The hillock of Tamrod's nobly shaven bare pubis gleamed smooth and proud, making Sindi ashamed of her own bushy blonde jungle.

Now she rubbed the panties over her breasts, gasping as she felt her big strawberry nipples stiffen. She rubbed the panties on her belly and quim, shuddering as she moistened and dreaming of her own lost *noblesse*. She looked at her tan body in the glass as she prepared to don her garments: the big, almost melon-sized breasts (not that mere slaves were permitted to eat melons, whose red juice might drip only from the lips of noble ladies), which

9

the other girls liked to tease and touch in the bathhouse, painfully flicking her nipples between finger and thumb – though if the intrusion was too painful Sindi would fell her attacker with a knee to the groin, then sit on her and pummel the girl's breasts with her fists until the teats were bruised blue, for Sindi's body, toughened by work, rippled with hard muscle.

Although fighting was a whipping offence, in practice the female guards, sleek in their uniform banana-leaf skirtlets, enjoyed two slaves grappling, for they could bet cash on the likely winner. Many dinars were won and lost over slave-fights. Daring girlslaves liked to tweak Sindi's big pubic bush, too, their lips curled in envy, for her forest was bigger by far than any other girl's. The golden hair dangled in shiny tufts, well below her thick pink quim lips.

Soon the whipman would shave her pubis clean, before her ritual whipping. A whipped slave was briefly permitted a clean pubis, in mockery of her lowly status, but later she must wince, as the sprouting hair itched and her forest grew back. How Sindi longed, like all girlslaves, for her own pale body and shorn hillock to return to her, away from the torturing sun, and her skin ripen with swelling cosmetic muscle like that of a noble. Like Tamrod Gazee's . . .

Sindi's muscles were tougher, she thought, than any noble's, but sinewy tough, like whipcord, not the bulging, honed beauty of Tamrod. It was Sindi's distraction from her task of properly tonguing the bathing lady, and her impertinent murmur of envy, that had earned her the noble lady's anger and her sentence to whipping. '*Sale petite chienne!*' That hurt, more than any lash could. Yet being lashed meant she could have the delight of briefly wearing panties and stockings.

Sindi rolled the pink panties over her loins and slid the white wormsilk stockings over her thighs. She gasped in pleasure as the thin fabric caressed her legs and sex. She stroked herself through the panties, feeling her sex moisten, then, quivering with pleasure, ran her fingers up and down the stockings. But her pleasure was not to last long. A shadow covered her, the shadow of a man holding an oiled hide whip, nude, but for his black rubber helmet. His skin was darker than Sindi's gold, as dark as his mask, and his massive black penis was fully erect.

'It is time for your whipping, girl,' said the whipman. 'If you suck my penis and swallow my seed, to soften my anger, it shall go easier for you. And I shall give you one of my best cigars to smoke. '

A cigar! Only males and noble ladies were permitted to smoke.

'*Oui, monsieur,*' Sindi said.

She knelt, cupping the man's bare buttocks, and opened her mouth to take his huge man-shaft into her throat. Her heart raced as she tasted the acrid skin of the whipman's penis. Come dripped from her throbbing sex, soaking her panties. As she sucked, she watched the whipman light a cigar for her and blow a plume of blue smoke over her blonde hair and naked breasts. The cigar was huge, fragrant and black, like his penis. At that moment, Sindi wanted it, more than anything.

2

Whipman

Sindi winced as the whipman's razor scraped her mons. But that too was a delight, to be bare-mons like a noble. The blade passed close to her sex lips, and the whipman's eyes glinted in amusement beneath his black rubber mask. Between the swollen vaginal folds her clito stood stiff, pink as her new panties – which were strung between her knees, over the shiny white stockings. Her wrists were tethered to the wooden gibbet from which she was suspended. Her bare ankles were stretched by blocks of stone from the mountains so that the toes dangled in the air, a thumb's length from the floor of the gibbet. She was already in pain, even before the whipping of her buttocks began. Her only pleasure was the cigar perched between her lips, and the fragrant smoke which she luxuriously inhaled and exhaled. The taste of the cigar mingled piquantly with that of the black whipman's sperm, which hung heavy in her stomach. Whipmen were always of the deepest ebony and were chosen for their muscular beauty and their large balls and penises, so that they could serve the *dames nobles* with copious ejaculations. The whipman had spermed so much that she had to fight to swallow every drop of his hot cream. His grunt of satisfaction when his spurt had finished gave her pleasure, as did showing off her fine underthings – with a frilly garter belt, too.

Tamrod and her noble friends sat on gold-painted mahogany chairs beneath the gibbet to watch Sindi's whipping, attended by their boyslaves. For the occasion, as was customary, to mock the flogged, nearly naked slave, the *dames nobles* wore only their boots and stockings, belted daggers, silk hats jingling with rings of bells or whirring with little tops, and three- or four-tiered necklaces of pickled bulls' pizzles. The bigger her pizzles, the grander the lady. The boyslaves carried ostrich fans to cool their noble mistresses' bodies. Their faces were grave, for their penises threatened to stir at the sight of the ladies' bare skin, and each slave knew a flogging awaited him if he allowed himself to become erect. That, too, was part of the pleasure of the *grandes dames.*

'Mark her hard, whipman,' hissed Tamrod Gazee, puffing on a cheroot. 'I fear that my sentence of twenty strokes – *la pleine vingtaine* – was not enough to tame that cheeky young lemur.'

Sindi, strung in pain, gazed at the full, sensuous, purple-painted lips of the noble lady who had sentenced her to flogging. Tamrod's bare breasts were almost as big as her own, the nipples – also painted purple with the dye exuded by the murex snail – erect in anticipation of the whipman's lash cracking on the helpless girlslave's naked croup. There was a drool of moisture at Tamrod's swollen quim lips as she eyed the whipman's newly and enormously erect black penis.

Sindi spat cigar juice at Tamrod and the brown fluid landed on the nipple of her right breast. The noble lady howled in shame; her companion, Lady Qimon, more slender but more feline in her grace, snarled; a boyslave lowered his fan and licked the cigar juice from his lady's nipple, until her breast was clean.

'Whipman,' she shrieked, 'whip that bitch raw! I want her buttocks bruised to black, black as your sex! No, more than that, I want her filthy little arse to squirm, and I want to hear her scream!'

Sindi spat again, this time, landing a mouthful of tobacco juice on Tamrod's gleaming sex hillock. Qimon laughed, and the slaves could not repress smirks.

'Do your worst, *Mademoiselle*,' she snarled, as Tamrod's boyslave licked the tobacco juice from his mistress's sex.

'You'll pay for that, you slut,' hissed Tamrod, having suffered severe loss of face.

As the boy's tongue touched the fragrant flesh his penis stirred, and tears came to his eyes as he became fully erect.

'I beg pardon, mistress,' he blurted.

Tamrod's eyes glinted.

'You shall have pardon, boy, after you are punished.'

She unsheathed a dagger from her belt.

'No, mistress, please! I didn't mean . . . *Ahh!*'

Tamrod grasped the boy's stiff penis and her knife flashed as she began to beat his glans and peehole with the flat of the blade. He screamed and fainted.

'Take this worm away,' she ordered another trembling boyslave, his own bare penis limp with fear. The whipped boyslave was hauled away by his ankles, his body gouging a furrow in the ochre dirt.

'The sentence to Sindi was twenty strokes, madam,' intoned the whipman. '*La vingtaine* was decreed. I must obey the law.'

Although drained of sperm by Sindi's agile tongue, his huge penis was again proud. There was a hurried conversation among the noble ladies, all of them licking their purple-painted lips at the sight of the whipman's stiff penis and rustling their ornate headdresses, some with ostrich plumes and tiny whirling windmills. How different from home, Sindi thought scornfully, where she had inherited her mother's wedding headdress of real elephant tusks, the white ivory trimmed with tiger fur. It was agreed that the law of Madagascar was the property of the prince himself, and that a noble's sentence, once spoken and enshrined in the archive of the realm, could only be changed by the prince's own dictate.

'Well, after that bitch's disgraceful insult, I want her sentence increased to ... oh, at least a hundred lashes ... so we must beg the prince for his attendance,' said Tamrod, licking her teeth and leering cruelly at Sindi.

'But how ...?'

'We are naked, are we not?' said Tamrod. 'The prince cannot resist ...'

The noble ladies giggled.

'Especially if our nipples are hard and our sexes wet in his honour.'

The nude noble ladies began to stroke their breasts. When their nipples were standing and their thighs were slick with seeping come, Tamrod decreed that they were in a fit state to approach His Royal Highness, Prince Een, and a messenger was sent.

'And it would help if our naked bottoms ... you know.'

'Red as our nipples?'

'Exactly.'

Each lady spanked the other on the naked buttocks until their fesses glowed deep crimson. Tamrod's spanks were the harshest, yet her fesses the fieriest.

'Oh! It hurts!' cried the lady Qimon, who was Tamrod Gazee's best friend.

'The prince will be pleased.'

'I am pleased. It feels so good. My croup hurts and tingles, and ... oh, couldn't the whipman ... that luscious big sex ...?'

'No! He must not dissipate his corrective strength, and shall attend only to the wicked slut,' Tamrod snapped. 'She had the nerve, the audacity, to envy my body!'

'That will never do,' murmured Qimon, her fingers rubbing her sex as she stroked her clito, masturbating discreetly, and gazed at the whipman's rigid black penis. 'Do you think my croup beautiful, Tamrod?'

'You know I do. Are you frigging for me? For my love?'

'Yes. Yes.'

Tamrod bent to kiss Qimon's spanked buttocks. Her tongue penetrated her anus.

'That is so nice. I'm going to come!'

'Come, then.'

'Ah . . . ah . . . oh! Yes!'

Qimon's belly heaved in spasm as Tamrod now applied her mouth to the nude woman's quivering sex and sucked her juice. Tamrod licked her lips as she swallowed the girl-come.

A purple robe, of duckling down dyed in murex, brushed Tamrod's naked buttocks.

'Oh!' cried the noble women. As one, they knelt and pressed their lips to the dirt.

'You may rise, ladies,' drawled Prince Een, after stroking and pinching their bare buttocks for several seconds. 'What brings me here?'

Trembling in the prince's presence, Tamrod stuttered to explain. A girlslave lit a cigar for the prince, who briefly extinguished the match (one of his family monopolies) on her bare nipple.

'Thank you, Highness,' she gasped, fighting back her tears.

'A new one, eh? And tasty. One of those lusty Antarctique specimens, I'll warrant. A hundred lashes?' the prince said, after Tamrod, head bowed and buttocks upthrust, her lips kissing the prince's feet, had explained her sentence. 'Is that all?'

'Begging your Highness's pleasure, I think it shall be enough to make her faint and piss herself,' stammered Tamrod.

Een's eyes darkened.

'It is not a girl's task to think,' he said.

'No, of course, Highness,' the noble ladies chorused.

'Those tasty fesses of yours could take another of *my*

whippings, naughty Tamrod. And a nice painful enculement.'

'If your Highness pleases.'

'Not for the moment. Let the punishment begin, then,'
said Een. 'We shall indeed see the girl faint, perhaps, and
the whipman, in whom I have complete faith, shall decide
when the punishment is sufficient. He is one of my best
whipmen, a Kenyan. It is not for some *girl* to decide
matters of punishment. But that slut is attractive. I want
to see scars on her bottom. A girl, any girl, deserves to
be striped on her buttocks and endure the sweet pain
therefrom. She has no right to be blessed with such
beautiful fesses, therefore must be punished for her
bottom's beauty. Now, I wish to be seated.'

Qimon, crouching with her face in the dirt, immediately presented her naked buttocks, upon which Prince Een
sat. He had finished his cigar and stubbed it by applying
it delicately to one of the drips of moisture from Qimon's
quim, so that it sizzled. Summoning a naked boyslave to
bring him a fresh cigar, Een flicked the lit match on
Qimon's nipple, to extinguish it. Qimon winced. The
prince's purple robe sheathed her. He lit a second match
and stubbed it on her clito.

'Thank you, Highness,' she sobbed, her open sex
oozing juice.

When a boyslave smirked, the prince lit another match
and flicked it on the boy's naked peehole.

'Whipman, flog her well,' the prince ordered. 'She is
too beautiful, too blonde – I want to see those naked
buttocks marked well.'

'Yes, Highness,' said the whipman.

Vap!

'*Ahh!*' Sindi screamed, the sound jarring in her tortured
throat and her breasts quivering as the whipman's first
stroke streaked across her naked buttocks. She knew it
would leave an ugly weal; she could feel the smarting.

Vap!

17

'Oh, no!'

Vap!

'*Ahh!* Please!'

Sindi's bare croup was clenching, writhing; her dangled toes tried to find the floor, but could not. She was helpless. Tears gushed down her cheeks. Vap! The whip lashed her tender haunches.

'*Ah! Oh! Ahh!*'

Vap! A stroke to her cleft, the whip's tip touching her vaginal lips and her clito.

'*Oh! Oh!* No, no, *no . . .*'

Vap! A crimson bruise on her wriggling thigh backs.

'*Ahh!* Oh, God . . .'

The scaly crocodile-leather thong was merciless, as it striped her squirming croup, not sparing the top buttocks, thigh backs or underfesses. Droplets of come shone beneath Sindi's shivering quim lips and trickled down her threshing thighs. The whipman knew his work. Tamrod laughed.

'I do believe the bitch is enjoying it,' she purred.

Prince Een ordered a girlslave to bend over and spread her buttocks, then masturbate herself to wetness; when she was dripping, the prince inserted his half-smoked cigar between her thighs and watched with delight the cloud of hissing steam. Then he ordered her to light a fresh cigar for him, first inserted and rolled in her vagina, so that it was well moistened with her juice. To suck a cigar soaked in girl-come added to the pleasure of smoking.

Vap! The whipman's lash relentlessly stroked Sindi's naked globes. The golden skin squirmed in agony.

'Oh, it hurts!' she screamed. 'Please, no more!'

The prince laughed.

'Fifty lashes, at least, for *those* superb fesses,' said Prince Een, as he smoked his cigar. It was made of smuggled black Congolese tobacco, a sign of his exalted status, even though the Madagascar tobacco was his monopoly. He chortled as Sindi's bare buttocks writhed under the whip.

'*Ahh!*' the girl shrieked.

'Those buttocks!' the prince mused. 'And the wormsilk stockings! I could *eat* them. Chew that silk, Let it slide down my throat. Her teats, too. Nipples big as nectarines, and so crimson. Toes shapely as prawns from the ocean. Softer and better than prawns. Buttocks like melons. Chew and gnaw and suck them. Quim flaps sweet and thick, like slices of unleavened bread. Suck them till they're dry. Belly like a thick loin of boar. I could eat all of her. Drink her come, a good glassful, heated by my fire of Zanzibar charcoal. And her clito! A feast to chew on. I shall spare her and keep her for my own use. She is too beautiful. Whipman, how many strokes has she taken?

'Only thirty, sire,' said the whipman.

'Well, on reflection, it is enough. Tamrod, my dear, I am afraid I must confiscate this girlslave and make her my queen consort. Whipman, truss the slut, and have her conveyed to the Palace of Toleara.'

3

Bitch Queen

Sindi, the queen consort, sat immobile on her throne in the palace of her lord and master Prince Een, high over his capital, the southern port of Toleara. Sometimes he sojourned at his secondary capital of Rivo, in the mountains, when it was too hot, but he preferred Toleara, with its cooling sea breezes, where he could watch the ships setting forth for his profit with their cargoes of cloves, vanilla, hemp, corn, crustaceans, tobacco and tortoiseshell, and, above all, dusky, full-buttocked girl-slaves. Toleara girlslaves bore a guarantee of satisfaction, having been subjected to rigorous disciplinary and medical tests. Sindi had been no exception. She had few pleasant memories of Prince Een to sustain her in her aching stationary ordeal, least of all her recent medical examination, conducted by a doctor and nurse who were nude but for stockings and presided over by her drooling consort. Her body still ached from it. The memory lingered, her shame and joy . . .

Nude, on a plain wooden table, she was ordered to masturbate and obeyed without hesitation. If that was all they wanted, she could put on a show.

'I admire her prowess,' said Dr Jatt.

She and her nurse peered at Sindi's slit, their noses inches from the clito, which Sindi's fingers had brought to erection. Come dripped from the flaps of her sex, as her fingers penetrated the inside of her pouch. She gasped, writhing as she frigged, her back arched, thighs spread wide and toes clutching the edge of the table. Her legs and belly quivered as her quim poured shiny come on to the wood, wood that was stained by much previous fluid.

'She is a seasoned frigger,' said nurse Bilin.

'Pleasantly shameless,' added the doctor. 'I particularly like her manipulation of the clito, while at the same time thrusting inside the vagina.'

'She juices heavily,' said Bilin.

'And an exhibitionist,' said Jatt.

Sindi blushed, for it was true. Shamefully, she was enjoying her display. Jatt's fingers crept beneath the watching Prince Een's robe, and idly masturbated his penis.

'She is better at self-pleasuring than any other girl we have had. Note the rhythmic thrusting of the fingers inside the pouch. Three fingers spanned, so as to stretch the quim walls, with the nails at her wombneck. The thumbnail stroking and scratching the nubbin. That is *art de noblesse*, combining pain and pleasure.'

'I have never seen a girl juice so much,' gasped Bilin.

Sindi thrust her buttocks up and down, jabbing her pouch, as she rubbed her clito. Eyes closed, she moaned, drool seeping from the corners of her mouth, which was tightened in a rictus to bare her teeth.

'Uhh . . . Uhh . . .' she panted.

Bilin licked her teeth, her face blushing red. She pushed damp strands of hair from her brow.

'The girl obviously needed to masturbate,' she said, 'to relieve the stress of her new role. Look, she loses herself in her own pleasure. I wonder what she sees in her fantasy as she frigs.'

'Tell us, Sindi,' said Een, smiling, as Jatt's fingers caressed his balls.

21

Sindi began to moan and roll her head, causing her breasts to spill from side to side. Her fingers twitched, pounding the swollen wet lips of her quim, as, eyes closed, she masturbated faster.

'The male comes, big brute of male, oh please, no, no, don't spank, it hurts me on the bare, my bottom is so sore, oh yes, more, penis so hard, split me, oh, yes, big penis meat, how I need it ... spank my bottom, make me squirm, master, whip my bare to ribbons, please fill my hole, burst my bottom with your stiff sex ... whip me!'

The medical girls looked at each other, their faces beaded with sweat and their blonde ringlets dancing in the breeze from the whirring ceiling fan.

'Anal fantasies,' murmured Dr Jatt. 'Together with fantasies of spanking.'

'And more,' added Bilin, pressing her thighs together. 'It's making me wet.'

'Whip me on the bare, make me wriggle,' Sindi gasped, as her quim jerked and her fingers frotted her dripping lips. 'Whip me hard, oh, so good, hurts so much, encule me, master, take your girlslave and make her grovel. No shame is too great for me. Yes, yes ...'

She grasped her pubic bone, squeezing her quim, her thumb pounding the nubbin and all four fingers reaming her slit.

'Mm ... mm ...' she gasped, 'come all over me, girl, sit on my face, crush me with your thighs and fesses ... sir, split me with your tool and sperm mightily in me ...'

Bilin and Jatt rubbed themselves between their wet thighs, their fluids already staining their stocking tops.

'Proceed as you wish, ladies,' said Prince Een, his face flushed and his stroked penis rigid.

They smiled. Bilin reached towards the rack of disciplinary intruments, her hand passing over each one until Jatt nodded again. Bilin took down a boarhide strap studded with nutshells along one side. Without removing her boots, she vaulted on to the bed and squatted over

Sindi's face, before lowering her buttocks so that her quim and perineum squashed the masturbating girl's mouth and nose.

'Mm . . .,' Sindi moaned, her face trapped under the nurse's buttocks, as her fingers frotted her quim faster.

'My,' gasped Bilin. 'The little hog has her tongue right into my anus.'

Bilin's clito was stiff and extruded amid her bushy mane, her sex lips swollen and oozing juice. She touched her clito and stifled a gasp. She shifted forward so that her quim was directly over Sindi's lips and her bottom raised slightly to present its entire nudity. Her quim began to writhe as Sindi tongued her buttocks and clito, while Bilin vigorously masturbated. She made Sindi raise her legs straight up, affording a view of buttock and thigh, then lifted the strap and brought it, whistling, across Sindi's bare. Whap!

'Mm!' Sindi grunted, as a wide pink weal appeared on her skin.

Whap!

'Oh, yes . . .' she moaned, frigging her engorged nubbin, as Bilin's nates crushed her face.

Dr Jatt was masturbating as she fully bared her lord's penis and frotted the glans and shaft. Two more livid bruises from the nurse's strap appeared on Sindi's bare, which began to squirm. At the sound of each stroke, Sindi's loins and croup jumped and she moaned, her fingers rubbing her clito and cooze lips. Come dripped from Bilin's gamahuched quim, wetting the masturbating girl's upturned crimson face. Whap! Sindi's whipped bare nates flamed crimson, the puffy, blotched bruises darkening to puce. Weals covered her buttocks and soft thighs, which shivered and clenched as the strap cast its shadow on the striped globes, throwing the ridges of welted skin into stark relief.

Whap! Moaning, Sindi frigged hard as Bilin's quim squashed her face. Her tongue delved into the nurse's wet

23

slit, while with nose and teeth she frotted the clito pressing on her. Whap!

'Oh,' moaned Bilin, 'I'm going to come, all over her Highness. Ah . . . ah! *ahh!*' she shrieked.

Sindi gasped, gurgling in the come that drenched her mouth, and her quim writhed as she fingered her erect clito, to bring herself off in time with the writhing cooze atop her face. Her climax was heaving and noisy. Bilin continued to whip her on the bare, and as soon as the girls' shuddering wails had ebbed to gasps and sobs, Bilin crouched on the floor with her bottom up. Dr Jatt, still masturbating her master, mounted the naked Bilin, who moaned and continued to frig. As the doctor rode her like a pony, heartily spanking her buttocks, a heavy stream of pee hissed from Jatt's quim, splashing the nurse's body. She knew what Een liked.

'Ahh . . . yes . . .,' gasped Prince Een, 'piss on her . . . oh, yes!' – as Jatt rubbed his stiff sex.

The masturbating nurse's legs quivered and she gave little staccato yelps as she orgasmed again, her bottom dripping with Jatt's golden piss. Her rider dismounted and curled her lip, while running her fingers over the welts on Sindi's bruised bare bottom. The whole expanse of buttock flesh was lividly bruised by the strap; her face was red and twisted in a grimace.

'It's Sindi's turn,' panted Prince Een.

Bilin remounted Sindi's upturned face and pissed into her mouth and nose, making her splutter as she was drenched in acrid fluid. The nurse dismounted. Dr Jatt masturbated both herself and Een, who, as Jatt orgasmed, ejaculated over Sindi's soaked face. Sindi began to cry and raised herself, wiping her face of the mingled fluids. The doctor smiled at Sindi as she wiped her wet quim with her hair.

'Enough,' said Prince Een. 'She'll do.'

That memory alone was enough to make her shudder, yet, could she only admit it to herself, her humiliation had thrilled her. Here on her throne, her blonde hair cascaded down her pale, jutting, bare breasts, but she was forbidden to lift a finger to smooth it, or to move any muscle at all; even to wipe the tears that seeped from her wide green eyes, or the sweat that dripped from her body in the stifling heat. Her sweat mingled with her perfume, for she had been rubbed all over with vétiver roots, to make her fragrant. None of that was pleasant, apart from her desire to exhibit her naked body, and the plant's scent.

Though his queen, she was yet Een's slave, subject to daily purgative bare-whipping, six stingers, with extra strokes or a gibbet suspension if she committed the sin of shifting even slightly on her sacred throne. Twice a week she had to sit motionless all morning, while the nobles, priests and augurs scrutinised her face and body for omens. A twitch here, a blink or a shiver, could augur a good cucumber harvest, a new lode of copper – or the opposite, some disaster, a storm, a ship laden with valuable cargo lost amid icebergs in the south. A gibbet beside her throne reminded her and the assembly that, shorn of her nipple rings and regal baubles, she was a naked girlslave.

Tears sprang to her eyes when she thought of her home in which, at the age of nineteen summers, she had been mistress of slaves, ruling them with her own cruel whip. Nineteen brief summers in her young life, now ruined for ever. Antarctique summers were short and wondrous, for in the cold highlands ice melted and lichen grew on the exposed rock. It was the job of girlslaves to squat and wipe the lichen from the rocks with their quims. The slimy mould, when absorbed through the girl-orifice, was considered healthy medicine, but girlslaves were forbidden to masturbate using the mould; surplus lichen was scooped from the girlslaves' pouches and applied to those of noble ladies, who masturbated with their slits full, wiping their nubbins with the slime mould, their spasms of orgasm thought to absorb fully the wondrous powers of the growth. Noble Antarctique ladies, including Sindi, received their sacred summer solstice floggings with their naked buttocks coated in lichen.

Now her master Een would flog her as pitilessly as she had flenched rebellious slaves with thongs made from the skins of dog, bear and seal. Gone were her bear furs and sealskin boots, her tortoiseskin whips, her bronze and silver nipple rings, quim pins and necklaces, her carriage pulled across the Antarctique plains by a dozen girlslaves of her private guard, panting under her whip in their eager obedience. She herself was now a slave for the flenching – yet the fire in her breast burned, making her believe that her slavery would not be forever.

Slavery had taught Sindi much. At home in Kerguelen or Antarctique, she scarcely questioned the provenance of the spices, tulipwood, copper, tobacco and wine transported by vessels from afar. It was only when traded as a slave that she had learned how many places there were, deserts and jungles and snowy mountains. Antarctique girlslaves, blonde like Sindi, were the most precious cargo, their firm young breasts and buttocks deemed most whipworthy; for a lord's pleasure and prowess on Earth were expressed in whipping skill on a girl's croup, as he sacrificed her weal-striped buttocks to the power of the sun.

Kerguelen exported few slaves, but Antarctique girls sold at the highest premium in silver dinars. Everywhere on Earth, girls were preferred as labour slaves, being less truculent and rebellious than boyslaves, who were bought for the size of their penises and generally kept for domestic pleasure work. Constantly despermed by their lustful mistresses, they were docile and grateful. Sometimes the ladies of Madagascar liked to castigate their boyslaves on the bare buttocks, perhaps savagely, but never so savagely as girls, whose buttocks were worshipped, objects of veneration in the cult of the sun; like all sacred objects, they must be severely punished by whip, in adoration.

Thus Sindi knew her fesses to be sacred, images of the sun, which assured life on Earth and had to be appeased with constant sacrifice: ritual chastisement of girls' buttocks, the girls secured with intricate cords. The knots binding the whimpering sacrifices were themselves of sacred symbolism and were tied by priests who had spent years studying the science of girl-binding to achieve the prized rank of knotmaster. The priests and slavemistresses of Antarctique scoured the mountains, valleys and slave mines to find girls for export whose croups were in celestial harmony with the sun. Bitter irony, that she had once been a slavemistress . . .

She had thought it good luck to fall at last into the hands of Een, but now she knew that the life of a queen in Madagascar was the worst form of slavery, despite her crown, necklaces and nipple rings, her sumptuous robes of crimson and blue and yellow, the repasts of crustaceans, eels, turtle soup and, delicacy of delicacies, raw hedgehog liver. Even despite her sumptuous array of silk stockings. She must sit stock still for the priests, and in the evening endure Een's ingenious whippings on her bare rump, before parting her thighs for a full anal penetration, another sacred form of buttock-worship, by his painfully massive organ.

She wondered how long it would be before Een tired of her and disposed of her as a slave to the cattle fields or copper mines or vineyards, or traded her to some other prince and an uncertain destination – perhaps to one of the other cruel and savage nobles lurking in the far interior, in the unknown north of Madagascar. Those were men who pleased themselves in devising ever more subtle tortures and brutal whippings of the girls in their power, for thus they imagined the appeased sun would excuse their other crimes. Involuntarily, she shivered violently at the thought. At the sight of her unquiet body, the trembling of her breasts and thighs, there were gasps from the priests, shaken heads and a rustling of the books, to consult the scriptures inked on ancient hide.

'You worthless whore!' cried Een. 'A blasphemous ill omen! Knotmaster! Strap her to the frame. You shall be strung and whipped at once, my beautiful Sindi, and your squirming buttocks may atone for your infamy.'

Shuddering, she rose from her throne and presented herself for punishment at the whipping gibbet, obediently raising her arms, for her wrists and hair to be roped by a knotmaster, in an intricate, painful *mélange* of bowline and ox-hitch knots, to the top of the heavy wooden frame. The cord binding her hair stretched down her back to penetrate the cleft of her buttocks and pierce her anus with a harsh, pointed wooden plug, while further slender cords tautly bound her ears to her nipple rings, the cruel fastenings serving to keep her head erect. Yet they were unnecessary, as Een knew, for even under the harshest lash his consort maintained the regal bearing of a princess.

He raised her until her tiptoes just touched the floor, whereupon the priest bound her ankles with strands of rope tightened on each toe. Her body dangled helplessly, her buttocks and breasts quivering, the nipples stiffened by fear and their rings jangling as she trembled. The king took a sealhide whip, over an arm in length and two fingers thick. Vap! The thong laced her squarely in mid-fesse, and she groaned. Vap!

'Uhh . . .'

'Silence, my lovely blonde bitch queen,' snarled Een.

Vap! Vap! She wriggled in shame and anguish as the whip striped her buttocks crimson and raw. She wanted desperately to piss but knew better than to displease her lord further by pissing under punishment, although her belly was bursting. Only after nine strokes, when his queen's bottom was striped in a patchwork of crimson welts, did Een lay aside the thong and order the sobbing girl released. She resumed her position on the throne, trying to keep still, despite the smarting agony of her bare bottom and the bursting of her piss-swollen belly.

'Your illicit movement, your blasphemous twitching, mean that something is going to happen soon,' he growled, 'and it bodes no good.'

'Oh, no!' Sindi groaned, and pissed a steaming golden stream all over her throne.

4

Slavesnatcher

Monsieur Loleelo the slavesnatcher hummed to himself as he drove south from the silver city of Igfal, in the far north of Madagascar. His wagon, its giant wheels the height of a man, puffed steam from the copper boiler mounted at the rear, as it proceeded at slightly more than walking pace. A retinue of girlslaves rode alongside on six-legged black boars, twelve hands tall, leading two extra beasts for their master's use. His own master was the Rubberlord, who owned the vast northern plantations of rubber trees, tapped by girlslaves, and the silver and tin mines, where less fortunate girlslaves laboured naked, cruelly thrashed in the intense heat. Silver was transported to the domains of Prince Een, who styled himself the ruler of all Madagascar but in truth was more of a nominal overlord; rubber, however, as a material for war, was withheld, being sent overseas instead. Frequent wars did not interrupt the smuggling trade in slaves, silver, tin and fish.

Inside the house-on-wheels were stored dried and salted hedgehog meat, pemmican cakes and water, bronze swords and artefacts of cattle horn and hides, silk stockings, crossbows and arrows with rubber pads for shooting giant hedgehogs in ditches (or escaped slaves down from their trees), and mesh nets for trapping them. Also sugar, wine, blocks of miraculous rubber, clothing, boarfat soap, silver weights and lemur furs, together with a bed and chairs, bronze plates and spoons, and everything for his comfort or use on his lengthy journey to the south, including a selection of canes, whips and other disciplinary tools.

He was a pious man, so there was a gibbet fixed to one wall from which a miscreant slave might be strung, a rack on which her body might be stretched, and beside it a cowhide flogging-horse on wooden struts, over which she might bend, bottom raised for beating, in honour of the sun. Monsieur Loleelo himself wore a short silken tunic with a collar of hedgehog fur and a headdress of dangling silver miniature windmills to denote his noble status. He was shod with cowhide sandals. The steam engine, Monsieur Loleelo's own invention, powered a wooden-bladed fan on the ceiling, for coolness in the sweltering jungle.

Although his lord's soldiers manned observation posts at regular intervals along the southern road, right up to the borders of the lord's domain, and each post contained a lodging-house with food and beds, the slavesnatcher preferred the comfort and exclusivity of his own accommodation. He was a handsome, heavily muscled young man with a fine head of long silken hair, lips curled in a haughty, amused smirk and the pleasant manners of power and supreme confidence.

From time to time the party stopped so that the slaves could restock his vehicle with wood and water from the placid vermilion streams of the jungle. He chewed on dried beans, fruits and cow-meat while a fire was made and the girlslaves cooked his soup of freshly caught fish in a copper pan. After they had basted it with juice freshly extracted from their frigged quims, he loaded it generously with precious pepper, for he liked salt and fire in his belly.

Monkeys howled, giant hedgehogs growled in their lairs and parrots chirped in the high trees as the party made its way along the well-beaten pathway, although the slaves had to use bronze scythes to cut away the crawling roots and tendrils obscuring the red earth, pressed flat by the constant commerce of wagons loaded with cargo on their way to and from the lord's silver and stone palace. There, timber was weighed and stored, imported wine cellared in earthen ewers, cattle penned, tobacco and furs and jewels locked away.

There were two cities of silver in Madagascar, the other being the rival city of Warebb, by the northern ocean. Both realms prospered as well from precious stones, timber, cattle and dried fish, and fruits, meats and insects culled from the teeming jungle. The sweet fruit called the pineapple came from Warebb, and the Rubberlord of Igfal loved to torment a flogged girlslave by scraping her weals with a pineapple's spiky crust. Unlike his master, who was loath to venture from his sumptuous chambers and pleasure dungeons, Monsieur Loleelo knew both cities, for the world lived by trade, and nothing could stop trade. In both places slaves were a precious cargo, for the Rubberlord, *Le Sieur du Caoutchouc*, like his rival *Monsieur de Warebb*, had an inexhaustible appetite for tender teenage girls as whipping meat.

Although the jungle river tribes provided plentiful nubile girlslaves, most prized were females from far to the north or south, whose strangeness excused or provoked their enslavement. Their distant provenance meant that in whipping and enculing them their owner sapped the power of their home realm. At frequent intervals the lord of a city had to assert his right to rule by a sacred flogging of innumerable girlslaves; rival contenders for the throne were obliged to compete in a trial of strength, publicly whipping and enculing girls, to determine which male could bring the most to climax without spurting his own seed. Thus had the Rubberlord won his throne.

When he had scarred a girl's buttocks with sufficient whipmarks and stretched her young anus with his massive tool, and if she survived his cruel hunting game, he sent her to be a field slave, under the lash of his male overseers, or entrusted her to Monsieur Loleelo, who conveyed her to a used girl auction on the distant border of the realm, near Prince Een's domain. Prince Een's writ did not run as far as he would have liked. A trading arena was a no man's land where outlaws gathered, wielding whips and swords and speaking a babble of dialects; they bargained, drank and diced while their mud-crusted girlslaves, groaning in their tight leashes, filled their wine cups or parted their legs to offer succulent quims and buttocks in payment of their masters' gambling debts. Jail-sweepings, gallows-birds and scapegraces, mutineers, thieves and assassins, girlslavers were grizzled brutes who flitted between kingdoms and were beholden to none.

Foreigners from other parts of Madagascar were barred from the Rubberlord's realm, nor might his subjects venture abroad; instead, there was a complicated system of exchange at the border, where goods to and from Igfal were bartered and transshipped. Heavy duties in silver dinars applied to all goods entering or leaving the realm. None of that affected his slavesnatcher-in-chief, who could go where he pleased, keep his own slave-stocked estate in the forest, away from Igfal, and trade as he wished. He made sure he was on the best of terms with Monsieur Haroon, the master of excise, always reserving a few choice girlslaves for him, and for Monsieur Abatt, the treasurer, who transferred the customs monies to the silver palace. All the Rubberlord's officials were loyal and honest, for they feared the penalties of betrayal: cast out as prey in the game or, worse, a boyslave's punishment, made into girls. There was a market for such creatures, as bizarre pleasure slaves.

His escort girlslaves were clad all in black rubber, moulded tightly to their skins, with black masks and hoods, even in the fierce tropical sunlight dappling the trees. They had a mild form of porphyria, common amongst primitive dwellers in remote jungle or mountain, and were sometimes called vampires. They fed excessively on animal blood or raw mice, rats and lizards, and could not suffer the light of the sun on their skins. Human blood, however – even the sight of human blood – was totally repugnant to them, as was fish blood, and if they ate fish it must be thoroughly cleaned. Abnormally (or ravishingly) slender, they had white skins, yellow tiger's eyes and purple lips. When they ate meat, tearing the carcasses to pieces with their claws, it was devoured raw by sharp pink teeth, kept permanently filed to sharp points. Their master liked to watch them squat naked and urinate, for their piss was a rosy pink or mauve.

Pan was the leader of his pack, tall, svelte and once blonde, a tribal princess from the northern silver mountains who had been captured in a raid by rogue slavers and sold in the market of Warebb, which Loleelo visited incognito, pretending to be a merchant. (Among his talents was the gift of mimicry, and as well as speaking perfect French and English he could adopt any realm's Austronesian dialect.) Her slim body rippled with muscle; she had firm, conic breasts and a bottom of pear-shaped fullness, so large that it seemed a magical outcrop somehow erupting between her narrow waist, and long colt's legs.

Struck by her beauty, he had kept her for himself. After purchasing her with a cask of vintage wine from far Maroc, he shut her up in darkness in a mud hut on his estate, regularly whipped every inch of flesh on her body and fed her on rat, sloth and hedgehog blood, until her tan skin paled to alabaster white, her lips darkened to purple, her eyes became yellow pinpoints and her tongue furred. She was a virgin, as befitted a princess. After every raw meal and every whipping, he enculed her, bringing her to several orgasms, so that after two weeks she was his devoted, submissive slave, addicted to animal blood, his whip and enculement. As an afterthought, he took her vulval virginity, not something he particularly cared for, but a useful method, he found, of enhancing a girl's affection and loyalty.

Monsieur Loleelo did not need to use his whip too often on his slaves, for their obedience was assured by their weaned addiction to blood. He whipped them for piety and his pleasure. Many lazy forest hunters became vampires, drinking their prey's blood with its meat, at first to spare them extra forays but soon for preference; they were too fearful of crocodiles and water ghosts to fish for their food. Therefore, some girls were already porphyriac when enslaved, but it was easy to turn a new slave into a vampire, feeding her raw bats or mice, hedgehogs, tree sloths, lemurs and guinea pigs. With appetite grew submission.

Their pallid faces, pearl-white bodies and dark lips gave these vampire girlslaves an unearthly beauty. It was a piquant pleasure, doing homage to the sun, to take down a girl's rubber panties and whip her bare buttocks, so deliciously white (he was also fond of stretching her nude on the rack, while flogging the soles of her feet), the translucent skin showing a tracery of tiny blood vessels, those in the buttocks blossoming to pink sponges as he whipped; as if one could see right through the flogged girl, into her heart and her pain. Then he would penetrate her nether hole or her mouth, filling the orifice with copious sperm. If he spurted in a slave's throat, she must swallow every drop; if in her rectum, she must excrete the hot man-fluid and gratefully lick it from her fingers.

Size of balls and sex organ was a mark of nobility in Igfal – the male organ was worshipped second only to the sun – and Monsieur Loleelo's balls were like pears, his penis inferior in size only to his master's. He was gifted with the ability to control its movements, to make it rise or wilt at whim, or swivel and point, for awed girl onlookers. He could experience orgasm without ejaculation, spurt instantly or delay ejaculation at will.

35

To have a vampire suck his penis was pleasant, for her sanguinary diet made the lips and tongue very tender and at the same time more pliable, so that a vampire's befurred, blood-swollen tongue caressing his glans was like a delicate whipping with hot silk. Pan, his favourite vampire, not only craved his whip – her kind readily became addicted to bare-whipping, to inflame their blood-dulled passions – but was adept at the art of fellatio. Like all vampires, numb of feeling, she preferred the stimulation of anal sex, and he would let her sit writhing on his lap, with his penis filling her rectum, as he drove.

Monsieur Loleelo was on a special mission. Spies had brought to his lord's attention the presence, at Prince Een's court, of a young girlslave, Sindi, of wondrous beauty, her buttocks and breasts as perfect as the sun, haughty as ice, and with snow-blonde hair. The ice bitch, she was called, in envy, contempt and awe. Ice was a precious commodity in Madagascar, hauled in huge ships from the giant land far to the south, which was half covered by ice and half by forest and lush grassland, and whence they also carried cargoes of fish, krill, bear fur and penguin meat. Een had become so enamoured of the ice bitch that he had made her his queen in Toleara. She had once been a *dame noble*, but was now a slave. The Rubberlord decreed he must have her, not least for the malign desire to deprive another lord of his queen and thus humiliate him. He desired to possess this mysterious blonde girl from afar – 'Antarctique? Where can that be?' – whip her naked body raw and pierce her vulva and rectum with his penis (he would mime lustily) until she screamed and wept, as token of his ownership. Mr Loleelo was wise enough not to correct his lord's ignorance of the world, for his own knowledge of distant lands beyond the seas gave him power.

'Consider it done, *Altesse*,' he purred. '*C'est bon.*'

From the treasurer, Monsieur Abatt, he drew a quantity of silver dinars sufficient for any bribery or purchase and equipped his vehicle for the long trip south. Chortling at the terror of slaves who fled from his puffing, clanking carriage, he set off towards the frontier.

After three days' travel, he ordered his girls to tether their boars and follow on foot. He abruptly turned off the pathway and into a clearing, leading to a bend in the vermilion river where the waters widened into a pool. He called this place the fish farm, and knew that the forest girls came here to bathe. On a slavesnatching mission he liked to whet his appetite, and test himself, with an easy capture. Sure enough, a handful of naked brown jungle maidens were splashing in the water. They drew back in fear at the sight of the house-on-wheels, which stopped by the water's edge. Mr Loleelo descended, holding out a sheaf of sugar sticks. The sugar came from a hot realm in the north, beyond Warebb.

'I come from our master, *Son Altesse* the Rubberlord,' he called. 'Who would like *du sucre*? Lovely sweet sugar?'

Uncertainly, the girls eyed the glittering sugar sticks, as he began to suck one.

'Mmm . . .' he said, smiling.

Suddenly, the girls were on the bank, clamouring for the delicacy. Speaking their Austronesian dialect, he ordered them to squat, with their thighs apart, and when they had done so, he handed out the sugar sticks. While the girls sucked, he strolled amongst them, inspecting their bodies. He allowed his tunic to fall open, revealing his dangling member, and willed it to stand half-erect. He made his penis stand rigid, go limp, then at once rise again; quiver from side to side or back and forth. The girls were in awe. They reverently eyed the massive tube of flesh, mindful of its sacred power, and some whined a prayer. At length, he pointed to one of the girls, a young one, with hard and pert upjutting breasts domed with huge, soft, plum-sized nipples, a flat belly and a narrow

37

waist, ripening into superbly large buttock pears, sleek, muscled thighs and long feet with dainty toes. She was most desirable; he asked her name.

'Fafni, master,' she said, with sugar juice dribbling down her chin onto the points of her tender young breasts.

'And how would you like to be a servant of the Rubberlord, in the silver palace of Igfal, bathe in scented pools, wear fine dresses and have all the sugar you can eat? And . . . wear silk stockings?'

Fafni glowed.

'Stockings! Oh, I want them so much. Your offer does me such honour,' she stammered. 'But I fear you are teasing me.'

'Not at all,' he purred. 'Just step into my wagon, and I will show you what luxury awaits you. *Ah, le luxe dont tu vas jouir!*'

'Why not?' she cried, licking her lips. 'Silk stockings . . .!'

She followed him into the house-on-wheels, with two vampires behind her. Pan and the girlslaves promptly overpowered her, knotting her in tight ropes, while he closed the door and propelled the wagon back to the pathway. The girl squealed and struggled but was helpless. The vehicle stopped by the side of the track and the vampires, apart from Pan, regained their boar steeds. He told Fafni this abrupt treatment was for her own good, that she must pass a test, a spanking test, before being admitted to the Rubberlord's household.

'Oh . . . surely no, master? I promise to be a good girl!'

'No girl is good. Bend over.'

'Please . . .'

'Do you refuse to be flogged, for the sun?'

Her eyes widened in terror.

'I, blaspheme? Oh! No . . . no!'

The shivering nude girl burst into tears, but did not resist as Pan pinned her belly to the flogging-horse.

Monsieur Loleelo lifted her feet and sucked each in turn, savouring the girl-grime between her toes. Then he stooped, put his tongue between her buttocks, and inserted it a little way into her anus, which he began to lick; then he did the same to her quim, its young mound sleek with delicate downy hairs. His penis stood stiff, and he obliged the pinioned girl to take it into her mouth and suck it. She gagged, as he pushed his glans deep into her throat, humming to himself as her tongue worked on his penis.

Withdrawing, and stroking his erection with a satisfied smile, he took off a sandal and began to thrash her bottom. She sobbed and squirmed as her skin reddened, but he did not stop, until her flesh was deeply blushed, after a beating of over sixty slaps. Next, Pan handed him a wide-thonged cowhide smackwhip, which he applied to the glowing buttocks, his strokes cracking cruelly, yet the broad tongues not raising sharp welts. Fafni must be delivered pristine of buttock to her new owner. Vap!

'Ahh!' she whimpered, her bare bottom writhing in pain.

Vap! The whip's tongue wrapped lovingly around her naked haunch.

'Uhh! Uhh! Sir! I feel strange . . .'

Vap! Vap! The thongs raised deep crimson blushes on her thrashed bare globes.

'Oh . . . oh . . . it hurts so . . . I'm going to . . . going to . . .'

Vap! He allowed the tip to flick between her legs, lashing her moist vulval lips.

'Ahh!' she screamed, but copious juice oozed from her swollen sex lips, and she cried out 'Ah! Ah! . . .' again as she shuddered, panting in orgasm.

Pan held her legs apart, while her master mounted the girl from the rear.

'Sir! I am a virgin,' she wailed.

'What? You have not known pleasure-spasm from penis?' the vampire hissed.

'Only by my own fingers, or when whipped,' she bleated.

'Then you must be broken in, for the Rubberlord's comfort,' snarled Pan, rubbing the crotch of her tight rubber skin and gently masturbating her vulva.

First, his huge penis penetrated the moaning girl's wet cooze, piercing the virgin membrane, upon which she shrieked, and after a few thrusts bringing her to a shuddering, gasping orgasm; then he transferred his dripping member to her anus. Though lubricated by her generous come, it took some effort to penetrate the tight channel.

'Ah! It hurts!' wailed Fafni, her fesses bucking, as he enculed her with deep, savage strokes. 'Ah! Ah! You're bursting me. You're too big, you'll split me in two, sir.'

He kept up the buggery of the tender young maiden while she groaned, drool oozing from her mouth. Pan masturbated more and more voluptuously as her master's penis stretched Fafni's anal elastic with loud, squelching thrusts.

'Ahh ... by the sun ... don't stop ...' Fafni groaned. 'Yes! I'm wet! I'm going to spasm again ... ooh!'

She writhed in further climax as Mr Loleelo released his cargo of sperm into her rectum, and Pan rubbed her groin to her own grunting orgasm. At once, the vampire knelt and applied her mouth to the buggered girl's anus, sucking her master's sperm from the hole. When her mouth was full, she kissed Fafni on the lips and squirted the fluid into her throat, so that, gagging and sobbing, she swallowed almost all Mr Loleelo's ejaculate.

'She'll do,' he purred, wiping his dripping penis on Fafni's long dark hair.

Pan slung the new slave on boarback, the girl's glowing bottom up and visible to the sun. The vampires cooed and howled, licking her wealed crimson buttocks, before the croup was smeared with healing zinc balm of Loleelo's own concoction. Pan instructed a girlslave to ride back to the palace with Fafni and present the prize of new girlmeat to the Rubberlord, as a token of loyalty and esteem; Monsieur Loleelo was always eager to deliver extra. The vampire trotted away on boarback, sitting on Fafni's body as a saddle. Loleelo whistled to himself, then lit a smuggled Congolese cigar, before driving his vehicle and his tribe of slaves on towards the frontier and his prey, Queen Sindi.

5

Prince Een's Palace

Mr Loleelo hid his vehicle in the Forest of Sacred Rocks, two leagues above the port of Toleara, and left three of his vampire girlslaves to guard it. It was a wide, blackened plain of massive granite extrusions worn over the millennia into the shapes of grotesque human faces, ten times the height of a man, and with a floor of solidified lava. The inhabitants of Toleara shunned it, believing it to be infested with evil spirits, ghosts of the old people, who lived in the stone faces, with their long or hideously bulbous skulls, and glowed in the dark. Some said they came from another planet, although priests decreed there was no such thing as a planet, only the earth, sky, moon and sun. Heretics said it was a punishment from the sun, to warn what awaited if they, too, adopted the follies of the obliterated northern world – but few believed such fancies, or indeed in any northern world.

It would be foolhardy to take his vehicle into Toleara. For one thing, the jumbled streets were too narrow; besides, the southern Madagascarians were ignorant of the wheel and the steam engine, and would undoubtedly kidnap and torture him to learn the secret. Instead, he mounted the biggest and sleekest boar. With a bulging cowhide bag, he led his slaves at a canter to the market square below Prince Een's palace, which was built of gleaming grey rock, with glass windows where candle lights glittered in the twilight.

In the centre of the square stood a row of sacrificial whipping gibbets, mounted on a platform. Two were occupied by nude girlslaves, one dark and one pale of skin, and both well filled at buttock and teat. Monsieur Loleelo's practised eye identified one as a Zanzibarian and the other from the mysterious southern realm of Zuid-Afrika. They were strung by wrists, ears, nipples and quim lips with crude bowline knots and clamps on their tender parts, their flesh livid with purple whip weals. Their long manes were wrenched taut, knotted to the crossbar of the gibbet. The girls sobbed, trembling in their bonds and mewling, as the clamps tugged at their delicately stretched intimate flesh.

Smiling and raising his eyebrows, with an approving murmur Mr Loleelo passed by and selected the most opulent of the several inns that fringed the square. He entered a large, comfortable taproom, with easy chairs and a floor of granite flagstones, already thronged by wine-bibbers. Some were seated on benches, eating with their fingers from dishes of roast agouti at a communal table, strewn with jugs of red wine, while brightly hued gobbler lizards strutted the floor, pouncing on discarded scraps and bones. It did not take long, with the payment of a silver weight, to secure for himself the house's best room, with a view towards the palace. When they had carried his heavy cowhide bag upstairs, and he had approved his quarters, he washed from the jug, pomaded his hair, then changed his clothing to a richly embroidered hemp robe. He descended to the taproom and ordered his slaves to be taken to the slave quarters and roped next to his boars for their night's sleep.

'Do you serve guinea fowl?' he said.

The landlord nodded.

'And chameleon?'

'Of course, sir. We serve the best chameleon in Madagascar.'

'Then, guinea fowls and chameleons for my slaves. Uncooked and unskinned. They will find other food. If you have mice and rats, which I am sure you do, you will have fewer by morning.'

He ordered a jug of red wine for himself and took a seat at the communal table, where he began to nibble small pieces of succulent smoked chameleon from one of the platters.

'Honoured sir, there is the dining room for gentlemen,' said the landlord, somewhat agitated at seeing a slave-owning man of Mr Loleelo's status and fine dress. 'We serve the finest soups, including soup of oysters with genuine Antarctique girl come, from the choicest freshly whipped slaves. And there is entertainment for gentlemen.'

'Quite so. Perhaps later,' he said.

The lusty diners argued and boasted of distant lands they had visited, girls they had enjoyed, marvels they had witnessed, secrets they had learned: the tall stories of sailors and wanderers.

'. . . I tell you, they have girls with no heads! They are work slaves and pleasure slaves, who cannot feel pain, grown in the earth, with huge fesses, like hams of raw beef, four milk teats and three slits. Their holes are tight and silky, and suck you like snakemouths! I know, for I've had them. The wise men control them by power of thought. Some are twenty or thirty hands tall . . .'

'. . . in the Afric desert, they have an army of girls with tails! I swear it's true! The best poke on Earth! But vicious, the cruellest warriors . . .'

'. . . penis-gobbling girlslaves with gills, who can breathe underwater, like fish . . .'

'. . . a whole city under the sea, with underwater ships . . .'

'. . . the wise men told me all the lands of Earth float on a lake of molten rock, and they are coming closer to

44

each other; soon there will be only one sea, and only one land . . .'

'. . . in old days, there were machines that flew like birds and carried people through the skies . . . and to other planets!'

'Planets? Don't let the priests hear you talk heresy, or they'll turn you into a girl!'

There were roars of laughter.

'That's rich, eh? Where from, friend?' said the guffawing man seated next to Mr Loleelo.

'Why, from Antarctique,' he lied. 'I am here for the slave auctions.'

'Antarctique, eh. I've heard wondrous tales of that place. They say there are she-dragons of ice, monsters, girls with sharp teeth in their quims.'

'Some of the stories are not untrue.'

'You're selling? Antarctique bottoms are the juiciest to whip.'

'Buying. At home, we have such slaves aplenty, but variety is welcome and profitable. I seek ebony girlslaves. I believe there is an auction soon.'

'Next auction is the day after tomorrow, my friend, here in the market square. The prince will be there. He always is, and gets first pick of the girls. But there are plenty left to feast the eye on. The slaves on auction here have the slimmest waists, longest legs, firmest teats and the most whippable fesses, like ripe peaches, begging to be lashed, and so succulent, you'd expect them to burst under your rod, and shower you with the bitch's sweet juices! As for the rest, they are warranted to have the tightest of pleasure holes . . .'

He licked his lips, making curving gestures with his fingers, then the motions of spanking and, with two fingers, repeated stabbing gestures upwards, into an imagined vulva or rectum.

'I believe Prince Een has a very beautiful slave queen,' said Mr Loleelo.

'He does – the most beautiful woman under the sun, and the whole of Toleara gathers here to witness her sacrificial whippings on the prince's balcony. The prince himself gives her his rod, on her bare bottom. How prettily she wriggles! But you won't see her at the slave auction, either as spectator or merchandise. The prince is too enamoured of her.'

'Every girlslave has her price,' he murmured. 'Is there no chance that Een will sell her?'

The man shook his head.

'*Sell* her?' he gasped. 'No chance at all. He may tire of her, and demote her to drudge, but he will never sell any girl, once she has been his trophy.'

Mr Loleelo discovered that Sindi remained in her palace most of the day, her room being the one on the balcony overlooking the square, which was permanently draped with curtains. She would occasionally emerge, nude but for yellow, green, red or blue silken stockings, held up by a garter belt, to be ceremonially caned a few strokes on her bare, to the ecstatic applause of the public.

Rising from the communal table, he made his way to the gentlemen's dining room, where he was greeted by merchants dressed as richly as he was and invited to join a tulipwood table laid with silver. There, he was served good Tunis wine, fishes and a variety of soups, one composed of living bivalves sauced with pepper, lime and tasty Antarctique girl come, which pleased him greatly. There was a sumptuous buffet. In the corner of the room stood a flogging-horse, with cuffs at the end of each strut. Into these cuffs a nude brown girl was fastened, her belly draped over the horse and her bottom thrust up by a leather pad. Her long raven tresses hung down to the floor, obscuring her face. The host filled her quim with fiery red pepper sauce, making her squeal, then rammed a handful of shucked clams into her passage.

'There, gentlemen,' he said.

Whooping, certain of the merchants knelt – though not Mr Loleelo, who knelt for no one – and sucked the clams from the girl's quim. At the buffet, as well as tasty soups, there was smoked lemur, hedgehog and chameleon; slices of roast guinea fowl, partridge, heron, ibis, flamingo, egret and cuckoo. There were honey-fried butterflies, locusts and maggots, as an *amuse-gueule*, as well as snake and crocodile fritters, black bass, grouper, tuna, shark, whiting and numerous live molluscs. The deep-fried coelacanth, the oldest fish on earth, was most prized.

Each diner took his turn to cane the victim girl's bare buttocks with a thin, whippy wand of tulipwood. Such implements were supplied by the house, but most gentlemen wore their own whips or canes at their belts. By the end of the meal the girl's squirming globes were a mass of crimson stripes, and she sobbed uncontrollably, in woeful, gasping hiccups. Mr Loleelo, not wishing to let his turtle soup get cold, gave her buttocks four rapid strokes, which made the girl scream. He was applauded.

Most of the merchants were there for the slave auction. Loleelo said that he brought gifts for the prince, and hoped it would not be difficult to gain an audience the next day. On the contrary, he was assured, the prince was always avid for gifts or plunder. When the last of the soup had been consumed, the merchants threw seven-sided dice to determine whose penis should possess the whipped girl first. Loleelo won by deftly cheating. Joining in the wine-flushed laughter, he parted his robe and revealed his penis, massively erect, drawing gasps of astonishment and more applause as he showed how he could make it waggle up and down or from side to side.

'*Formidable!* Are all men in Antarctique built like that?'

'Most,' he purred. 'But our girlslaves' – pressing thumb and forefinger – 'have holes *that* tight.'

Briskly he penetrated the girl's writhing wet quim and began to thrust with hard slapping motions, withdrawing his penis fully and tickling her quim lips and clitoris with his glans, before slamming into her again. She wept and howled as he swived her. She was perfumed with sandalwood, which excited him.

'No! No! Sir, it's too big. You'll split me. *Vous me percerez jusqu'aux tripes! Ahh! Arrêtez, monsieur!'*

Happy at this homage, he swived keenly, delivering playful spanks to her striped buttocks, and taking care that his glans frigged her hard little nubbin. Thus he brought her to a loud, gasping orgasm, but himself refrained from ejaculation. Then he sipped wine, lit a cigar, and watched as all the other merchants possessed the squealing girl, until their mingled fluids trickled down her thighs.

After his dinner he slept contentedly with his cowhide bag beside him on the quilt, which was richly embroidered with scenes of girls, nude but for stockings, strung to gibbets and flogged. Similar quilts were on sale in the market place, as examples of the folk art of Toleara. There were innumerable paintings of nude girls reclining in stockings and masturbating, and pictures of stockinged legs alone. The populace could not legally own stockings, but they could have pictures of them. Bearing gifts, he would pay a visit to Prince Een's palace in the morning.

Refreshed by his night's sleep, untroubled by the hooting of ships in the port and the rumbling of the volcano under which he and the prince slept, he breakfasted on swan's eggs, then donned his most sumptuous furcollared court robe and jewelled sandals for his visit to the palace. Accompanied by two vampire slaves, he rode his boar the short distance across the square, dismounted and left his steed in their care. He entered the main portal, accompanied by Pan, carrying his bag of gifts, and explained his business to the guards, menacing in their uniforms of barracuda skin and helmets of shark's jawbone. He was a lord and high priest of Antarctique, and followed the noble calling of a merchant besides. Each guard received a copper coin. They bowed, recognising a nobleman, and bade him enter.

As Monsieur Loleelo entered the palace vestibule, he heard faint screams. In fact, Sindi was being caned on the bare buttocks by Prince Een, upstairs in the royal chamber. The prince, sipping his morning wine, wore an informal, lustrous robe, for he had not yet breakfasted. His slave queen was strapped in hard-knotted cords to a flogging-horse, her head lowered and bobbing up and down at each cut of her owner's cane to her helpless, squirming bare. A solemn circle of brown girlslaves, their hard breasts quivering in excitement, witnessed the punishment, standing behind a line of boyslaves, all erect above smooth-shaven pubis and balls. In Prince Een's palace boyslaves were permitted, indeed encouraged, to be erect. They were enslaved at the age of eighteen and freed at twenty-one to become the free population. In this way did Prince Een ensure the loyalty of his subjects, most of whom were his freedmen. Girlslaves, however, were never freed.

Sindi shuddered under the lash, as tears ran down her cheeks. Vip!

'*Ahh! Ahh!*'

As her flogged buttocks jerked and clenched, quim juice, oozing from her sex lips, glazed her thighs before dripping into a jewelled silver *vinaigrette* or come pot.

'Beating excites you, slut,' hissed Een. 'Admit it.'

His robe bulged from his massive erection.

'Ohh . . . yes, my lord, I admit it,' she whimpered.

Een took her to six strokes, then laid aside his cane.

'Thank you, my lord,' Sindi sobbed.

The girlslaves unstrapped her, then fastened her anew on a long surgical table, with her arms and legs raised high and spread, wrists and ankles attached to pulleys hanging from the ceiling. Her quim, gaping open to show the wet pink pouch meat, was at the height of Een's head.

A boyslave entered, bearing a tureen from the kitchen. The pot was crammed with tiny live pea crabs. He put it down and ladled red pepper sauce into Sindi's quim, making her squeal and wriggle. Several pinches of ground salt followed.

When her slit was brimming with sauce, the slave began to shovel the tiny crustaceans inside her, until the sauce overflowed down her come-streaked thighs. Prince Een licked his lips. Sindi jerked and squirmed as the crabs scampered and fought inside her gash. Een lifted her *vinaigrette*, and swallowed its viscous contents in one gulp, then pressed his mouth to her vulva and began to suck out the tiny crabs, dripping with come and pepper sauce, which he crunched and swallowed, while liberally refreshing himself from his wine goblet.

As her pouch was emptied, the kitchen slave shovelled in fresh loads of crab, until the tureen contained no more. Prince Een sucked the last of the pepper sauce, then drained his wine goblet, rubbing his belly to indicate satiety. He ordered his girlslaves to lower Sindi on her pulley to waist height. Flinging open his robe, he plunged his stiff penis into her anus, and began to thrust vigorously.

'Crabs and Afric pepper are best to restore the sleep-dulled passions,' he panted.

His hips slammed against her thighs and his penis sank into her rectum, right to his swollen balls, which pressed against her wealed buttocks. At length he grunted in triumph and filled the moaning girl with sperm. Then he withdrew with a loud squelch and motioned to one of the girlslaves that she was privileged to suck and swallow his sperm from the queen's brimming pucker. Eagerly the girl stooped to her task, pressing her mouth to Sindi's anus and with loud slurps delightedly swallowed her master's sperm. While this was happening, a boyslave entered, and said that the prince had a distinguished visitor from Antarctique, bearing gifts, waiting in the secondary chamber.

'*Des cadeaux?*' said Een, licking his lips and clapping his hands. 'Why, indeed we shall receive him.'

He gave orders that Sindi was to be sponged, clad and perfumed with attar of roses and essence of ambergris and civet cat. When she was ready, they descended to the chamber where Loleelo stood, accompanied by his slave Pan, bearing the gift bag. The visitor introduced himself as a priest-merchant of Antarctique. He planned to attend the next day's slave auction and purchase heavily. He had been travelling to diverse countries and brought a humble selection of gifts. Een embraced him and invited him to be seated beside him. He ordered wine to be served, and the men toasted each other and the eternal friendship of Madagascar and Antarctique.

Sindi stood humbly, in clinging pyjamas of yellow silk, and as he opened the gift bag Loleelo discreetly scanned the swelling curves of her young body, the tender breasts and buttocks thrusting against the thin cloth. *Yes*, he thought, *she's what my lord or any man wants*. The prince's eyes glittered as Mr Loleelo presented him with treasures, one by one, until the bag was empty: drinking horns, cut from the head of a bull, and adorned with intricate carving; a silver-handled bronze dagger; silver plates and wine goblets; a jacket of cowhide; a bronze dildo (at which Een licked his lips); a large sheet of thin rubber.

'What is this for?' asked the prince.

'A trampoline, my lord.'

He stretched and teased the rubber, letting it twang.

'It comes from an obscure princedom far to the north of your country. The prince there pleases himself by stretching it between poles, and making his girlslaves bounce naked on it. Their shrieks of dismay, and the wobbles of their girlish parts, are most pleasing to his lordship.'

Een roared with laughter.

'This I must try!' he cried. 'Monsieur Loleelo, you shall be my honoured guest in my pavilion at the auction tomorrow.'

51

For the rest of the day Loleelo visited the markets, buying gifts for the Rubberlord: wine, quilts, soapstone statues of nude girls, carved *vinaigrettes* of silver or sealbone containing imported Antarctique girl come, salted fishes and a bone chess set. He also strolled around the port, making notes of the ships at anchor and the troops guarding them. One could never possess too much information. Meanwhile, Prince Een heartily amused himself and his slaves by throwing naked girls on to the stretched rubber sheet and making them bounce up and down, two or three at a time, arms, legs and breasts flailing, until they were hopelessly giddy. Gleefully watching, he thought, *What a splendid fellow is this Monsieur Loleelo.*

6

Girl Auction

Under a scorching sun, Monsieur Loleelo sat beside Prince Een in the cool of his pavilion, a gaudy tent with flags flapping, overlooking the auction ring but cordoned from the main square. The ring was thronged with traders and simple onlookers, come to watch girlslaves tested by the whip. In its centre was a low stage for the girls, and at the centre of the stage stood a gibbet. The prince was surrounded by slaves, some with fans, others to serve wine and food. He had first choice of any female but preferred to bid through an anonymous agent on the floor, communicating with him by secret hand signals. This was a sop to his subjects, to show his fairness and benevolence.

'Queen Sindi does not care to witness slave auctions,' chortled Een, slurping wine, 'for it reminds her too painfully that she herself is a slave. Besides, this morning is audience morning. At this moment, she sits immobile on her throne while the priests scan her body for omens.'

'I don't suppose you would ever sell such a treasure,' said Mr Loleelo affably, clinking wine glasses.

'Certainly not,' retorted the prince. 'I keep my old girlslaves and work them as drudges, but out of my sight, for I can't bear to think that I once enjoyed *that* wizened hag. Although it was my tool that wizened her.'

Both chuckled, men of the world. A row of naked girls, roped together at the waist, was led on to the auction stage. At once, ringside purchasers surged onstage and, under the beams of the auctioneer, began to poke, pummel and tweak the merchandise. They squeezed breast and buttock, fingered anus and shaven quim, opened jaws to examine teeth and scanned the sweat-glistened young bodies for any blemish. The girls maintained stony faces as the men kneaded their flesh and poked their intimate orifices.

'All young virgin flesh, my friends,' bellowed the auctioneer. 'Choice unused *viande* from exotic lands.'

At length, cracking his whip, he opened the auction. The first girl up, a slender ebony creature of sultry beauty, with huge, firm breasts and large bottom, sobbed as she was strung in the flogging gibbet, her wrists secured by crude knots but her legs unfettered. There was a murmur from the buyers. Sobbing, so early in the proceedings, was not a good omen. Prince Een explained that each girl had to be tested for her endurance under the whip before the bidding started. She would take twenty lashes and the buyers might judge her fortitude by her wriggles, gasps and squeals. Silence would attract a high price and thus a rich owner, who might sustain her in some comfort, although some perverted buyers sought shriekers and weepers.

Vap! The whip cracked on the black girl's voluptuous buttocks, which clenched fiercely, and she gasped. Vap! A stroke to her shoulders. Vap! Another to the croup.

'Ahh!' she cried.

The girl began to squirm as the whipstrokes rained, and by the fifteenth stroke she had pissed herself. As golden fluid streamed down her ebony legs, there was a hum of disapproval from the crowd. After her body had been wealed by twenty expert, pitiless strokes, the sobbing girl was released and put up for bid.

'A pisser! She won't fetch much,' said the prince. 'Though there are some rogues who like a girl to piss into their mouths. I take a stern view of such debauchery.'

Een was right. Despite the auctioneer's pleas, bids were slow, and she was eventually knocked down for a mere thirty dinars, to a roguish, unshaven fisherman, whom Loleelo recognised from the inn as the man who had seen fish-girls that could breathe underwater. By quirk of fate and the will of the sun god, girlslaves might live in luxury or abject misery, and a tough life awaited this black girl. The next fared better; she was dusky of skin, but with straight hair, firm breasts, a taut, muscled bottom and long, coltish legs. Under the whip she squirmed and gasped but did not cry out until the seventeenth stroke, when she screamed. For her last three lashes, she kept up an unbroken wailing, until she was untied. The bidding was lively, and she was sold for seventy dinars to a minor lord of the interior.

The next was a full-breasted girl from the north of Africa, with fawn skin, cropped brown hair on a long skull, a prominent beaked nose and a succulent taut croup well scarred by whipmarks. Zanzibarians trans-shipped wine from Maroc and Tunis, brought across the desert in casks, carried on the backs of dromedaries, and with wine came pale slaves. Slavers argued that walking across the burning sands made the girls sleek and muscular. Monsieur Loleelo put in a few discreet bids to show his good faith but did not purchase. As the girl squirmed under her lashes, a fever of enthusiasm swept the crowd and bidding rose to a hundred and fifty dinars. The girl smirked in triumph, a valuable property.

The next girl, a mulatto, whom Loleelo thought the tastiest, had nipples the size of plums and voluptuous buttocks. She took her whipping in shuddering silence, and was bought by Een's agent for two hundred dinars, after an elaborate game of chin-rubbing and nose-scratching by the prince.

Warmed up, the crowd cheered the second batch of girls. All were blonde, with flat bellies, long feet and superb breasts, thighs and buttocks. The auctioneer boasted they were guaranteed genuine specimens, bought or captured in Antarctique. All took their whippings with no sound but gasps of agony, until their pale bottoms were crimson with welts. Bidding was fierce, reaching a thousand dinars, and the prince bought two of the blondes. Halfway through the line-up, Loleelo asked the prince's permission to be excused for a few minutes, as he had forgotten some urgent papers. Scarcely noticing him, and drooling lustfully into his wine, the prince waved his hand in dismissal.

Loleelo collected his slaves and animals from the inn and rode along the far side of the square to the prince's palace. Once more he pressed copper coins on the guards and lied that the prince had given him permission to witness Queen Sindi's audience. He moved his beasts to the back door of the palace under slave guard, and with Pan and two other slaves ascended to the audience room. There were almost no soldiers in the palace, for most were attending the slave auction.

Once inside, they beheld the nude Sindi quivering as she tried to stay still on her throne, while a throng of robed greybeard priests squatted on the floor gazing at her. From under his robe, Loleelo drew a net. Pan and her vampires rushed to the throne, pinioned Sindi and carried her to their master, who swiftly bagged her in the net. The priests were too astonished to move. Loleelo and his slaves fled along the corridor to the back stairs, from which they speedily descended, leaving by the slaves' door, where their boars awaited. As in most successful military operations, speed was of the essence, and it was over before the victims had time to react.

Sindi was secured with ropes to the back of a boar and the party of kidnappers left at a thunderous gallop, scattering unwary pedestrians and rapidly concealing themselves in Toleara's mesh of alleys and lanes, until they broke on to high ground above the city and made for the Forest of Sacred Rocks. Loleelo unroped and lifted the netted girl from her steed – the unearthly rock faces seemed to scowl and sneer at them – and carried her into his wagon, which the waiting slaves, on his instructions, had already fired up at a given moment on their sundial. Pan gagged the prisoner with a rubber harness, trussed her wrists and ankles in cords and knotted her hair tightly to a stanchion. Helpless, she could only weep and wriggle as Pan ordered her to silence with vicious cuts of a twig on her bare bottom.

The party set off at full speed, the vehicle spurting steam, along the main road to the north. The slave-snatcher was confident that the forces of Prince Een would not follow, because the prince would believe them to have embarked for Antarctique, and because his forces had dogs but no large riding animals. After several leagues, he signalled a halt by a river. In the shade the vampires stripped off their rubber skins and bathed, playfully mock-wrestling, their snow-white bodies glinting in the dappled shadows of the trees as their raven tresses danced.

'Let me go!' Sindi cried, her sobs having calmed. 'Where are you taking me? This is an outrage.'

Yet she could not help finding her captor strangely exciting.

'I shall free you from your bonds if you promise to behave,' he said. 'Do not think of escape, for we shall be travelling through deep jungle, and you would soon be eaten by a giant lizard.'

'I want to walk around,' she moaned. 'It was torture, sitting on the throne for hours, unable to move a muscle.'

'Consider yourself sold at auction, which could well have happened. Have no fear: I am taking you to live in luxury with a powerful lord, who has long admired your person from afar. I shall loose you, but if you make trouble I shall have to rope you for our whole journey, which is a long one. Accept that I am your new master for this time.'

She said coolly that she had no choice but to accept her enslavement. Whoever her master, one day she would gain her liberty.

'You are a slave, the only fitting state for a girl of your beauty.'

He allowed his robe to fall open, showing his nude body and erect penis. Her eyes widened as the monstrous tool softened and rose again, rigid and engorged, then waggled back and forth, up and down. She licked her lips, panting, as she gazed at the heavily muscled body, the massive nudity of the moving penis and balls, and felt moisture seep in her pulsing quim.

'How do you do that?' she gasped.

'I have rare and superior ancestry,' he said. 'There are not many of us among humankind. I am of the old people, called the longskulls, who invented books and wondrous machines. After I have broken you in, it is up to you to prove to your new owner that you are the most beautiful girl under the sun.'

'Luxury, then. What luxury?' she demanded.

'Things of your dreams. Jewels, ornaments of silver and bronze, stockings soft as a spider's web.'

'Huh! I had such things in Antarctique. What, anyway, is a spider?'

Yet the thought of stockings brought a glint to Sindi's eyes and made her lick her lips. He told her the legend of giant furry spiders in the jungle, which stung a girl into immobility, then ate her, slowly, piece by piece, beginning with her vulva. They gnawed through her belly and there laid eggs, shrouded in a cocoon of silk. That silk made the finest stockings.

'Shall I be whipped?' she blurted, her brow wrinkling in fear, eyes wide with awe at the huge naked penis dancing before her.

'Unlike spiders,' smiled Loleelo, 'discipline is unavoidable.'

For her first flogging she was strung quite simply, her wrists stretched by pulleys on the ceiling of the vehicle and her body dangling a few fingers off the floor. Pan, having removed Sindi's nipple and quim rings, threaded rubber cords through the pinholes in her vulval flaps and nipples and attached heavy stones to them, while her master doffed his robe and selected a long, thin cane fashioned of pickled baobab bark.

'Will this suit?' he asked politely.

'Oh . . .' she groaned, her flesh wrenched by the stones, yet her eyes riveted to her master's erection. 'Please, no. It hurts.'

'The stones, or the cane? Let's see.'

Vip! The cane streaked across her bare buttocks, causing her to shudder, and the stones danced, bouncing on the rubber cords.

'Ah!' she shrieked.

Pan stood before her, licking lustful purple lips and openly masturbating her crimson clito as she watched the girl's agony. Vip! Vip! Sindi's face creased, scarlet with tears, as the beating continued, her legs jerking rigid beneath her at each cut of the cane on her bare bottom. The stones smacked against her bare thighs and belly. Often he delivered two strokes in rapid backhand and forehand.

Vip! Vip!

'Oh! Please! Enough!'

Pan thrust two fingers into the whipped girl's sex and announced that she was juicing; her come shone as it oozed from her petals down quivering thighs. Vip! Her master directed the cane between her legs, striking her vulva.

'*Ahh! Ahh!*' she screamed, and a flood of golden piss hissed from her slit, making her sob in vile shame; yet when the torrent of piss ebbed, the dribble of come from her sex became a flow.

After four more strokes, Pan lowered the flogged girl and the master took her from behind, in the piss-wet quim, which gushed come over his pumping balls, while the vampire knelt to lick the girl's clito as the giant penis moved in her squelching pouch. As he thrust, his penis brushed against the vampire's furry tongue. He brought Sindi to orgasm while Pan masturbated to her own climax with fierce jabs to her sex and clito. Then, in the whipped girl's sight, he turned Pan round and enculed her to another orgasm, spurting his sperm copiously. Released from her stringing but still encumbered with her nipple and quim stones, Sindi had to kneel and lick the vampire's thighs, then suck the sperm from her anus and swallow it. Monsieur Loleelo said he hoped she had an appetite for supper. He applied ointment to her bruises, and the two dined heartily, with wine and fresh fried hedgehog liver, cooked by Pan. Loleelo was smiling, kind and attentive. Pan ate her meal raw, outside with the other vampires.

To Loleelo, cruelty to girls, and especially the striping of bare buttocks, was both art form and solar religious sacrament. He fed Sindi well between punishments, often making Pan spoon food into her mouth when she was trussed in rubber thongs and hooded in rubber. Otherwise, she wore slave's nudity, even during the cold nights, when her wrists were bound behind her back and her tresses knotted to the foot of her captor's bunk, although sometimes he would cover her with a rush mat. For insolence, she was 'baked', tightly bound while wearing a vampire's rubber costume that was too small for her, in which she sweated, until she pleaded to be whipped instead. Punishment, he explained, was to teach her proper slavehood, to relish submission and the pain of whipping.

Her innocence of any crime made the floggings more piquant: she was whipped for being a girl, and for the beauty of her buttocks. Piously, he concentrated the attentions of whip or cane on her croup, an offering to the sun, often inviting her to choose the implement of her correction. After each flogging he penetrated her anally, taking her to orgasm though rarely spurting himself, then anointed her body with a paste of river mud, containing precious zinc and iridium, powdered herbs and gel of the aloe plant, which healed her bruises quickly, so that her bottom became once more satin smooth and ready for fresh welts. She thanked him for the salve by kneeling to kiss his feet, then taking his penis in her mouth to lick and suck it. Tasting her master's penis was a reward for bravery under his lash. After several minutes of her worship, his penis rose and he penetrated not Sindi's but Pan's anus, spurting his sperm into her white body, with Sindi, complicit in her own distress, obliged to watch.

She would be strung by her wrists, hair, pierced quim lips and nipples, weighted by the stones from breasts and slit, to receive ten or twelve cuts of the cane on the buttocks. Sometimes he would cane her rump, while Pan used a delicate little scourge, from the workshops of Zanzibar, of six thin rubber thongs, like a fly-whisk, to whip her bare breasts, with special attention to the nipples. She could not help weeping as she shivered under the lash, for the pain of suspension, wrenching her arms, hair, nipples and quim petals, and the stones scraping her thighs and belly, was almost worse than the sting of cane or whip.

Pan would poke her fingers into Sindi's sex and announce gleefully that she was juicing. At that, the master would take the stockinged vampire from the rear, enculing her as she applied the lash to Sindi's bottom and the tops of her thighs, both inner and outer. Pan particularly liked to whip her sulcus, the tender zone between buttock and thigh. The vampire's beatings were always harsher when her own rectum was filled with her master's penis. After such a beating, Loleelo would withdraw from Pan's anus and penetrate Sindi's, thrusting strongly until she came, gasping, to orgasm. Thus did Sindi reach the desired understanding that whipping led to ecstasy.

Often she was stretched face down on the rack, to the point of pain but before the point of damage, to be flogged. Monsieur Loleelo let Pan administer the lash to her buttocks or, most painfully, to the bare soles, while he took her in the throat, sometimes ejaculating and making her swallow the copious draught. He interrogated her during her punishments, wanting to know about her life in distant lands, especially her prowess in whipping her slaves in Antarctique. She groaned proudly that her flenched girlslaves called her *La Cruelle.*

Sometimes Pan caned her so hard that she nearly fainted, and then she would feel Pan kissing and sucking her welts and masturbating her quim with deft fingers. During these shameful caresses, their master would take the luscious vampire girl from behind, making sure Sindi knew when he ejaculated. She realised he was trying to make her jealous of Pan, who received far more of his sperm than she did, and she *was* jealous of the svelte young pale beauty. Pan received more and bigger cigars than Sindi did. But when Sindi smoked the fragrant black tube, all her pain and suffering seemed to disappear for a few magical moments.

They frequently stopped by a river, where the vampires would bathe and catch fish for their master, diving to snap them up in their jaws, and mice and water spiders for themselves. On these occasions Sindi was given a cleansing lavage, or enema, with a curious pump of Loleelo's own invention, which sucked up muddy river water and forced it through her anus into her rectum and colon until she shrieked, bloated with pain. Tiny snapping fishes entered her with the water and their wriggles caused her further distress, to her master's amusement. But, docile by now, she obediently held the liquid inside her swollen tripes until he permitted her to void, a blessed relief as she squirted the brown fluid in a fierce jet from her anus.

Once she mischievously squirted her fluid all over Pan, who had just bathed, and the vampire's body was slimed with mud from her anus. Shrieking, Pan fell on her and the two nude, spattered girls fought, punching and gouging, while their master smiled, contentedly smoking a cigar. Sindi got the upper hand, squatting on Pan's face while she rained blows on her defenceless teats, belly and vulva, clawing inside the tender pink pouch, while Pan yelped under her crushing buttocks. She was noble again, dominant and in control. But the vampire's tongue entered her quim and began to flick the nubbin, and Sindi groaned as moisture spewed from her cooze over the girl's face.

She heard slurping as Pan drank her come, and leaned forward, squirming, to plunge her face into Pan's open wet sex. The two girls caressed each other, punches giving way to a tight embrace, gasping with pleasure, until they had tongued each other to orgasm, each sucking and swallowing the other's flowing quim juice. To climax with a girl, Pan required a hard chewing of the clito and a clawing of the pouch walls, for porphyria had dulled her senses.

Vap! Their master lifted his long cowhide whip and dealt a severe stroke, wrapping the thong around both bodies. While his slaves watched, eagerly masturbating, he flogged the girls, writhing in the muck, until they were exhausted and sobbing in agony. After a good dozen lashes, he permitted them to rise and ordered them to prepare a fish for his supper. The fish was to be wiped thoroughly inside both their quims, to absorb their juice, prior to cooking. He was fond of come-fried fish.

'Yes, master,' Pan gasped.

'Thank you, master,' said Sindi, bowing.

7

Rubberlord

Sindi stood nude and trembling before her new owner, the Rubberlord, who was seated on his silver and tulipwood throne. Monsieur Loleelo held her by a copper wire that passed through her pierced nipples. Her ankles were hobbled in bilboes, which kept her legs apart and her shaven sex open to view, the lips slightly parted to show her wet pink slit.

Her body was pure of whipmarks, although she had been beaten vigorously by Monsieur Loleelo during the voyage north, not for any misdemeanour – for Sindi, having herself been a slavemistress, well understood her degraded position as girlslave – but purely for his pleasure, in reverence to the sun. As well as applying his healing salve, her captor had latterly used a whip with wide, flat rubber tongues, which brought Sindi's squirming bare flans to a deep crimson glow but left no lasting marks that would displease the Rubberlord. One had to keep up *les apparences*. Monsieur Loleelo knelt, shuffled forward to the base of the throne and presented his master with the ends of the nipple-tethering wire.

'I hope she gives satisfaction, my lord,' he purred.

'Rise, Monsieur Loleelo, my faithful servant,' said the Rubberlord, licking his moist, fleshy lips and puffing on his cheroot. In a moment of automatic vanity, he smoothed his black locks, waved and shining with pomade of myrrh and perfume of iris. 'She gives satisfaction indeed. Come close, my slut.'

Sniffing perfume from his *vinaigrette* – the little silver container carrying a piece of Zanzibar sponge soaked in vinegar, sandalwood and lavender – he tugged Sindi's nipple wire, stretching her breasts, and the girl was obliged to hobble towards the throne. The Rubberlord's hand emerged from his mouseskin robe, under which he wore only a skirtlet of woven pubic hair from blonde Antarctique girls, and squeezed her breasts painfully. Then he stroked her belly, kneaded her buttocks and thrust two fingers into her quim, reaming the pink slit until she began to moisten.

'Excellent,' cried the Rubberlord. 'I think we may dispense with the ankle hobble, Monsieur Loleelo. You are not going to run away, are you, slut? You know who is your master now.'

'Yes, my lord. I shall be an obedient slave.'

A slave unlocked her ankle hobble and the Rubberlord withdrew his fingers from her slit. They dripped with shiny come, which he licked off with murmurs of satisfaction. He ordered her to part her thighs, then inserted the two fingers into her anus and pushed hard, as she grimaced, until he had reached her arse root.

'So tight, moist and silky! *Quel trésor!* What a treasure you have brought, Monsieur Loleelo,' he murmured, chewing on a betel nut. 'You shall be well rewarded.'

He began a slow fingering of her rectum and Sindi, shutting her eyes, moaned as come seeped from her slit.

'*Un joli cul!* A good tight hole,' said the Rubberlord, withdrawing his fingers and wiping them clean on her belly. 'And she juices well at the cooze, when stink-fingered. How much more shall you juice, my bitch, when my tool fills your holes fore and aft!'

He thoughtfully licked his finger, then raised it, summoning a boyslave, who wore a tunic of pressed balsa bark. The boyslave sprang forward with his head bowed.

'Take the girl to the slave baths, by one of the scenic routes,' he said. 'She is fit to serve at supper.'

The Rubberlord's palace was a dark and curious place, full of dimly lit corridors which seemed to go nowhere until at the last minute a doorway, barely large enough to accommodate a person, was revealed behind a tableau painted on the wooden wall. The painting was in fact the door to the next corridor, or to a room painted on ceiling and walls with *trompe-l'oeil* open-air scenes, so that the tiny room seemed open to the skies and much larger than it really was. Several times Sindi bumped her head in one of these rooms, provoking laughter from her guard, who was wisely stooping.

Many of the rooms were empty, or contained whipping frames and other machines of correction, covered in dust and cobwebs. Obscene paintings and sculptures decorated the walls, showing creatures who were half man, half boar or hedgehog, penetrating screaming nude girls with monstrous scaly or furry penis, or flogging their bare buttocks to a jelly. Once she stumbled into one of these derelict pieces and found that the dust was not real dust, but some kind of powdered rock, and the cobwebs were not real cobwebs but finely woven rubber filaments which sprang back into place after she thought she had torn them. In one corridor there was a flapping noise and a hideous squeaking, as a creature like a leather-winged rat dropped from the ceiling, teeth bared, on to her head. Screaming, she beat it off, only to see it bounce back to the ceiling on its rubber cord.

Frightened, she was glad to reach the baths. She gasped in surprise, for nothing could have been more different from the grimy murk of corridors through which she had passed. The baths were roofed with a dome of rose-tinted glass, allowing muted sunrays to flood in. The walls were also of glass, permitting the bathing slaves to gaze at the splendour of the Rubberlord's domain and the spired city beyond, as they wallowed in hot water perfumed with frothing unguents and soaps. In Antarctique only the nobles were privileged to use soap, which was made from seal or walrus fat, and smelly stuff at that. These soaps were perfumed with flowers.

There were ice-cold baths as well as steaming hot ones, and a good complement of naked girlslaves at their ablutions, switching from bath to bath, between hot and cold. There were also wooden sweat cabins, from which girls emerged pink and dripping with sweat to plunge into the largest of the ice-cold pools. A fountain played in the centre of the huge chamber. Her boyslave guard lifted Sindi bodily and threw her into one of the hot bathtubs with a huge splash, which made all the other girlslaves laugh and cheer. She emerged from the frothing water spluttering, and wiping her eyes.

'Hello,' said a girl's voice.

Sindi was not alone in the tub. Beside her lolled a tall, dusky girl, with long dark hair, thrusting breasts and the biggest, softest nipple plums Sindi had ever seen. The girl caressed her breasts contentedly, like a cat, as she contemplated Sindi, and the nipples swelled and stiffened.

'Mm,' she said. 'I'm Fafni.'

'Sindi.'

'You're new here. Where from?'

'Antarctique, I suppose – I used to be the slave queen of Prince Een, in Toleara, but I was cruelly captured by Monsieur Loleelo, who whipped and enculed me on the long journey here. I had to make love with his vampire girls, for his pleasure, and' – seeing the amusement curling Fafni's lips – 'oh, what's the use? I'm here now. I was cruelly enslaved, then made a queen, which was a worse form of slavery. I think I prefer being a simple girlslave. It is our lot to be the slave of men.'

'We have all tasted Monsieur Loleelo's penis,' murmured Fafni, 'and his whip. A queen? All girlslaves tell fantastic stories, not to be believed, but you do indeed

67

have the fabled beauty of Antarctique, of which the traders on the road told us in our village, when they came to buy fish and girls. I never believed them, or that such a strange place could exist, let alone have people in it. May I touch?'

Fafni began to caress Sindi's bare body under the water, tweaking her nipples until they rose, then inserting her fingers into the already juicing sex. Sindi's clito began to stiffen, and she saw that Fafni was languorously masturbating herself, caressing her erect brown nipples and fingering her nubbin. There was a faint jingle of metal within her pouch.

'I'm quite new myself,' said Fafni, eyeing Sindi's breasts as she squeezed them. 'Monsieur Loleelo kidnapped me, but I've stopped complaining. Once you are over the first shock, slavery to a strong lord is desirable. And if he approves of you, he will whip you properly. A girl unwhipped, her buttocks cold and not glowing from the lash, is sad. As well as opening your thighs and buttocks to his penis and baring your bottom for caning, you have to bounce on his rubber trampoline and learn to play other games, like hide and seek, in those fearful ghostly corridors. The only thing is' – she glanced around cautiously – 'the really big game is the girlhunt, where a slave is cast out into the jungle to run for her life, pursued by the Rubberlord and his friends with whips and nets. Few girls return alive from the jungle. Some girls say they are captured by vampires.'

'Ugh!'

'But it's only a rumour, and I certainly don't believe it. Perhaps girls escape to the city of Warebb. I do know that we have to masturbate as much as possible and fill our *vinaigrettes* every night, for girl come is a great delicacy, and very valuable on the market.'

Sindi gave the details of her capture by Monsieur Loleelo, and Fafni whistled in admiration, saying that to be thus selected was a great honour.

'Slavery is what most jungle girls dream of,' she said. 'To be fed and bathed and have a place to sleep, far from the wild animals. Has the Rubberlord poked you?'

'Not yet. Monsieur Loleelo, of course, used me in every way, on the journey here. He whipped me and poked me in the anus and also my virgin sex, and made me come so hard I couldn't stop coming. It was ecstasy, even though my punishments were vile and so very painful. Yet I learned a lot. The size of his tool! Such power, filling my rectum with his sperm! The Rubberlord has felt my body thoroughly, and has approved.'

'I've learned that some men like dirty, sweaty girls, with crusty, stinky toes and holes. Monsieur Loleelo does. But the Rubberlord likes us clean and perfumed, so we must bathe. And there are so many bottles of fragrances! Essence of ylang-ylang, attar of roses, lavender, oh, a hundred lovely things! Let's masturbate together – don't be shy, all we girlslaves frig our pippins – here, you can borrow my copper balls.'

Reaching into her slit, Fafni produced three shiny metal balls linked by a chain, enough to fill a girl's pouch. She showed Sindi how to insert them in her quim, and make them move around by a gentle oscillation of the belly.

'Oh, that's gorgeous!' cried Sindi. Her fingers probed Fafni's engorged sex lips and her thumb pressed the girl's distended clito. Soon both girls were eagerly frigging, with little gasps and moans of liquid pleasure. Fafni's thumb was on the nubbin, rolling the stiff little clito round and round, while she had three fingers poking Sindi's pouch, her nails scratching the hard wombneck. Sindi, too, rubbed her new friend's clito but preferred anal penetration, making her gasp as her fingers reamed her warm, moist rectum and colon. Both girls let their heads swoop to bite each other's breasts and tongue the big erect nipples, Fafni's nut-brown and Sindi's glowing pink.

'I'm so wet,' gasped Sindi. 'I'm going to come ... oh! oh! yes!'

Her belly fluttered and heaved, as her slit oozed come. Fafni's orgasm followed not long afterwards, and she suggested a water-plunge. Dripping suds mingled with quim juice, the girls padded to the ice-cold pool and dived in. The familiar cold was joy to Sindi and she remained a long time, splashing in the icy bath, while Fafni sat on the edge, dangling her feet in the water.

'This reminds me of Antarctique,' Sindi gasped. 'It is what I really like and yearn for, my cool homeland.'

'In our compound by the fishing river, there were stories about foreign lands,' Fafni said, 'but I thought that meant just the Kingdom of Toleara to the south, where the traders go, and the islands of Réunion and Comores, and then Mauritius, after which you fall off the edge of the world.'

Sindi was glad she had not mentioned Kerguelen, which would only complicate matters.

'Here there are two silver cities, of which this is one, and a girl who is ritually whipped through the streets of both has a chance of regaining her freedom. Yet no girl has ever wished to give up her slavery. I believe in those lands I have heard of, and the two cities, but it is hard to imagine there are any others.'

Sindi told her about Antarctique, its salt and furs and seaweed, but she said she couldn't believe such stuff. How could people live in a dark, cold land? Sindi asked where she thought the salt on the Rubberlord's table came from, if not Antarctique; the pepper, from Zuid-Afrika; or, from myriad lands, the tobacco for his pipe and the wine for his belly. Fafni admitted that she was only a simple jungle girl who had never worn clothes or shoes, and though she could hunt rats and hedgehogs, or dive deep and catch a fish, nevertheless she knew little.

For example, she had never heard of a wheel before, until she saw Monsieur Loleelo's wheeled wagon and he explained what the big round discs did; and that there were kingdoms beyond the sea was undreamt of by the riverine girl in her sensuous simplicity. Sindi, carried in a brutal merchant ship with its cargo of girlslaves, had heard stories of many such lands, where there were timber and whale blubber and white bear fur for sale, and of scorching Niger, with its peppers and tomatoes, packed in Antarctique ice on the ships; and Maroc and Tunis, with their wines and their naked girlslaves roped in herds to cross the burning desert sands.

Fafni, pouting, retorted that everyone knew the sea was a giant waterfall, and that if you reached the last island you would fall off into the abyss. The dispute was ended only by a whistle, at which all the girlslaves lined up at the doorway, where a guard wheeled in a wooden cart, bearing piles of costumes in shiny powdered rubber. Fafni said the girls must put on their uniforms to serve the Rubberlord and his guests their supper in the great hall of the silver palace. Eagerly they bathed and perfumed themselves, to smell sweet while serving the lord's food.

8

Slave in Rubber

The great hall sparkled with its walls and ceilings of pure silver and rubber. Outside the large blue glass windows – the glass was imported from the island of Réunion – it was darkening to dusk, as Sindi, perfumed in musk, iris, sandalwood and her own quim juice, wheeled her cart full of steaming dishes down the table. The Rubberlord, who sat at its head, and his guests thumped their silver wine goblets and laughed at each other's obscene jokes on the subject of the mulatto girlslave who was strung naked by her wrists to a gibbet. Her head was covered in a black rubber hood which left apertures only for her nose and mouth, while her ripe naked breasts and buttocks and her muscled belly quivered in fear; her extruded nipples were stiff. Monsieur Loleelo sat in a place of honour beside his lord. Each male had his *vinaigrette*, to overcome the stench of inadequately perfumed slaves. The only female at table was the schoolmistress, who ate sparely, her fingers stroking the oiled wood of her cane. She spoke seldom, and then only a few acid words, but when she did, the table hushed.

Sindi, like Fafni, wore a maid's costume of black rubber: a flimsy skirtlet that scarcely covered her unpantied quim lips, and a very tight rubber top that squeezed her breasts up, clearly outlining her nipples, stiff from the friction of the thin rubber. Her belly was bare above a thin corset, also of squeezing rubber, which pressed her waist to a painful thinness. Her legs were sheathed in black rubber stockings, making her sweat, and her feet teetered on high ankle-bootees of lizard skin, with pointed toes and spiked heels of tulipwood. But she loved the feel of the black rubber stockings. Rubber seemed a bizarre fabric, certainly less sacred than silk, but there was something exciting about the way the latex clung to her bare legs. And just to have stockings again – ah, such a joy for a girl. She liked the corset, too, even though it squeezed so painfully. It was unnerving to see the girlslave strung for her punishment, but Sindi was sure she must have done something to deserve it. If nothing else, the beauty of her body, her bulbous teats and buttocks, deserved punishment.

Awaiting his dinner, the Rubberlord wore nothing but a short skirt of blonde pubic hair from Antarctique girls. He had a selection of such garments. His lips, toenails and nipples were painted purple, and his shaven head covered in a blonde wig of Antarctique girlhair. He made no secret of his massive erection under his hair skirt as his rubber-clad girlslaves served him. The wine slaves, however, did not wear rubber, but were barefoot and bare-breasted, their loins clad in skirtlets of hedgehog hide with the bristles pointing outwards. If they erred in their service they would have to reverse their skirts and smile through the spiking pain.

The serving of food was quite easy, just a matter of ladling, because most of the dishes were soups and stews or sliced fish. Hedgehog stew, heavily spiced, was a favourite. There was grouper, tuna, shark, sardine, whiting, crayfish, crabs, shrimps, mussels and oysters, and a dazzling variety of fiery sauces, which the boisterous males enjoyed pouring over a wine slave's breasts.

The Rubberlord's wine poured, he gave the signal for the hooded girl's flogging to begin. A boyslave, penis erect, lifted a long thin cowhide whip and began to lash

73

the girl across her buttocks and back. The very first stroke left a pencil-thin pink stripe across her naked fesses, which clenched; the second marked her back, and she moaned long and loud under her hood, the lords chortling as they quaffed.

Beside the gibbet was a large rubber sheet fixed in a frame, and on this trampoline the wine servants took turns at bouncing, in the full nude, for their hedgehog skirts must not mar the rubber. It was difficult to control one's motion on the trampoline and the girls' limbs flailed helplessly, their breasts jiggling and thighs helplessly open, to show their quims, which added to the spectators' amusement. Fafni whispered to Sindi, as they sweated in rubber, running back and forth to the kitchen, that they were lucky to be mere food slaves. One wine slave, an elfin Congolese girl, made a mistake in pouring, and had to turn her skirtlet of hedgehog bristles inside out, the quills pressed to her quim lips. Grimacing, she continued to serve wine, as was her duty. The girlslaves labouring in the kitchen sweated profusely, their bare bodies splattered painfully by grease and hot olive oil (the best, brought from far-off Libya).

The high point of the meal was the serving of a huge coelacanth, last of the hundred-million-year-old deep sea lobefish, together with a giant clam in its shell that weighed as much as three men and offered a barrelful of meat. Sindi had to learn from Fafni how to carve the coelacanth and serve the succulent steaming morsels into the mouths of the lords – who would grope her rubbered bottom cleft while she did so, pushing their fingers into her anus and afterwards licking them. The liver was reserved for the Rubberlord himself, who washed it down whole, bathed in a sauce of cow-butter, sea salt and wild garlic, with a draught of wine. After that, he ate the eyes and sucked the head of the fish until it was empty. The giant clam did not have to be carved, for it was swallowed raw, doused in lemon and pepper, the lords gouging the living bivalve with their fingers. All this time the moans of the whipped girl served as musical accompaniment to their meal.

After that, there were other entertainments. Drenched and slippery in pungent olive oil, two girlslaves wrestled, gouging and biting and kicking, until one submitted in tears. Two more girls boxed bare-knuckle, punching each other in breast, belly and groin, until one was knocked unconscious by an uppercut. Two boyslaves boxed until they staggered and one fell, not to rise. The winner was permitted to encule the winner of the female boxing match. The Rubberlord, Monsieur Loleelo and the lordly guests applauded, as the boy took the girl in the anus and savagely buggered her, while she squealed in pain. When his sperm had spurted in her anus, the loser of the female boxing match had to kneel and suck it out, then kiss the winner of the girls' wrestling contest on the mouth and share the boy's sperm with her. Both girls were rewarded with a copper coin from the Rubberlord when they had swallowed the boy's cream.

Then there was a game of 'painball', where naked boys fought naked girls, the object being to get a weighted cowhide ball into a net. There were no rules in this game, all violence being permitted, and the boys and girls shrieked as they kicked, gouged, bit and punched each other. If a boyslave got a girlslave pinioned, he could pause to encule her or swive her between her thighs. Of course, this left him with less energy for the game, and the schoolmistress would punish him with a bare-caning if he failed to perform well.

The schoolmistress was in charge of the education of boyslaves, intellectually promising or otherwise, and especially of their physical correction; she was one of the most feared personages in the Rubberlord's palace. Clad in a black silken gown, black rubber boots and white stockings, under which she was naked, she taught classes in philosophy, poetry and history, the fabled history of times long past, before the mushroom-cloud wars (for she possessed ancient secret books), and the worship of the life-giving sun. At other times she prowled the corridors, searching for lazy boys to whip. She had the right to whip or otherwise chastise any boyslave she deemed miscreant. A painful, hard caning of twelve strokes on the bare, before his fellows, was not unusual for a boy she accused of 'skulking' or 'ignorance', although the definition of those terms was entirely within her own remit. Even the Rubberlord was in awe of the schoolmistress; perhaps because of her arcane knowledge, perhaps because of her cane. Both knowledge and cane meant power.

Meanwhile the hooded girl sobbed under her flogging until the lord ordered her cut down. She had taken twenty whipstrokes and her body was livid with welts. Her buttocks were well scarred and her supple back horribly striped. Her duty now was to crouch, suck the penis of every lord present and swallow his sperm through the mouth aperture of her rubber mask. She did so and, with the sperm of several lords dribbling down her mask, was rewarded with a copper dinar. She pushed the coin into her dripping slit.

'Thank you, my lord,' she gasped.

The Rubberlord grasped Sindi's soiled panties, moist with her fluids, and sniffed them with a smile of voluptuous delight.

'This whoreslave will be my companion tonight,' he said. 'You may take Fafni, Monsieur Loleelo.'

Fafni was right; when the Rubberlord summoned Sindi on that and subsequent nights, to slake his lustful thirst, he wanted only to take her in the anus or have her fellate him. By day, she was nude and pulled a cart, whipped on by a senior girlslave. By night, she dressed in rubber, perfumed her anus with myrrh and oil of sandalwood, powdered her face with chalk and a drying powder of magnesium from the mines of Zuid-Afrika, and attended the Rubberlord. It seemed strange to her that he did not wish her to be in her normal slave-nude for these adventures, but preferred her to dress in full rubber costume of skirt, blouse, panties and stockings.

The rubber panties had a hole at the anus, and the Rubberlord would make her bend over, spank her on the panties, which hurt less than Sindi expected, then insert his penis into her through the aperture for a hard ramming into her rectum, which made her groan and gasp in agony. When he had spermed at her colon, he would take off her boots and sniff them and lick her toes, for the rubber stockings had a buttoned opening at the tip. But mostly he would make her bare her breasts or her buttocks, freeing them briefly from rubber, and have her masturbate him until he spurted his sperm over the naked flesh-globes.

'That is what men really like to do,' he said, licking her toes. 'And we also like to present a girl that we own – it is all about ownership, my dear – to our friends, for their pleasure. It is highly pleasant to watch a girl you own taken in her anus. Especially by a young boyslave.'

The next night, the Rubberlord promoted Sindi: that is, she was allowed to serve dinner in the nude. She introduced the *plat du jour* but did not have much to serve, for it was raw oysters, presented in the sexes of girlslaves wearing only thin stockings of pink Zanzibar latex, who squatted on the table so that the lords could suck the food from their slits. The lords of Madagascar liked to spank the bottoms of the girlslaves as they sucked the bivalves from their open quims.

At a signal from the Rubberlord, three boyslaves presented themselves, curtsying. They were smooth and brown, shipped from Mauritius, and their large penises were already erect at the sight of Sindi's body. The schoolmistress set about each one in turn, striping their buttocks with her cane, punishment they took without flinching, to eight or nine cuts. After they had sucked the oysters from the girls' quims, the lords had a dessert of red grapes expelled from their anuses. The whistle and slap of the schoolmistress's cane on the boys' bare bottoms encouraged Sindi to masturbate, hoping she was not observed, and she rapidly brought herself to orgasm.

'Dereliction of duty!' cried the schoolmistress. 'We shall have to teach you a lesson.'

'No! Please, my lord!' Sindi cried, as the boyslaves pinioned her, but the Rubberlord nodded with a benign simper, and her protests were to no avail.

9

The Schoolmistress

The schoolmistress was vigilant, stroking her wooden cane, watchful for any failure of virility on the part of her students. She patted her long blonde tresses and stroked her stiffened clito under her gown, as she watched Sindi enculed by the three boys, one after the other. Sindi had followed without protest the Rubberlord's suggestion that, as punishment for unseemly behaviour, she 'perform' for the schoolmistress – in fact she was thrilled at this strange new exhibitionism.

The schoolmistress liked caning girls and, even more, boys, and knew those boys' fesses well. She liked seeing their penises rise as she caned them on the bare and they gasped in anguish. And she liked to masturbate them if they had been brave under punishment. She loved the feel and the taste of their sperm, and her feeling of power as they gasped in orgasm under her nimble fingers or lips. The schoolmistress could not help feeling jealous of Sindi's own blonde tresses, and pleased at her distress, under a boy's vigorous penis. She remembered her from her own girlhood in Kerguelen; even then she had been jealous of Sindi's proud body, the more so because Sindi had enjoyed such prosperity in haughty Antarctique.

'Ahh!' Sindi groaned, her pounded buttocks squirming, as she was buggered. 'Oh, please, no!'

Yet Sindi's quim was juicing, and as each boy's penis penetrated her rectum she was frigging her clito.

Meanwhile, hot sperm splattered her writhing body and the buttocks of her buggering boy, for, following the example of their host, who had doffed his pubic hair skirtlet and was as naked as any slave, each of the lords had his cloak open and his penis bared and was allowing a girlslave to masturbate him over the enculed girl's writhing bare flesh.

The schoolmistress approved Sindi's distress. She was adept at devising thoughtful punishments for her charges. One of her favourites was a 'lard-caning', in which a cylinder of solid boar lard was inserted into the anus of a boyslave – or, for a girl, two cylinders, one in anus and one in quim – and the miscreant, wriggling frantically to melt the fat, was caned an indefinite number of cuts until the lard had trickled away. Sometimes this took a caning beyond fifteen strokes.

She used this punishment with particular relish when a group of girls were discovered with illicit stockings smuggled from Zanzibar. The girls would have stocking parties, rolling the silky hose over their legs, swapping the stockings as they became progressively soiled and smelly, and smoking smuggled cigars as they did so. There were often boys with them, for it seemed boys loved to ogle the girls as they paraded in their stockings, and some boys liked to wear stockings too, especially those well perfumed with a girl's sweat and bodily essences. However, it was impossible to get information as to the provenance of the stockings, save that they were bought from some unknown, a criminal type, in the market. It was rumoured that a black girl named Gunn, an escaped slave, ran the importation of smuggled stockings and cigars from a remote jungle lair, and that she controlled an army of slaves and was probably in league with Monsieur de Warebb, as well as Prince Loro.

While the schoolmistress loved caning boys, watching their organs stiffen even as they writhed in agony under her lash on the naked buttocks, her most piquant pleasure was making them confess under lash that they *wanted* to be whipped by a cruel mistress. Not by a slavemaster or whipman, for that was shaming and disgusting, but by a beautiful girl.

'Yes, please whip me, mistress!' they would groan, as their flogged bare fesses glowed and squirmed, and it was music to the schoolmistress's ears. 'Oh, how it hurts! Oh, yes!'

She had learned that boys liked, and needed, to be whipped by a beautiful girl. And the schoolmistress *was* beautiful. She knew that, and reminded herself of it as she masturbated every day, often several times, gazing at herself in the looking-glass and caressing every part of her nude shaven body. Shaven, that is, apart from her long blonde tresses, which cascaded over her ripe breasts and caressed the big pink domes of her nipples. And nude but for the silk stockings which, with the apparatus of suspenders, were often her only raiment. She was a slave, of course, but one of the few permitted to wear white silk stockings, with a frilly suspender belt and garter straps. This gave her immense power. Sometimes she would cast off her gown and, in white stockings and black rubber knee-boots, parade through the labyrinth of the Rubber-lord's palace, carrying only her cane, pressed to her nipples.

Another source of power was her competence in the art of photography, which scared the Rubberlord and even Monsieur Loleelo, although he was keen to learn its secrets. She had a simple device called a box camera, and would procure silver halide film by ship from a former owner of hers, Mr Patel the slave-dealer in Madras, who had a small circle of photographer clients; or else she would make her own albumen paper or glass plates, coating them with the whites of ducks' eggs and sea salt. She had her own darkened room where she would develop the photographs she took and make them into prints, on glossy Turkish paper that she got from another former owner, Mr Erevan the slave-dealer, in the walled city of Antioch.

A few hundred leagues north of Antioch, at the great rocky desert formerly called the Black Sea, the known world ended, and there was only an unending expanse of blackened rubble and fused magma, still glowing and sparking after all the centuries since the great destruction, and stretching to the edge of the universe. The schoolmistress knew these things from her books, as well as from popular wisdom imparted by Mr Erevan. He, like Mr Patel, had owned her briefly before she was sold to the Rubberlord at the auction of used girls on the slave island of Socotra. She had learned much from those two gentlemen.

Her photographs were of naked slaves, sometimes whipped, sometimes copulating. When she delivered a caning, she always made her victims wait, whimpering in agony, while she photographed their scarred bare bottoms. She would make them masturbate and photographed them – while masturbating herself. She would not reveal the secrets of her picture-making process, and that was how she maintained her power. If you owned an image of a person, especially a person shamed and naked, then that person was in your thrall.

One of her devices was to sit a girlslave on a looking-glass and photograph a double image of her body and her open sex. She sent the photographic prints by trade-ship to Mr Patel, who in return sent her more silver halide film, and himself made a profit by selling the explicit images to wealthy collectors. Images of her own nude body featured in her 'private collection' and were sold for many dinars. In those images she fellated boyslaves, or had two organs plunged into her quim and anus, while she sucked a third; masturbated herself with a cucumber or even a mango; captured herself pissing on a slave's face, or a succession of boyslaves pissing all over her own naked body. There was nothing the schoolmistress would

82

not do. She supposed that the wealthy collectors masturbated, looking at the images of her, either in power or degradation – which was just another form of power – and this gratified her.

Her name was Nathalie d'Ortolan and she had been captured by Socotran pirate slavers from her temperate home island of Kerguelen, in the southern ocean, where she lived in the finest house in Port-Raymond. She was twenty years old, and her fate was not much different from that of Sindi. It was the destiny of beautiful blonde French girls to be kidnapped by slavers. One had to make the best of it. It was when she was paraded in the slave market of Socotra that she first became introduced to the beauty of stockings – the girlslaves at auction were exhibited nude, save for the most elegant gossamer stockings.

She loved the feel of the delicate fabric as it slid on to her bare thighs, and as she pulled the tops up, almost reaching her already juicing quim lips, she thought it was not such a bad thing to be a slave. She loved to waggle her naked breasts at the buyers, loved to let her bare bottom sway for their lustful eyes. If only a girl could find the right master! In the Rubberlord Nathalie thought she had indeed found him. She was owned, but she had the power of the whip. And she had stockings to wear . . .

By the time of her nineteenth birthday, Nathalie had made love with almost every boy on the island of Kerguelen. Some of them had possessed Sindi, too, of course. She had seduced and made love with most of the girls, too. Nathalie liked being taken in the quim, and also the anus – how she loved to writhe in pain as she was buggered, awaiting the hot spurt at her colon – and she loved to fellate a stiff penis and swallow the gluey sweet sperm. She also loved to be naked with a girl and lick her sex while she writhed in the onset of orgasm. *Elle avait du chien*, as the boys said – a hot bitch.

If a boy was man enough, she would order him to spank her bare buttocks, and if he was even more of a man, she would spank his. The bare-bottom spankings were serious, extending to two or three hundred smacks. In a double-spank session, with both croups glowing hot as fire, the love-making was ecstatic. Sometimes, she thought her enslavement was punishment for this lustful behaviour. Yet she was wise, had achieved a diploma at the renowned Collège de Kerguelen and knew several languages, including English and various Austronesian dialects, and much ancient booklore describing the destruction of the northern world and the survival of Southern Earth, properly known as Gondwanaland. This made the Madagascar priests jealous of her.

Her last boyfriend had been Gaston, a krill fisherman. He would take her out on his boat in the southern ocean and, after work, make her suck his penis, or else encule her. He made her dive naked into the ocean and scoop up armfuls of the krill which swam near the surface. These tiny crustaceans, small as a grape seed, were thrust living into Nathalie's quim, producing an agreeable tickling sensation, and Gaston and his crew would suck them, sauced with her come, from her pouch filled with stinging Indian pepper sauce. Likewise, they sucked oysters from her crammed anus.

Nathalie grew to like this sport, act of consumption or act of worship; she was *mademoiselle la casserole*. She devised ingenious concoctions of salad, fruit or fish, which the men could suck from her holes, and as each male took his fill she replenished herself, laughing mischievously. When their meal was finished, she would crouch, presenting her food-slimed buttocks like a dog, and Gaston and several of his crew members would enter her in the places where they had just eaten. Nathalie usually gave them an excuse to spank her bare, or even whip her with a fishing-rod. She enjoyed being flogged on the bare, liked the sting and the glow of the cane, just as she liked flogging males on the bare. *Peu importe* who squirmed in pain, as long as there *was* pain. The males seemed not to like it so much, and their wriggling was unfeigned; that gave Nathalie another glow, as she frigged her clito, watching their bare bottoms writhe in distress.

When Mathieu, one of Gaston's deckhands, had committed some trifling offence of negligence, Nathalie suggested that the others hold him down while she gave him a whipping. The boy's complaints ceased when he saw Nathalie strip off her clothing and prepare to whip him in the nude. She said it was a custom, from the priestesses of olden times, that a punisher must be as shamed as her victim. Mathieu had previously spermed in her rectum, of course, and eaten from her stuffed quim. It seemed only right that Nathalie should have a modest revenge. Her sex moistened as she saw the boy become erect while she swished her fishing-rod in the air. Then – vap! Her naked breasts bounced and her quim lips dripped come, as she laid a lash across the helpless boy's bare fesses with all her might.

'Ahh!' he shrieked.

His buttocks clenched, as a crimson stripe darkened them. Vap!

'Ahh! Oh! Oh! Please, don't!'

'Silence, you stupid whale!' she snarled. 'Or it will be worse for you. You want two dozen strokes, instead of one?'

Vap! Gaston and his crew laughed as they held the boy down for his flogging. His buttocks jerked and writhed as Nathalie's cane lashed him. The fishing-rod was very heavy and very whippy – the vap! vap! sang into the sky – and Nathalie's sex juiced copiously as she saw what pain she was inflicting. She stroked her clito between every stroke, and by the end of the boy's whipping she had brought herself to a sumptuous, gasping orgasm. That was when she decided to become a schoolmistress.

Her role as whipper on board Gaston's ship grew in importance, and she learned that boys actually relished being punished by a girl, especially a naked girl, though they would resent punishment by another male. They did not mind being stripped for a whipping on the bare by a girl; indeed, they wanted to be. But that role ended when pirates invaded Gaston's ship, stole his cargo of krill and took her and a number of others as slaves.

When the pirates found she was no virgin, they knew she was damaged merchandise, but she was still strong and beautiful. So, after rapidly selling the krill, they took turns to penetrate her every day on the long sea crossing from the southern ocean to Socotra. If she made a fuss, she was strung naked and whipped. In the slave auction she was presented as a pleasure slave, not a virgin slave; however, there were plenty of men, and some rich widowed ladies too, who liked that. They wanted girls who knew how to perform. And Nathalie performed.

She took boyslaves in her quim, in her anus, in her mouth, and the noblemen of Socotra applauded, while their penises were sucked by black girlslaves and the noble ladies masturbated discreetly under their short skirts, which rapidly became stained with come. Mr Patel bought her and shipped her to Madras. He had several wives and did not wish to enter her but to photograph her as she sucked the quims of his young brides while he masturbated. Thus it was that Nathalie learned the art of photography. Mr Patel was friendly with Mr Erevan from Antioch, who visited, selling glossy photographic paper, and eventually he sold Nathalie to him.

Although he was fond of masturbating over her nude body, Mr Erevan *did* like to encule Nathalie, very hard, and she learned more of the secrets of photography from him, especially how to construct a box camera. By now there were photographs of Nathalie everywhere around the Indian Ocean: Nathalie penetrated, caned or masturbating, with her thighs apart and her pink slit gleaming under her tapping fingers; Nathalie with Mr Erevan's penis deep in her throat, as she sucked him to orgasm.

The Rubberlord acquired several of these photographs and communicated with Mr Erevan. At the next slave auction in Socotra, Nathalie was the one he wanted.

'Ohh . . . Ohh . . .,' Sindi groaned.

Her multiple buggery was almost complete. She was aware of being photographed, and her buttocks rose and squirmed a little more than her painful enculement would demand. Her heart raced, both at the thrill of being penetrated by boyslaves with huge penises, and at the excitement of exhibiting herself for this mysterious thing, the camera. Men would see the pictures of her degradation, and might even be driven to masturbate, desiring her, although their desire would be impossible to achieve. It was unbearably exciting. As the last boy, a Mauritian boyslave with an outsize penis, spermed at her colon, she frigged herself to a shuddering orgasm. Nathalie's box camera clicked its last shot as Sindi's buttocks writhed.

'*Très bien!*' Nathalie cried.

'Oh!' Sindi gasped. 'Oh, I liked that.'

'Liked being enculed, or photographed in the nude?'

'Both, *maîtresse.*'

10

Sexe Nu

Slaves had their rewards, as well as their torments. At Sindi's next exhibitionist session – she chided herself for looking forward to it – the otherwise nude Nathalie, with a cigar dangling from her lips, unbuckled her silk stockings, unrolled them from her legs and handed them to Sindi.

'Put these on, girlslave,' she commanded.

Sindi was eager to obey. The stockings were smelly with Nathalie's pungent fragrance, but Sindi's quim moistened as she rolled the hose up her legs. It was so thrilling to be wearing stockings, just like a noble lady. The hot sun beamed fiercely through the big open windows of the photographic studio, casting a vivid chiaroscuro of light and shadow. Nathalie casually removed her frilly garter belt and straps and ordered Sindi to don them, in order to hold the stockings firmly in place. She was not to have panties, of course, but to remain *sexe nu*: that was the whole point of the photographic session.

Nathalie herself, divested of stockings, put on a pair of skin-tight lizardskin boots with sharp tin toecaps. They reached almost to her naked sex lips, so that they looked almost like stockings. The boots had high spiked heels, carved from crocodile ribs. Nathalie thrust a heel into Sindi's navel and ground her skin for a few moments, laughing at her groans and the moisture that seeped into her eyes. Then she thrust a toecap fully into her pouch and rammed her for several seconds, while Sindi moaned and writhed. Nathalie had conceived a deep loathing for this girl who, she feared, was the more beautiful, but her loathing was coupled to a powerful attraction, a desire to dominate and possess that gorgeous pale body.

'Now you are going to perform,' she said. 'Monsieur Loleelo will be here at any time with Fafni . . .'

The door burst open and Monsieur Loleelo led in the girlslave by a thin chain attached to a new piercing of her quim lips. Chewing on a raw dormouse, Pan followed him, herself followed by the other vampire girlslaves. Fafni grimaced as her master's chain wrenched the lips hard, and Pan laughed. With a pink silk ribbon tied round the boy's balls, she led in the Mauritian slave who had buggered Sindi so cruelly with his massive penis. Sindi's quim flowed with juice at the sight of his enormous brown tool, trembling half stiff in that pendulous, promising state so exciting to a girl. Nathalie's fingers crept to her quim lips and she began a discreet rubbing of her clito. Her power as photographer, like her power as caner, never failed to make her sex moisten. Sindi obeyed Nathalie's instruction to crouch like a dog and spread her naked buttocks.

Fafni looked with envy at the stockings. She was handed a cane and ordered to whip Sindi's bare bottom, with the strokes spaced every ten seconds, holding the cane in place so that Nathalie could make a photograph. Jealous of the beauty of Sindi's stockinged legs, Fafni was more than ready to obey. Vip! The cane bit Sindi's bare bottom and she groaned as the fesses clenched. Vip! The camera clicked, as each new crimson stripe appeared on her flesh. Vip!

'Ahh . . .' she groaned, her bottom squirming.

Come trickled from her quim lips, moistening her stocking tops; her nipples were stiff. Vip!

'Oh!'

Fafni aimed the cane between her thighs, striking her quim flaps. Vip!

'*Ahh!*' Sindi screamed.

Monsieur Loleelo lit a Congolese cigar and smoked, smiling, as he watched Sindi's flagellation.

'It is said that in times past there were moving pictures,' he purred. 'A thing called the *ciné*, and a box people had in their homes, called a *téléviseur*. That is what the priests say, but of course it is probably just priest-talk. Would it not be wonderful, though, to watch Sindi's flogging again and again, at leisure?'

Vip!

'Oh! Oh! Stop!' she sobbed, yet her quim still juiced as her flogged fesses writhed under Fafni's cane.

The Rubberlord entered, wearing one of his skirts of girl's pubic hair, and proceedings stopped while all crouched in obeisance. Smiling at Sindi's quivering bare nates, he nodded and ordered the caning to continue to fifteen. Fafni, panting, lashed her friend as instructed, whereupon both girls were handed beakers of chilled cucumber juice to refresh them. However, Sindi's photographic ordeal was not over. On Monsieur Loleelo's instructions, a boyslave brought in a dish of sawtooth and snipe eels, which he stuffed into Sindi's quim, and then Fafni was ordered to eat the live eels from her friend's pouch.

Sindi moaned as the eels squirmed inside her, but Fafni, glad of the food, quickly consumed them. Then a load of tiny live hermit crabs was stuffed into her quim and, groaning at the almost unbearable tickling of the tiny crustaceans, she spread her thighs for the Rubberlord to eat his fill. The Rubberlord was pleased to be photographed at this treat, especially as Pan was sucking his penis, and he soon spermed into her mouth, the vampire swallowing his copious ejaculate. After that, Sindi lay back and parted her legs, thighs tilted back to her ears, for the Mauritian boyslave to take her anally. The Mauritian boy's penis, quite the biggest among the crew of slaves, and the object of Sindi's desire, was rock-hard, and he moistened his glans with her come before piercing her anal bud. She groaned as he straddled and enculed her.

'Masturbate!' Nathalie ordered, herself masturbating vigorously. 'Frig your clito, slave!'

As the boy enculed her, Sindi obeyed and brought herself to orgasm, even before she felt the spurt of his hot cream at her colon. It was so copious that it bubbled over her anal lips and slid down her thighs into the stockings.

'You've wetted my stockings!' Nathalie hissed. There'll be hell to pay for that. But first, you must masturbate with this salt cellar. Both you and Fafni. The ancients knew how to design things well.'

'It is very old and very valuable,' said Monsieur Loleelo, whose penis was being sucked by a small, svelte girlslave.

He gave Sindi a gilded dish, where a naked god and goddess – sun and moon, it seemed – faced each other with legs apart, he erect, she obviously moist. The bodies of both god and goddess resembled outsize male sex organs; between them, two domelike salt pots suggested male balls.

'It is called a Cellini,' he added. 'Only a few were made, it seems. It is from the Rubberlord's collection. One of the mysterious prizes from the world before Time.'

Obediently, Sindi inserted the head of the golden god inside her pouch and began to rub her stiff clito. The god's head was made to fill a girl's pouch perfectly but because of its size, painfully. As Sindi masturbated and the girlslave fellated him, Monsieur Loleelo licked salt from the tiny chambers between the god and goddess. With a gesture, he ordered Fafni to take the goddess into her sex.

The girls obeyed, Nathalie, masturbating her stiff pink clito quite openly, clicked her camera as the girls writhed on the two ends of the salt cellar and Monsieur Loleelo licked his salt from the metal space between their juicing quims. *Sel d'Antarctique* was a special delicacy in Madagascar. He accompanied it with fingerfuls of snipe eels. When he had finished his saltlick, he withdrew his erect penis from his girlslave's mouth and sucked the bulbous nipples of his fellatrix, while she masturbated with a banana doused in raw powdered ginger. Pan sat in the Rubberlord's lap, her back to him, and his stiff penis impaled her anus.

Monsieur Haroon entered, bearing a pair of white wormsilk stockings – the tiny windmills adorning his conic fur cap whirling in agitation – and the Mauritian boy paled.

'We found *these* under the palliasse of this Mauritian,' blurted Monsieur Haroon. 'Illicit for any slave, and besides' – his brow wore an accountant's frown – 'no excise duty has been paid.'

'Smuggled stockings,' hissed the Rubberlord. 'Where did you get them, boy?'

He babbled that he had bought them from a freed slave, a black girl, very tall and muscular, who travelled widely and, from those without money or spices to barter, exacted a price of sperm for the stockings she sold. A slave had no money, so had to penetrate her quim to obtain the coveted, though illicit, product.

'A freed slave?' snorted Monsieur Loleelo. 'There is no such thing. An escaped slave, more like. I think the boy is in league with the renegade Gunn!'

'Well, we can whip the truth out of him, sire,' murmured Nathalie.

With languid fingers Nathalie felt his bare and pronounced it ripe for flogging, so the Rubberlord ordered the boy strung, as a subject under whip for Nathalie's camera. The schoolmistress licked her lips.

'No!' Sindi cried. 'Please, my lord, don't mark him. He is so beautiful.'

The Rubberlord glowered.

'What's this? Love among slaves?' he drawled. 'That will never do.'

He sniffed perfume from his *vinaigrette*.

'*I'll* take his punishment, my lord. Just please don't scar those lovely buttocks,' Sindi pleaded. 'I admit it ... they were *my* stockings.'

'You are a liar, like all slaves,' he snapped. 'You'll both take punishment! Monsieur Loleelo! Have your girlslaves string them both, then whip them soundly.'

Sindi grimaced as Pan and her girls seized her, bound her wrists and ankles with rubber cords, and hoisted her to dangle helplessly from the gibbet. The Mauritian boyslave beside her suffered the same treatment. Sindi's quim could not help moistening as she looked at his massive penis, again tantalisingly half-erect. She shuddered as she saw Pan lift a nine-tongued rubber quirt, then screamed, as – vap! – the thongs lashed her buttocks. Yet there was something thrilling about being whipped in stockings. She wriggled helplessly in her bonds as the strokes fell, while beside her the Mauritian writhed under a similar quirt wielded by Fafni. He groaned in agony, yet his penis still trembled, semi-stiff.

As the floggings continued, Nathalie, masturbating openly, continued to photograph the wealed bare bodies wriggling on the gibbet. Weeping, the boyslave protested that he did not know the identity of the ebony girl whom he had tupped in exchange for the pair of stockings. He had met her in the brush and she had seduced him with both the stockings and her body. The boy sobbed as his flogged buttocks squirmed. After both he and Sindi had taken twenty lashes, the Rubberlord called a halt, saying that he accepted the boy's story. He was just an ignorant slave, after all – the culprit was the mysterious Gunn, the stocking-smuggler. He ordered the flogged slaves cut down, and then noticed that Nathalie was rubbing herself to a noisy climax. The Rubberlord frowned.

'I did not give you permission to frig, schoolmistress!' he snarled. 'You forget that you, too, are only a slave. Seize her.'

In an instant Fafni had Nathalie pinioned, while Sindi unrolled her stockings and wadded them in the girl's mouth, muffling her squeals of protest. Pan sat on Nathalie's back, herself frigging – although the Rubberlord did not seem to mind *that* – while Sindi seized Nathalie's cane and began to lash her bare buttocks. Nathalie squirmed and wept until, after fifteen hard cuts of the cane, the Rubberlord indicated that she should be released. Nathalie d'Ortolan rose, flushed, weeping and livid with anger, and unravelled the stocking gag from her mouth. Her caning had reminded her that she was indeed merely a girlslave. She gazed at Sindi, her eyes burning with hatred, and snatched her cane back. The symbol of her authority, it was still hot from her own buttocks.

The Rubberlord ordered her to crouch and lick Sindi's quim to orgasm. His own penis was between the fingers of the elfin girl, who was skilfully rubbing him to new erection, as he tweaked the big thimble-sized nipples of her pert breasts. Face contorted in pain and rage, Nathalie obeyed, kneeling before Sindi, who parted her thighs and cradled Nathalie's blonde tresses as the schoolmistress tongued her clito, swallowed her copious juice and brought her rapidly to a belly-fluttering climax. The Rubberlord spurted his sperm into the elfin girl's palm just as Sindi gasped in orgasm.

'My lord,' Nathalie said, rising and curtsying painfully, 'thank you for my punishment. But I have enough photographs of this blonde slut. I fear she is incorrigible. May I suggest you send her on tomorrow's girlhunt?'

'What do you think, Monsieur Loleelo?' drawled the Rubberlord.

'I think she would make excellent prey,' purred Monsieur Loleelo, whose penis was now dallying between Pan's squeezing thighs.

'Keep her in chains until tomorrow, then,' said the Rubberlord.

He looked at Fafni, who blushed, for she had been discreetly masturbating as she watched the spectacle, but could not hide the tell-tale trickles of come on her quivering bare thighs.

'The other one as well.'

11

Rain Forest

It was so unfair. Before the start of the girlhunt, Sindi and Fafni had been given a lord's breakfast of crabs, raw beans and crayfish, heavily spiced with salt and chilli pepper, and jugs of maize beer to drink. They had wolfed this fare, so different from slave's porridge. Then, nude, they were whipped off into the brush, with a five-minute start on their pursuers: the Rubberlord, Messieurs Abatt, Haroon and Loleelo – trundling in his strange steaming wheeled vehicle – and Pan with her troop of girlslaves, all wielding nets and vicious long whips of crocodile hide.

They ran, panting and sweating, and suddenly Sindi understood what her salty, spicy breakfast had been all about. It would slow her down; she must take time to void her bowels and bladder and, more important, because she was desperate with thirst from the beer she must find waterholes and pause to drink. The pursuers would be heading for the waterholes to ambush them. A couple of times Sindi and Fafni had to hide in the scrub, squat and excrete, grimacing, as the fiery peppers passed through their bowels. In the brush, they listened to the hoots and trumpets of their pursuers and the strange growl of Monsieur Loleelo's house-on-wheels. Exhausted in the savage heat and dazed by thirst, they could scarcely contemplate what fate awaited them if caught: all they knew was that few slaves returned from a girlhunt. Sindi's parched throat burned like fire.

'We must find a waterhole,' Fafni gasped. 'I'm dying of thirst.'

'Me, too. But they'll be waiting at the waterholes,' Sindi said.

'Not all of them. It's worth the risk. If we collapse from thirst, we'll be caught and . . . what? Sold to Zanzibar, but that's if we're lucky. I hear it whispered that Prince Loro is the cruellest of all masters. If we're *unlucky* . . .'

Fafni shuddered.

'We must get to the rain forest,' she gasped. 'It's our only chance. We'll be safe there.'

'But there are monsters, giant insects, wild animals!'

'Who do you think is pursuing us, then? Do you want to be tortured in Loleelo's pain-chariot? There's water to drink in the rain forest. Oh, no, I need to go again. If I survive, I'll take no more pepper.'

They ran on through bush and scrub, but always with the trumpets of their pursuers growing nearer.

'Wait,' said Fafni. 'I've an idea. Let's double back, and retreat towards the Rubberlord's palace. They won't expect that. They'll overtake us, going the wrong way, and then maybe we can work out another roundabout route to escape to the rain forest. We could risk crossing the empty savannah.'

Sindi agreed and the girls doubled back towards the terrifying hoots and trumpet blasts of their pursuers. They climbed an enormous baobab tree and hid in its branches, with parrots and monkeys squawking and howling all around them, while beneath them passed the Rubberlord and his hunting party, braying and whooping and drinking much Maroc red wine. The trunk of the baobab was wide as four or five men, and the branches, frequently as thick as the trunks of other large trees, formed a mass of impenetrably obscure foliage. Sindi helped Fafni climb up by pushing a fist into her quim, then Fafni pulled Sindi up by her wrists and wrenched her nipples to guide her to a safe branch. Despite their plight, both girls giggled. They were safe there. But they liked each other's touch and lingered, caressing.

The Rubberlord and the other lords were carried in mahogany chairs, in front of Monsieur Loleelo's huffing steam vehicle, while the whipper slaves and net slaves went on foot. There was a waterhole not far from the baobab tree, apparently unguarded by their pursuers. In the distance shimmered the towers of the Rubberlord's castle, to which they agreed they could not return; a girlhunt was not supposed to have survivors. In the other direction stretched the savannah, devoid of brush or cover, and at its end, misted by heat haze, the gleaming green mass of the rain forest. Yet the hunting party had gone the other way, through the scrubland and bush.

Could they make a dash across the unprotected savannah? They agreed that it was worth a try. They clambered down from the baobab tree and squatted by the waterhole, drinking their fill. Fafni plucked the fruits of the baobab tree, which were called monkey bread, a little like lemons, and fashioned leaf sacs in which they could carry both the fruits and water, for their trek to the rain forest. Sindi marvelled at the forest girl's expertise at these tasks. Soon each girl was equipped with a water pouch, a sunhat made of leaves, and a bag of monkey bread. They began to walk under the pitiless sun across the dry grassland. Vultures swooped overhead in expectation of their next meal. They were approaching the rain forest when the thump of footsteps surprised them. Before them, leering with hatred, stood Nathalie, brandishing her cowhide whip, backed by Pan, carrying a cane, and two others of Pan's girlslaves.

'Caught!' Nathalie panted, her nude body dripping with sweat.

'Not yet,' said Sindi, and kicked her between her stockinged legs, right in the crotch.

Groaning, Nathalie sank to the ground, while Fafni dealt with Pan, kicking her quim, then sitting on her and pummelling her breasts. The other girlslaves took fright and fled. Sindi grasped Nathalie's whip, bent it double and began to flog the girl's buttocks, while Fafni picked up Pan's cane and began to deal the slave a vicious bare-bottom thrashing.

'Ahh!' Pan screamed. 'Enough! Monsieur Loleelo shall hear of this.'

'Then we have nothing to lose,' hissed Sindi. 'Submit, Nathalie.'

Sitting on Nathalie's back, she took the beating of the schoolmistress's unprotected bare fesses to twelve cuts before Nathalie, her face in the dirt and her bottom squirming uncontrollably under Sindi's expert lashes, sobbed that she submitted. She offered no resistance as Sindi rolled down her stockings and stripped her of her suspender belt and garter straps. Sindi gave the precious underthings to Fafni to hold before continuing her assault. Her body heavy on her victim, pinioning her to the ground, Sindi rubbed her quim against Nathalie's, while Fafni sat on Pan's face and ordered her to suck her clito while she received a spanking on her shaven vampire's quim. Pan cried as her hillock was spanked, but stuck her tongue deep into Fafni's slit.

'This will teach you,' Sindi snarled.

'No . . . no . . .,' Nathalie moaned, yet her own sex was juicing as Sindi quim-frigged her. She pinched Nathalie's nipples hard, as she bounced her loins on hers, and Nathalie sobbed and cried, but was helpless to prevent the finger-torment of her nipples. Sindi's clito rubbed Nathalie's until both gasped in orgasm, just as Fafni shuddered under her climax, induced by Pan's captive but eager tongue.

'Now you've learnt your lesson,' said Sindi.

At whip-point she ordered their two would-be captors, now sobbing and crying, to run away. She and Fafni laughed as the two weeping huntgirls obeyed, their buttocks and breasts bobbing as they raced across the savannah. Before she fled, Nathalie sobbed, with a leer of defiance, that Sindi could never escape her slavery, for her photographic images would be in every port in the Indian Ocean.

The sun was going down as the two sweating girls approached the shimmering outskirts of the rain forest. Their water and monkey bread were long exhausted. They entered the dark canopy of tree branches and were suddenly in a different, cool world. Lemurs swung from branches, frogs croaked, parrots and monkeys squawked. Leafcutter ants scurried with their strange arboreal food. There were Venus flytraps, bladderwort and pitcher plants, trapping and eating any of the hordes of buzzing insects. The floor was of soft moss, mushrooms, lichen and orchids, on which their bare feet squelched. Above them soared coconut palms and a myriad other trees. Sindi said she was thirsty, but saw no rivers; Fafni replied that they could suck water from the moss or, better, drink the juice from a coconut. There were huge puffball mushrooms to eat, and the trees were coated in giant sulphur fungus, which was also edible. Figs, the fruit of the banyan tree, bananas, wild ginger . . . the rain forest was rich in food.

'Climb one of those trees?'

'Not necessary. We wait for a coconut crab.'

Sure enough, in a few minutes a giant coconut crab scaled a palm tree and descended, clutching the coconut it had clawed from its branch. Fafni effectively despatched the creature with a tree branch and took the coconut, which she cracked open to reveal it brimming with water. The girls drank thirstily. The operation was repeated four times, and then they sat down to a banquet of raw crab, mushrooms, ginger, bananas and figs. Fafni said they should proceed through the rain forest, for the

Rubberlord's party would soon be looking for them, and come out on the other side, by the port of Warebb. There they could sell themselves once more as slaves, and with luck take ship for India, Turkey or Yemen – or even Socotra.

'Why enslave ourselves?' Sindi asked, her lips dribbling with crab juice.

Fafni shrugged.

'It is for a girl to be slave of a master. We are nude. They will know we are slaves, and probably guess we are escaped slaves.'

'We do not have to be nude. Look at the leaves of these giant orchids. We can make skirts and tunics. And we have a lord's whip, a cane and a pair of stockings. One of us can be a slave, the other a mistress.'

Fafni clapped her hands in delight, then blushed.

'I shall be your slave, then . . . mistress.'

The two girls set to fashioning dresses for themselves. Once they were clad in rustling skirts of orchid leaves, they set off through the rain forest towards the port of Warebb. Sindi carried the whip, the cane and the stockings and suspenders, carefully parcelled in a mauve orchid leaf that was knotted by a liana to her waist. It was Fafni's job to obtain food and water.

Thus they walked through the rain forest for four days. They discussed their new plans, when they got to Warebb. Sindi could don her stockings and pretend to be a great lady and get credit for a passage to Réunion or Mauritius, where they would be free. Or she could simply sell Nathalie's stockings for a good price and buy their passage.

'We could keep the stockings,' Fafni replied, 'and sell ourselves.'

'But if we sell ourselves as slaves, we certainly cannot keep the stockings!'

'No, no, sell our bodies to lustful men. I mean, our holes. The lords in Warebb will pay many dinars to poke an aristocratic lady with her stockings on. Perhaps even Monsieur de Warebb himself. In the temple of Warebb, an ancient building called the Hôtel de Ville, there are sacred prostitutes of the cult of the sun. They make good money.'

'Good money!' cried a girl's voice. 'I like the sound of that.'

They looked up in astonishment and saw a statuesque nude black girl – nude, that is, but for a pair of shiny white stockings – swinging from a branch of a banyan fig tree. Instinctively they backed away but tripped over a liana strung across their path. They both screamed as a net scooped them up and held them imprisoned, dangling beneath the banyan tree. The girl whooped, dived down from her branch and seized Sindi's whip, cane and silk stockings, which she sniffed with a gleam in her eye and a widening of her nostrils.

'Most ripe,' she said. 'I'll have these.'

She stripped her prisoners of their orchid dresses – pronouncing them very tasteful – then took her whip and delivered three or four cracking strokes to the writhing bottoms of the netted girls. Vap! The cuts echoed wetly in the chirruping rain forest. She lifted the cane and lashed both girls three strong cuts across their nipples.

'Ahh!' Fafni screamed.

'Oh! Oh! Don't!' Sindi shrieked, as her fesses and breasts smarted.

'Just to teach you not to make trouble, or there is more where that came from. You are my slaves now.'

'Who . . . who are you?' sobbed Sindi.

'People call me Gunn,' said the naked ebony girl, her perfect white teeth exposed in a leer of supremacy. 'I live here. It is my domain. I am the queen of the mountains and queen of the forest. And queen of the stockings.'

12

Gunn

'Come this way, slaves.'

The nude black girl was so powerfully muscled that neither Sindi nor Fafni dared to think of disobedience; in truth, both girls were fascinated by the lithe, magnificent beauty of her body, rippling with muscle, the gleaming black breasts upthrust and the buttocks full and ripe, over long, powerful legs. They were agog to see what this new adventure would bring them. Gunn's head was cropped to a mass of tiny lustrous curls, but not a hair disfigured her smooth dark body. Her shorn pubic hillock swelled like a shiny eggplant, with pink slit flesh glistening between her ebony quim lips.

She led them through the whispering, chirping and cawing shadows of the rain forest, dark under its closed canopy of treetops, dripping moisture. Snakes slithered under their feet, which made Sindi jump, but Gunn said the snakes of Madagascar were not poisonous. Eventually they came to a huge clearing in the jungle, full of wooden huts, by the bank of a river, with numerous boats moored to the jetty by ropes. Their arrival attracted brief glances but little curiosity; Gunn's capture of new slaves was obviously a normal daily event. Towering above the huts was a mansion of wood, gaudy with crenellations – Gunn's palace, guarded by bare-breasted girls in uniform of black stockings and boots and skirts and armed with whips, with which they drove naked girlslaves and boyslaves to perform various tasks: unloading parcels of stockings and tobacco and spices from the boats, or climbing the trees to pick fruits and catch lemurs and monkeys.

The compound was a hive of activity – literally, for at the far end was an apiary, where girlslaves collected honey from beehives. The bees fed on borage leaves, which the slaves were allowed to nibble. There were piles of coconuts, fruit and vegetables, tallied by guards who wrote on wooden boards. A row of girlslaves squatted, masturbating their come into silver or bronze *vinaigrettes*, while they idly watched the bare-caning of a boy and a girl, strapped side by side on a flogging-frame. Their plight did not seem to attract much attention. Their svelte bare bodies wriggled as the canes lashed their squirming nates, and Gunn explained that they had been caught copulating without permission.

'The only time slaves may copulate is when I want a show,' she drawled. 'That is why I keep my plantation of those rattan palms over there.'

She licked her lips.

'They are an excellent source of cane, for making baskets and chairs and things, and for making very painful disciplinary canes, although some prefer the baobab twigs. You will be able to judge for yourselves, soon.'

Elsewhere in the compound, a variety of curious and cruel punishments were exacted by the girl-guards on the bodies of slaves who had evidently displeased. The least of these was the wearing of curious tin panties, tight and cruelly chafing, while the slaves did their work. Then there were strange wooden devices which Gunn said were called the stocks and the pillory; she had copied them from an ancient book she had stolen, or 'nibbled' as she put it. As Sindi was to learn, stealing, which was Gunn's way of life, was called 'nibbling'.

The stocks were a row of wooden clamps in which the victims' ankles were fastened so that they were helpless to avoid the whips of the guards. The pillory was even worse, for there the victim had to stand upright, with shoulders clamped and the entire body open to the lash, which the guards did not spare. In addition, their fellow-slaves would throw rotten eggs, fish and tomatoes at their imprisoned faces, which was thought great sport.

But there was worse. A girlslave groaned, weeping, as her body was agonisingly stretched face-down in the rack and her buttocks whipped. Several girlslaves shuffled around the compound hobbled in bilboes, which made their progress difficult and painful. Those were slaves who had been suspected of trying to escape. After a savage flogging at the pillory, of which their bare bodies bore the marks, as a warning to the rest, they had to wear bilboes at Gunn's pleasure. Many had rings clamped to their nipples and quim lips, and from these rings were suspended heavy rocks, which stretched the breasts and quim lips to a grotesque fullness.

Boyslaves were tethered by tight lianas around their balls, then bound to a tree with their hands tied around the trunk and flogged on their bare buttocks to ten or more strokes by the girl-guards, who seemed to take particular pleasure in flogging boys, especially when their tools stiffened in the excitement of being beaten by a girl. The groans of the slaves mingled with the chirping birdsong, yet the work of the compound continued cheerfully, as though the punishment of slaves was part of the daily round, as Sindi discovered it was. Even Fafni seemed not overly distressed.

A number of weeping girls, selected for flogging, were suspended upside down from the tree branches by the simple device of a cord knotted around their waists, with a further cord binding their ankles and wrists together. Their humiliating posture exposed their buttocks to the eager canes of the guards, which could scarcely have been more painful than the agony of the cord girdling the waist. A girl groaned, suspended on tiptoe by two clamps fastened to her nipples, her long dark hair tied to a tree branch beside her wrists. Gunn seized a stick and gave her five brisk lashes on the bare, ordering her to stop moaning. Her flogged bottom danced madly in her pain, and she did not stop moaning. Gunn laughed and threw the stick away.

'The rod is the only language slaves understand,' she mused.

Those unfettered and unpunished were simply glad to remain so. Slaves emptied buckets of crayfish into barrels, where they fermented, while other slaves pressed down on the lids to squeeze out a foul-smelling sauce, which was then potted or stored in *vinaigrettes*. Others pounded yam, to make slimy balls of maize fufu, to be eaten with the crayfish sauce or the fermented soya beans Gunn called *tempeh*, from another barrel.

Slaves beheaded, skinned and chopped mice, hedgehogs and snakes, roasted snails over a fire or grilled tiny elvers. They coated locusts and beetles in honey and roasted them too. Peanuts were crushed and roasted, then made into a paste. A permanent stockpot of soup simmered, bubbling with boars' snouts, fish heads, borage, sorrel, birds' skulls and other meat scraps and vegetables. Beside it stood a pot of maize porridge.

Lemurs scampered through trees, occasionally making a brief raid on the foodstuffs. From time to time, a slave who had performed good duty was rewarded with a platter of stew, or the leg of a giant crab. They cleaned their platters, bones and everything, boar feet and crab shells being crunched by eager teeth. Some of the girlslaves had pale white vampire bodies, very thin, with yellow eyes and purple lips, and ate raw whole mice, licking up the tiny trickles of blood.

Sindi was astonished at so much industry and satiety amid such cruel discipline, and even more that Gunn could climb trees and prowl the rain forest without damaging her pristine stockings. She watched a boyslave whipped on the bare with a cruel rod, while a girlslave crouched to suck his stiff penis and swallow his sperm. In the sunlight his buttocks glistened brown and moist with sweat, well striped by the rod. His fesses squirm prettily, Sindi thought, as he gasped in his climax, his penis plunged in the girl's throat right up to his balls. She moistened at the spectacle. Gunn's boyslaves all seemed to be chosen for their abnormally large penises.

'We eat everything here,' said Gunn, with a friendly – or suggestive – smile. 'Now, I wonder, what duties shall you perform?'

A bare-breasted coffee-hued guard, who had just finished caning the two weeping slaves, approached Gunn and bowed deeply to her. She carried a platter of roasted snails and a dish of stinking fermented fish sauce. Gunn picked up a handful of snails, and dipped them in the sauce, cracking each one between her teeth before swallowing the sliver of meat and spitting out the shell.

'Salo is a loyal servant from Somalia,' Gunn said. 'She is very strict. I shall put you two in her squad. She will tell you where to sleep, and where to work. And she will make sure you masturbate and fill your *vinaigrettes*.'

'The boyslaves must also masturbate every day,' said Salo, 'not for their sperm, which has no commercial value, for noble ladies must have their sperm fresh, but to keep them docile. Boys like masturbating, you see – they are quite incorrigible – so it is best to encourage them to do it. They don't really like to tup girls, although they imagine they do – in truth, *ils veulent se branler*. Of course, we girls are also incorrigible frots. The boys masturbate in company with the girls and, graced with the sight of a girl's opened, juicing quim, their spunk rises at the hope that one day they might enter such a tender vessel. But in my experience boys prefer to masturbate over a girl, spill their cream over her breasts, rather than penetrate her. They like the humiliation involved, and it is less hard work for the lazy devils. My girls, however, must frig to fill their *vinaigrettes* every day, for that liquor brings much money in the markets of Warebb. You, boy!'

She tugged a boyslave by the ear and he grimaced, his penis rising a little.

'What would you most like to do in the world, apart from having the danger of freedom?'

'Oh, Mademoiselle Salo, I . . . I . . . .'

'Answer me, worm. The truth. I know you are an obedient slave, and masturbate every day.'

'Yes, mademoiselle!'

'And what do you think of, when you are tugging your worm's member?'

'I . . . I . . . .,' he stammered, blushing.

'I'll deal with this,' said Gunn crisply.

Gunn squatted, placed him over her thigh and began to spank his bottom with harsh, rapid smacks, until the boy's penis rose to full erection. The boy sobbed as his bare fesses squirmed under her palm. Her huge breasts gyrated and her belly trembled, as, smiling, she spanked the boy. Her brown nipples were hard as walnuts.

'Speak, worm,' she ordered. 'Unless you want to be strung and flogged. Your greatest desire?'

'I . . . I . . . I think of you, mistress. Of spurting my sperm over your breasts. Over your belly, the bare hillock of your quim, over your thighs, over your stockings, or your bare feet . . . oh, you are the most beautiful woman in the world.'

'I know *that*.'

'The vision of your nude body . . . I cannot help frigging myself.'

'You impudent beast. I should have you whipped.'

After sixty smacks, Gunn ceased spanking. The boy's buttocks were flamed red and his penis was rigid.

'However, for your honesty, you may have your wish,' she drawled. 'Masturbate, and spurt over my nipples.'

It took only a few strokes from his trembling palm for the slave to spurt a huge ejaculation of hot cream over Gunn's stiff plum nipples. She smiled, raised her breasts and put her nipples in her mouth, to lick up the sperm.

'You see?' said Gunn, her lips glistening with white cream, 'boys like nothing more than to masturbate.'

She paused in thought.

'Of course, they like to be spanked, too.'

Salo was tall, slender and long-legged, not as muscular as her owner, her breasts pert rather than bulging, but nonetheless wiry and strong, with a certain raffish elegance. Fafni whispered that the people of Somalia were Nilotic, the name coming from the great mysterious river, the Nile, which traversed the Afric land on their borders. The powerfully built Gunn, on the other hand, was Bantu, from somewhere else, Congo perhaps, in the deep and unknown centre of the continent; Fafni was not sure where. Salo scrutinised her new charges, her sneer revealing pearl-white teeth. Her cane flicked the nipples of both girls, who winced at the sudden pain.

'I shall have fun with you two,' murmured Salo.

'That is what slaves are for,' said Gunn.

As she departed she raised Salo's skirt and playfully slapped her bare bottom three times. Salo's bottom was a coffee colour, the buttocks firm and taut, and they clenched, perhaps with some exaggeration, at each slap, while Salo smiled.

'Thank you, mistress,' Salo said.

13

Nibbling

Gunn went nude but for stockings, as an expression of rank. Salo, the sergeant, had to wear a pretty skirt of banana leaves, fresh every day, but remain bare-legged save for her boots.

'I love being bare,' said Sindi. 'Though a sign of slavery, it is wonderful to show myself.'

'Of course,' Fafni replied. 'Being nude is freedom. It is the normal and best state. It means we can feel alive and feel ourselves and fill our come pots, which we must. We must masturbate every night.'

'That is so,' said Salo. 'If you are at last called to spend the night with Mistress Gunn, you will be required to masturbate all night long, for her pleasure – *and* open your anuses to any boyslave she likes at the time. It's quite a task for them! Sometimes, when Mistress Gunn is in a good mood, she doesn't make them sex her girls, but orders them to cream over the girl's teats, or into her mouth, or over her hillock – almost as an offering. Boyslaves who have really offended her, after their whippings, have to masturbate *each other*, or even . . . *well, you can imagine*. Mistress Gunn gets pleasure from any spectacle of degradation. But now I shall have to give you both your first whipping, so that you will understand obedience.'

Gunn, smoking a cigar and stroking her stockinged thighs, watched with a smile as Fafni and Sindi were strung together from a gibbet, and Salo took a rod to their buttocks. The two girls, suspended by their wrists and hair, were bound at waist and thigh by tight rubber cords, so that their quims and breast-bulbs were mashed together. They sobbed and screamed as the vapulation proceeded, the wooden cane frisky as Salo wielded her strong, cruel arm. Yet as their buttocks striped and reddened and their nipples and clitos frotted, the clitos stiffened in a bath of moisture and come dripped down their shivering thighs. Gunn, legs parted, fingered her own erect pink clito as she watched the torment of her strung girlslaves. She ordered two boyslaves to crouch, bottoms up, and suck her toes, while she masturbated, caning them lightly and occasionally touching their stiff penises.

'A boy's croup is never so beautiful as when it is squirming under the cane,' she drawled, puffing on her cigar.

She was adorned with a necklace and waist-chain made of bleached bones and giant sharp teeth, which Salo said were from creatures called dinosaurs, who had lived on Madagascar millions of years ago.

When Fafni and Sindi were released, weeping, from their gibbet, after ten cuts on the bare, Salo rubbed a paste of cooling ointment on their bruises, then said that they would be sent to dive for white-claw freshwater crayfish, which lived in the river. They were like sea lobsters but smaller, and their succulent claw-meat was one of Gunn's favourite foods. It was messy work, for the crayfish usually burrowed into the banks of streams or ponds and fed upon live or decaying animal or vegetable matter. Salo was the expert in this, and she stripped and led the girls underwater, where she dived to the bottom of the shallow river and showed the mudbanks where the crayfish hid.

There was an equality of slave and slavedriver when each was nude, competing to see who could hold her breath longest and gather the most crayfish from their burrows. Sindi found she could hold her breath longer than the others and gather the most prey. After their first few forays, Salo no longer accompanied them underwater but waited on the shore with a troop of boyslaves, hobbled by lianas round their balls, who held baskets to take away the river's bounty. The girls wriggled in the water like the eels which eddied around them.

One day, Gunn was pleased when Sindi brought back a pair of slippery eels, which were hard to capture. Gunn skinned them and ate them raw. She rewarded Sindi with a loaf of black bread and some onions. She had fresh lime juice to drink, and shared her food with Fafni. As Sindi squatted in the dirt and wolfed her meal, she saw a boat come in, laden with gleaming bales of white silk stockings, from Zanzibar. Her eyes widened, at the magnificence of the spectacle, for there were stockings of every hue, every size and every design; she wanted stockings more than anything.

After their first whipping, Sindi and Fafni received merely token canings on the bare from Salo if, in the darkness of the slave-shed, they had not frigged sufficiently to fill their come pots. The bottled exudations of the girlslaves' quims were taken on to boats every day by the sumptuously robed merchants, who bought bales of smuggled silk stockings. As Sindi dived for water spiders, crayfish and eels, she saw the boats pass overhead and dreamed of her freedom, although being alone underwater was itself a kind of freedom, better than being a boyslave, sweating and whipped in the dirt.

The market for fresh, virgin and counterfeit stockings from Prince Loro of Zanzibar was buoyant, and Gunn's treasury was well filled with silver dinars from this unlawful trade. Only Prince Een's factories were allowed by law to make and distribute stockings. But there was another market, and when Gunn abruptly summoned

Sindi to her bed one night, she told her about it. First, Sindi had to lie back with her thighs apart and her feet at her shoulders, with Gunn's massive buttocks crushing Sindi's face. As Gunn tongued her clito to orgasm after orgasm, Sindi did the same to her owner, chewing the heavy swollen clito, while Gunn writhed and grunted in the pleasure, or pain, of her climaxes. To Sindi's surprise, between orgasms Gunn bent over and ordered her to spank her bare bottom with her hand. A slave had to obey, and she wondered what revenge would come of it, but none did. Gunn masturbated as Sindi spanked her bare, and brought herself to climax twice before she ordered the spanking halted at about the hundredth slap.

A well-muscled boyslave was introduced, trembling with fear. Gunn lifted her cane and dealt him seven stingers on his buttocks, which made him grimace, fighting back his tears. Then she ordered Sindi to crouch and take a spanking from him, similar to the one she had just suffered from Sindi's palm. She obeyed, groaning, as the boy's heavy, vengeful hand smacked her bare bottom for several minutes. With tears in her eyes, she then had to take his erect penis in her mouth and suck it, while all the time Gunn smoked cigars and masturbated.

When Gunn judged the moment was right and the boy's penis was sufficiently swollen, she ordered Sindi to crouch and spread her buttocks. Sindi wailed as the hard penis entered her anus and plunged into her rectum to begin a vigorous enculement. Nevertheless, as her rectum adapted to the thrusts of the organ and began to squeeze the stiff tool in welcome, Sindi's fingers went to her clito to match her ravisher's thrusts with her own frig. She heard his groans as he spurted a full load of hot creamy sperm at her colon, and then at once the boy was dismissed and she was ordered to resume her position with Gunn.

The ebony mistress put her lips to Sindi's anus and began to suck, until she had swallowed the whole load of her boyslave's sperm. Then they resumed their gamahuching. At dawn, after their sweating bodies had shuddered several times in orgasm, Gunn explained that Sindi had proven herself a worthy slave and would be accompanying her on a 'nibbling' expedition to the city of Warebb that evening.

'The noble ladies of Warebb hold stocking parties,' explained Gunn with a smile, 'where they show off their new stockings and exchange them. Sometimes they combine this with swapping hats made of lizard skins or Venus fly-traps in pickle. But it is the stockings that concern us. There is such a party held tonight, my spies inform me, in the Hôtel de Ville of Monsieur de Warebb. You see, slave, there is a very profitable market in *used* stockings and panties, for wealthy collectors. They must smell of the lady who has worn them and should bear her crest, if possible. Certain merchants – Mr Patel in Madras, Mr Erevan in Antioch, amongst others – specialise in this trade. And of course the garments must be stolen from the persons of the ladies, for that is part of the fun. So tonight we go to Warebb to invade the party and steal their smelly panties and stockings. And their *vinaigrettes* too. Oh, and their nipple rings.'

'Do have some more curried snake,' drawled the lady Giselle to the lady Sylvie, their faces illumined by the lights of Warebb harbour, sparkling beneath the *grande salle* of the Hôtel de Ville. 'There is swan aplenty, heron, broiled hedgehog with salad of palm hearts, alligator pears in vinegar . . . and a special delicacy, yellow potatoes fried in oil! Yes, real potatoes from Zuid-Afrika! And the yummiest sea lettuce soup, with crab and sea cucumber!'

All the noble ladies of Warebb loved soup.

'And this is fresh Zuid-Afrika wine.'

They loved wine too. Boyslaves, uniformed in clam-shell loinstrings, bustled to replenish the plates and glasses. Like the other ladies sprawled on divans, Giselle and Sylvie were nude but for sumptuous stockings of Zanzibar silk, the colours white, peach, crimson, blue, yellow or green, and hats adorned with fruits, furs, flowers, the skins of lizards and bats, and whole stuffed hummingbirds. Each lady was accompanied by her own silver *vinaigrette*, positioned below her quim lips, exuding herbal vapours, to perfume her private parts. Large silver rings dangled from their pierced bare nipples, which boyslaves washed with living perfumed sponges. They also used the sponges to wash the ladies' quims. During this service the ladies would clasp the boys by the balls to ensure the correct performance of their task.

In a corner, one boyslave, shorn of his loinstring, was being slowly caned on his naked buttocks by another, and his moans added to the ladies' enjoyment of their meal. Another boyslave blew a merry trumpet made from the shell of the giant triton sea snail. Most of the ladies had little furry lemurs perched on their naked shoulders. They were the sacred prostitutes of the sun in the Hôtel de Ville: enslaved in the service of Monsieur de Warebb, but accorded the title of *dame noble*.

'Well, I think it's time for some stocking fun,' Giselle purred.

She began to roll down her stockings and then her panties, revealing smoothly shaven legs and a perfect tan all over her body, including her satin-smooth pubic hillock. Although her public persona required the wearing of hose, in private she sunbathed in the nude. A delicate creamy tan, distinct from the nut-brown tan of an outdoor slave, was thought becoming to a noble creole lady of Warebb, for it showed the sun smiled on her. The other bare-breasted ladies – Taupe, Nafrage, Miaou, Peean and Chenne – giggled and began to remove their own underthings for the game of silk-barter.

Boyslaves stood naked and semi-erect at the spectacle – a half erection pleased a lady's eye, as it signified the beast within the boy – but they were not permitted to touch a lady's stockings, on pain of flogging. Yet the sight of a lady's legs and cooze emerging bare from their cocoon of silk was enough to make any boy's penis stand, and the simpering ladies would have been disappointed, and perhaps angry, had it not been so. That was the point of a boyslave – to have lovely red stripes on his whipped bottom, and that organ trembling and stiffening at all times, just at the sight of his mistress.

'Let's swap,' said Nafrage.

'Yes, let's,' said Chenne.

The ladies exchanged stockings and panties, rolling them up their bare legs.

'Isn't it such fun?' said Taupe.

'The very best,' said Miaou. 'I say, yours smell pretty ripe.'

'So do yours!' cried Peean.

They all laughed as they caressed their stockinged legs. At a signal from Giselle, boyslaves brought silver dishes of shelled saddle oysters in fermented sauce of *bêche-de-mer*, the sea cucumber, sometimes with a tiny parasite pearlfish inside, and each lady parted her thighs for the filling of her pouch.

'Oh! It's hot!' cried Sylvie.

'It's supposed to be hot,' replied Giselle. 'Now get down and eat from Peean.'

Soon, under Giselle's direction, all the ladies of Warebb were sucking food from each others' quims. Giselle had Sylvie's quim filled, and then her anus, and sucked her dinner from both holes. Nafrage supplemented her meal by fellating a boyslave. She clutched his tight, heaving buttocks, and took his penis right to the back of her throat before tonguing him to a groaning orgasm and swallowing his cream. Beaming and licking her glazed lips, she advised her colleagues that sperm was good for you, better even than rock lobster, and full of nutrients.

At that moment, Gunn and her gang burst in through the window. The ladies screamed.

'I see you're nibbling,' sneered Gunn. 'Well, we've come for our bit of nibbling. I say, is that sea lettuce soup? Mm ... stockings off, ladies, panties too, and be quick about it, or you get this.'

She swished the air with her cane.

'Guards! Guards! Oh, the drunken swine are asleep,' cried Giselle. 'You bitch! You can't just – *ahh!*'

She screamed as Gunn's cane lashed her breasts, making her nipple rings jangle, then, sobbing, obeyed the bandit intruder and began to remove her stockings.

'Rings and chains, too,' ordered Gunn. 'Or it's the lash for you all.'

She crouched and sucked Peean's quimful of sea lettuce soup, wiping her lips on the sobbing girl's hair.

14

Jour de Fête

'I'll have those !' cried Gunn.

She had Giselle by the hair, pulling hard, and Giselle was shrieking, her stockinged legs wriggling high in the air like giant worms. Gunn meant that she would have her stockings. They were pale blue – in fact, Giselle had just swapped them with Peean. What Gunn wanted, she wanted. It did not take long for Sindi and Fafni to overpower the timorous boyslaves. Boys, Sindi had learned, were always vulnerable to a threatened assault on their precious balls. Or, when a girl sat on his face for a minute or two, a boy always submitted.

'Monsieur de Warebb will have you flogged for this!' screamed Sylvie, as Sindi ripped off her pink panties and stockings.

Fafni was rolling down a pair of lemon yellow stockings, suspenders and stained panties from Nafrage's legs, and giggling at how smelly they were. She chewed Nafrage's bare toes, licked her smooth-shaven thighs and, unable to resist temptation, a concept unknown to forest girls, sucked her clito until Nafrage came rapidly to orgasm and groaned in pleasure and shame. Her thighs glistened with come but Fafni licked them clean. Then Gunn bent down and began to bite her knees. The raiders easily subdued the prostitutes of the sun, then packed their booty of stockings, panties and nipple rings into a sack. They heard the thump of feet approaching and, clutching their loot, prepared to flee through the window and escape into the thronged night streets of Warebb, the same way they had come.

'Pity you didn't have time to taste that soup,' Gunn said to Sindi. 'But there's plenty of food in Zanzibar, where we are going soon to pick up a bale of special stockings.'

'Too late!' cried Sindi.

The doors burst open to admit, not the guards, drunken or otherwise, but a sumptuously jewelled man in a purple silk robe, escorted by boyslaves. His hair glistened with aromatic myrrh from Arabia and he wore a monocle in his right eye, fastened to his silver buttons by a chain. The tinkle of bells accompanied his passage, for under his headdress of dyed ostrich plumes hung little silver bells whirling on chains.

'Monsieur de Warebb!' gasped Giselle.

'It is feast day, ladies, a *Jour de Fête*, in honour of the slave stars that attend our sacred sun, and you are all invited. But what have we here? Strangers? A scrimmage?'

'Oh . . . it is nothing . . .,' stammered Sylvie. 'They are our guests. We have been testing them for the priesthood of the sun.'

None of the girls wished to admit they had been bested by the robbers, or had indulged in lustful practices with them. Monsieur de Warebb squinted at Gunn through his monocle.

'I have a suspicion I know who you are,' he drawled. 'Well, you are all invited, and during the feast, I shall ponder how these strangers may be of use to me.'

Monsieur de Warebb absenting himself, saying that he would join them shortly, boyslaves led the excited girls through teak-panelled corridors to a vast banqueting hall where they took their places, each at her own small table, forming a ring around a platform where the dishes of food were placed. Some boyslaves poured iced water over their hands, while others manicured their feet; they sang at their work. Sindi demanded wine. In a trice, a boy was there, singing as he attended to her, and soon all the diners had brimming goblets of coarse red wine from Zuid-Afrika. There was a small band of boyslaves blowing triton snail trumpets.

Hors d'oeuvres were served when everyone had taken their places, except Monsieur de Warebb, for whom the throne at the top was reserved. The dishes for the first course included a bronze boar with two baskets, cucumbers on one side and seaweeds on the other. Over the boar were two pieces of plate, with Monsieur de Warebb's name and the weight of the silver inscribed on the rims. Miniature silver frames shaped like bridges supported dormice sprinkled with sugar and poppy seed. There were steaming hot boar-and-dormouse sausages too, on a silver gridiron, with plums and pomegranates, a *vinaigrette* full of fragrant herbs and, fried in batter, a huge tureen of goby fish a fingernail long; they lived inside sponges, and Gunn whispered that it took twenty thousand to make a plateful. There were sea cucumbers and steaming hot sea lettuce soup, which the girls devoured avidly. There were oysters on a bed of ice, and piles of limes, tomatoes and mangoes, with dishes of hot sauces, pepper and fermented fish. There was a boar's head, roasted, its mouth agape and stuffed with braised hedgehog livers. A giant spider crab, its legs two arm-lengths across, was draped across the table, with silver hammers to crack its carapace. And there were jugs of spiced red Libyan wine. For a while, only the sounds of eating and drinking could be heard.

Monsieur de Warebb, freshly bathed and perfumed, was carried in to the sound of triton trumpets and set down on a pile of cushions. His head was crowned in peacock feathers; his robe was of purple silk; his neck bore a knotted napkin with a broad purple stripe and silken tassels dangling. His monocle was newly polished, his hair freshly pomaded with glistening myrrh and other perfumes, and he was wearing a girl's lemon-yellow stockings. On the little finger of his left hand he wore a heavy gilt ring and on the last joint of the next finger a smaller one. His bare right arm was adorned with silver armlets in the shapes of snakes. On his head, a gourd of scented animal fat melted slowly, so that the perfumed grease dribbled down his face. Soon all the girls were similarly coiffed.

To the sound of song and trumpet, a silver tray was brought in with a basket on it. There sat a wooden broody hen in a bed of straw, its wings spread round it. Two slaves hurried up and, as the shell trumpets played, began searching through the straw and dug out peahens' eggs, which they distributed to the guests.

'I gave orders for that bird to sit on some peahens' eggs,' said Monsieur de Warebb with a simper. 'I hope they are not starting to hatch.'

They took up their heavy silver spoons and cracked the eggs, which were in fact made of rich pastry. Sindi nearly threw away hers, as the birdlet seemed already formed, but heard Nafrage whisper: 'There should be something good here.' So she searched the shell with her fingers and found a plump little songbird, with green head and yellow throat, covered with yolk and seasoned with pepper, herbs and wine. She sucked the fragrant fat from it, crunched the tiny bones and swallowed it all in one, finding it delicious.

Monsieur de Warebb, slurping wine, told the girls to drink as much as they wanted.

'This is fun!' blurted Fafni, rubbing the scented animal fat into her breasts.

Suddenly there was a blast from the trumpets and the hors d'oeuvres were whisked away. A naked girlslave came in with a broom and began to sweep up the scraps of food, which would be used to feed her and her

121

comrades – event the scraps that the sun prostitutes had mischievously pelted her with. Two long-haired Somalian girls followed, carrying small leather bottles, and poured scented vinegar over the girls' hands to clean them.

Carefully sealed and corked Maroc wine bottles were now brought, their necks hand-labelled in a barely decipherable script: *VIN DE L'ATLAS PREMIER GRAND CRU.* While the girls were examining the labels and wondering what they meant, Monsieur de Warebb clapped his hands and said with a sigh:

'Wine has a longer life than we do, you know. Wine *is* life. I didn't put out such good glug yesterday, though the company was of a higher class than mere pleasure-sluts. I had the ambassador of Réunion to dine. My, how he could drink!'

The girls drank too, and nibbled at further dishes of deep-fried baby frogs and lizards. Sindi missed no opportunity of admiring their host's elegant hospitality. In the middle of this a slave brought in a silver human skeleton, whose bones could be pulled out and twisted in all directions. After he had flung it about on the table once or twice, its flexible joints fell into various grotesquely amusing postures. When it had disintegrated, each girl was presented with a gift of a silver rib bone, while Monsieur de Warebb placed the gleaming skull beside his own plate. He said tearfully that the skeleton was over a million years old, and it was a *memento mori*, which no one understood; of course no one disagreed, though Sindi feared what the priests of the sun might say at the heretical idea that anything could be so old.

To applause, the next course was brought in. It was not as grand as they expected, but very novel. It was a deep circular grail, with the sun, moon and nine planets arranged round the edge. Over each of them the chef had placed some appropriate tiny dainty suggested by the planetary subject; for example, there was a goose over Venus, the planet of foolish love, and the only one Sindi

122

recognised, for she was ignorant of planets, which were not supposed to exist. In the centre was a bed of dark seaweed bearing a honeycomb carved in the shape of twin buttocks, and on top another in the shape of the sun.

'Is this all?' whined Giselle.

As the girls started glumly on this meagre fare, four slaves advanced in time to the music, and removed the dome of the great dish, revealing underneath plump guinea fowl, smoked chameleons, boars' udders and a hare with wings fixed to his middle.

Four little silver figures of a monkey were arranged to let a peppery fish sauce flow over some fish which seemed to be swimming in a moat. They all clapped in delight, and helped themselves to these foodstuffs, a far cry, Sindi thought, from slave-porridge. Then came the high point: the 'Congo Pig'. It was actually a giant roast boar, gutted and stuffed with a pig, which was stuffed with chickens, which were stuffed with deep-fried frogs. The enormous dish dripped with cow-butter, garlic, turmeric and herbs, and the creatures wallowed in a pond of steaming meat juices. Monsieur de Warebb ordered the carving to begin and insisted that all the girls finished their platefuls. Sindi, accustomed to jungle fare, accomplished this easily, as did Gunn and Fafni.

At last sated, Sindi turned to Giselle, who, full of wine, seemed to have forgotten the outrages to her person, and began to pester her for gossip and information. Who was running the place, while Monsieur was feasting and playing lustful games?

'Monsieur de Warebb is shrewder than he seems,' said Giselle. 'He rules a land far greater than Prince Een's or the Rubberlord's. He's sooo rich! To get honey, he ordered bees from Zuid-Afrika. And recently he ordered mushroom spores from Mr Patel in Madras. You see these cushions? Every one of them has silk stuffing, dyed with the juice of the murex shell. No one will ever defeat him.'

123

'I suppose not,' replied Sindi, po-faced, and smiling to herself.

Most of the girls seemed quite drunk, but Sindi drank sparingly. Spanking games began, with nude boyslaves viciously chastising equally nude girlslaves, a spectacle which had her quim juicing as she watched the firm buttocks and risen tools of the boys. The other girls reacted the same, especially when rubber quirts came into play, striping the slave-buttocks of either sex most painfully. Aware of this, and pawing the new girls' intimate parts, at which Sindi winced, Monsieur de Warebb spoke.

'You girls are superb physical specimens. You have shown spunk in daring to invade my Hôtel de Ville, and for that I think I have a better use for you than as field or domestic slaves. Therefore you shall join my elite private troop of guards. The discipline is fierce, for you must first be broken as slaves, and the fighting tough – there are bandits everywhere, like yourselves, who would rob me. You, in particular, interest me, *mademoiselle*' – chucking Gunn under the chin – 'for I think you must be the infamous Gunn. There are no other black outlaws in my domain that I know of through my spies. Admit it!'

Gunn nodded defiantly and spat.

'Yes, I admit it.'

Monsieur de Warebb clapped his hands.

'Capital!' he chortled. 'If you satisfy me as a guard, then I shall make you one of my wives and take possession of your wealth and your criminal enterprise.'

'As your bride, I wish to keep Fafni and Sindi as my slaves.'

'That is permitted.'

'And if I do not satisfy? What then?'

Monsieur de Warebb frowned and pursed his lips in a tight smile.

'I am afraid I shall have to dispose of you, my dear.'

15

Medical Exam

Sindi and Fafni had been meant to go across the ocean by night to Zanzibar, to collect a batch of stockings from Prince Loro's counterfeit factory. But the new developments interfered with Gunn's plan. They all had to take a hot shower – a giddying luxury – before their medical exam for the guards, under the supervision of a gruff Socotran corporal named Hamm. They delighted in frothing up clouds of soapy foam, which prevented Cpl Hamm from seeing that they were surreptitiously masturbating each other, although their gasps might have alerted her. Hamm, armed with a bull's pizzle, was a lovely but morose girl, fond of complaining about the Madagascarians, who, she said, hated foreigners, though they depended on them to perform the tasks they were too lazy for. She would begin, 'Another thing about these Madagascarians . . .'

They awaited the medicine woman in a hygienic-smelling chamber, where Cpl Hamm shaved their entire bodies, shearing their hair to the scalp, much to Sindi's distress. The medicine woman entered: Artabaxa, a tall, coltish Congolese girl with lustrous black hair braided in ringlets, which danced on her head like snakes. She had a rubber listening tube around her neck, dangling between her heavy naked breasts, through one of whose pierced nipples was pinned a silver coiled snake, signifying her medical status. She wore white rubber knee-boots with high pointed heels and a white rubber skirt hanging just above the knee, which clung so tightly to her firm thighs and arse-globes that she was obliged to walk very delicately. Her legs shone in peach-coloured silk stockings, and Sindi found the contrast between her ebony flesh and the ripe peach colour beguiling. Artabaxa sniffed and wrinkled her nose.

'I smell come,' she said promptly. 'You have been unlawfully masturbating, slave Sindi. Your clito is stiff and your thighs are moist. Your friend's quim is also wet, and I deem her the temptress responsible. You will touch your toes, Fafni, for a whipping of six on the bare. Hamm, you will administer punishment when I command.'

'But –!' wailed Fafni.

'Silence!'

Gunn smirked. The medicine woman made Sindi lie, thighs up and parted, on a mahogany table, then swabbed her quim and thighs dry with a cotton pad and inserted a pipette right up to the neck of her womb, placing its open end in a metal dish that was wedged underneath Sindi's buttocks. Fafni's face was stony as she bent over and touched her toes.

'Cane her as hard as possible, corporal,' ordered the medicine woman.

'Oh . . . no . . .,' moaned Fafni, as a stream of yellow pee hissed down her inside left thigh and wetted the pile of Sindi's hair clippings on the floor. The medicine woman watched in disgust while Hamm leered.

'After your beating, slave, you will clean the floor of hair clippings with your mouth,' ordered the medicine woman, 'then fill your vulva. Hamm, you may commence punishment.'

Vip! The first cut of Hamm's pizzle took Fafni on the tender top buttocks, which clenched as her body trembled. Vip! The second lashed the same welt and her buttocks began to squirm. Sindi did not take her eyes from the caned bottom, and the dish where her buttocks nestled was soon slippery with her own come. Vip! The third landed on the fleshy mid-fesse, as did the fourth, with the fifth and sixth cracking on the slender brown haunches.

Her caning over, Fafni sobbed uncontrollably, and after a prod from the corporal she crouched and began to collect Sindi's piss-soaked hair with her mouth, spitting the golden clumps on to the table. When this was done, she held open the lips of her quim and Hamm wadded every tuft of hair inside her intimate holes. A roll of green sticky palm leaf was passed across her perineum and slit several times, until Fafni's quim and anus were thoroughly bandaged. The medicine woman removed the pipette and the dish brimming with come from Sindi's vulva, and decanted the contents into a clay pot. A smile played on her lips as she gazed into Sindi's eyes, then down to her wet quim.

'Almost full,' she said. 'You are quite the heaviest juicer I have examined, slave. Fafni's caned bottom excited you.'

Sindi blushed but remained silent, and the medicine woman resumed her examination in silence. Tubes which she called speculums filled both vulva and rectum, and she was instructed to squeeze tightly. Then the medicine woman's rubber-clad finger poked into both Sindi's holes, and she measured her clito. After this, she ordered Sindi to rub herself to arousal and collected a further sample of come. Sindi wondered why only she was fully examined, and Gunn scarcely at all. After a few simple measurements, the sobbing Fafni, her vulval tape squeaking, followed Sindi back to the showers for their second cleansing. This time they stood in a communal cold-water shower stall, for hosing by the guards without soap. They had little time to inspect each other's newly shaven bodies before Hamm issued each with rubber sandals and ordered them, dripping wet, to follow her at the double across the darkening square.

They entered the guards' refectory hut, joining a line of girls, all still running on the spot and supervised by corporals cracking lively canes. The canteen slaves were nude like the others, but wore white turbans (supplied by Mr Patel in Madras) as chef's bonnets. At the food dispensary, Sindi, Fafni and Gunn were handed wooden trays, each of whose compartments received a slop of food, while the holder still ran in double time. Most of the food was spilled by the time the three reached their allotted places at the end of a bench and slotted their trays into grooves that ran the length of the table. Each table was supervised by a corporal, and Sindi felt Hamm's breath on her bare skin as she ate. The prospective guards ate rapidly and without looking up, pausing to take draughts of cold water copiously provided in tin jugs. Exhausted, Sindi picked at her food: some greasy stew, stale bread, soggy leaves ... Suddenly a whistle blew, and the corporals upended their tables: every food tray, emptied or not, slid down the grooves into a waste bin. Hamm leered.

It was dark outside, save for a sparkle of starlight, and they followed the snake of naked girls, still at the double, into a large dormitory, whose thick stone walls were pierced by slits that gave only feeble illumination. They kept up their double time while queuing for the latrines, where the three new slaves were issued with tree bark to clean their teeth. For evacuation, there was simply a trench dug into the baked earth, with a trickle of water to wash away the deposits.

There was no lights-out, for there were no lights. The girls were separated, each marched to a straw mattress on the bare earth floor, with a water jug between bed and wall. There were no coverings, either of boar skin or palm leaves. The girls lived, and slept, in the nude, packed together, their bodies of every hue and nationality united by their humiliation. A narrow aisle separated the facing rows of beds, just wide enough to allow a girl to pick her way to the latrines, after begging permission of one of the patrolling corporals.

Sindi lay on her back, not sleeping. There was no talking, no delicious whispering. Nor, despite the closeness of the straw palliasses, was there any touching. The corporals patrolled with lit candles. Girls constantly rose for permission to stool in the latrines. If this was granted, the corporal followed the girl, and sometimes there were two or three canestrokes, after which the girl, having dunged insufficiently or not at all, returned in tears, rubbing her caned bottom. Girls wishing to pee simply squatted at the foot of their straw and pissed into the bone-dry ground, which rapidly soaked it up.

Almost every girl masturbated. This was tolerated, or even tacitly encouraged, by the corporals, who ogled the spread wet quims and flickering fingers of their vigorously frigging prisoners. The air moaned with orgasm and was perfumed with come. Sindi's fingers crept across her bare belly, stroking for moments the nakedness of her pubic mound, before she too slipped fingers into wet slit and rubbed her clito to stiffness. She parted her fesses and poked her index finger, then forefinger, into her anus bud, getting the two digits all the way into her elastic anal passage as she rubbed her erect clito, while her fingers pinched the pulsing wet walls of her slit. She was not the only girl with fingers in anus as well as quim. After her first orgasm she rose to piss and emitted a thick golden stream, sparkling in Hamm's candlelight like drops of yellow rain. She held her quim lips wide open so that the corporal could see, and Hamm began to masturbate too.

Back on her palliasse, Sindi opened her legs as wide as she could and showily frigged, fingering her clito and pouch, until her come was a lake. The corporal's breasts and buttocks quivered and juice flowed from her own frigged slit. Sindi frotted herself more and more vigorously, threshing and sighing, but not allowing her body to stray from her palliasse, sodden with her come. Hamm stood, legs apart, masturbating as though transfixed, and when she shuddered in orgasm, Sindi spasmed too, her belly heaving. Her face wore a smile as she fell into a deep sleep.

'Did you masturbate in dormitory last night, slave?' asked Artabaxa the next morning. 'Hamm reports that your palliasse was soaked in vaginal fluid.'

'Yes, medicine woman,' said Sindi. 'I . . . I sensed that all the slaves masturbate regularly every night. I mean, it's tolerated.'

'You sensed correctly. It obviously does not distress you, since you admit to having joined them in masturbating.'

'A slave's distress cannot count for much, even though she hopes to become a guard.'

'Are you a frequent frigger? Your dossier suggests that you are, when male company is unavailable.'

'*My dossier . . . ?* Yes, I have always masturbated a lot, I admit.'

'How many times did you orgasm last night?'

'Only twice. I am surprised *that* isn't in my dossier.'

The black woman smiled and stroked her thigh, near her pubic mound.

'After a few days it will be,' she said. 'In my office, you are a subject of evaluation, who *happens* to be a slave, and I recommend the regime of discipline best suited to you, to enable you to obtain your happy goal as guard. You may stand at ease, slave. Your medical report' – inscribed on papyrus – 'indicates *sex obsession*, a strong addiction to bare-bottom chastisement and anal sex from males; yet you juiced heavily on watching your friend's bottom caned by a *female*. Most slaves fear the cane, which is why it is used to toughen and reform them. Yet you seem eager for bare-bottom caning, so I may deem it necessary to cane you on the bare at some point in your interview. My task is to find out if your fesses will come to *crave* caning by females . . . and their caresses.'

She rose and unbuttoned her white coat. Beneath it she was nude but for her peach stockings with frilly tops, secured by garter straps and suspender belt, also frilly. Sindi knew that these items were manufactured in the sweatshops of Zanzibar, for they were much in demand amongst Gunn's customers. Artabaxa draped the coat over her chair back. She was taller than Sindi, smoothly muscled, her dark skin swathed in a film of sweat. Her slender skull was the dome of a queen, not a slave. Her nose was proud and straight, her dark eyes wide, her breasts and croup swollen to perfect, firmly muscled ripeness. Her sleek body, with its jutting teats, softly rippling thighs and buttocks and massive bare mound, smelled powerfully of no perfume but her own. The teats wore silver nipple rings, not hanging, but one-inch discs pierced or sewn into the skin surrounding the areolae, so that the nipple buds were squeezed to a state of permanent erection, like berries. Her shaven quim bore a silver ring through piercings in the lips. From pendulous lobes hung earrings of black basalt, each in the form of an erect penis and balls.

'I shall interview you nude,' said the medicine woman, 'to study your reactions and allow you to tell me of your desires. Keep your thighs open so that I may observe your vulva.'

Sindi obeyed, her quim already dripping come as she gazed at the Congolese girl's nudity. The medicine woman fixed her eyes on her slit and smiled.

'We are equal, *Mademoiselle*. I sit bared for your inspection, just as I am inspecting you. We shall take tea before you make me an account of yourself.'

Two servants entered, bearing trays of tea and food, which Sindi eyed hungrily.

'We feed you muck, on purpose, in the training grounds,' said Artabaxa. 'But not in my office.'

One servant was male and the other female, both of Sindi's age, and their basalt black bodies were nude. The male's enormous penis was fully hard, with a high arch of erection. The female was a younger version of the medicine woman herself, the smooth globes of the fesses proudly jutting, the young belly flat over a hairless mound, although her breasts were more conic than Artabaxa's huge, shapely teats, and were topped with oversized brown nipples that seemed to cling like clamshells to the smooth bare flesh. Both servants had grave faces and their bodies were shaven, except for the female's mane of long straight hair, which flowed over her buttock tops. The wet flesh of her quim, the protruding pink clito, glistened in the folds of her silken black pouch. The buttocks of both servants bore deeply etched cane marks, arranged in a crossed pattern, like a tattoo.

Sindi accepted her tea and drank, her eyes closing momentarily and her flared nostrils savouring the herbal aroma. The girl put down a plate of baked breadfruit and yams sliced open, and her fingertips began to rub the huge glans of the male, whose eyes were fixed on the medicine woman's wet slit-folds. Casually, as if it were part of her duty, the girl frotted her clito while she masturbated the male, and her slit rapidly overflowed with come. Sindi's own quim juiced as she stared at the trembling of the male's helmet, the circumcised glans melding smoothly with the shaft of the giant penis, whose flesh was equally velvet, as though his penis was one long glans. Soon he groaned softly and his sperm spurted, to splatter on the breadfruit. There was sufficient to cream five of the fruits, and when he had finished, the girl took each one and, still vigorously frigging, pressed it against her slit, allowing her come to coat the breadfruit until it was gleaming. The medicine woman accepted a fruit and bit it in half; as she chewed, her tongue licked sperm and girl-come from her lips. Sindi crammed one into her mouth, wolfing it whole.

'You will note the slave Dird's penis: our Congolese custom is the African circumcision of the male, whereby the whole skin is peeled, not just the prepuce; it is, naturally, very painful, but leads to greater pleasure for the adult male. Masturbation, to my people, is a sacred ritual. Our women instruct both males and females in the masturbatory art from the moment of adulthood. Both are trained to experience multiple orgasm, the males without ejaculating but reaching the *coup de vinaigre* and maintaining themselves in an orgasmic state for many minutes, without loss of sperm; the females, to know the innermost secrets of their pouches, so that they can climax repeatedly, and juice copiously. Gano! Orgasm three times.'

The black girl parted her rippling thighs and pushed two fingers into her pouch, delving to the knuckles. She did not touch her clito.

'*Oh* ...,' she gasped, then, almost immediately, '*Ahh* ...'

She withdrew her fingers and grasped her distended clito, pinching its tip, kneading the nubbin and pulling it hard away from her body.

'*Ahh!*' she gasped again, her belly contracting in her spasm; come flowed down her trembling thighs.

'There are many techniques of female masturbation,' said the medicine woman, 'and time spent as one of Monsieur de Warebb's guards eventually instructs a girl in the effective enjoyment of her own body. Too many girls frig rapidly and impatiently, with simple clito-frotting, ignoring the slow and sensuous delights of caressed quim lips, the pouch itself, and of course stimulation of the nipples, anus and spinal nubbin. Masturbation becomes holy when female or male frigs during a bare-caning with the rod of the baobab tree.'

Sindi's quim was flooded with come, and her fingers strayed near her throbbing stiff clito, eyed lustfully by the medicine woman.

133

'Like the caning of six cuts which Gano shall now give you, *Mademoiselle*. The squirming of a whipped bare croup is the swell of the the river, the jungle or the ocean waves. The tears of a female flogged naked are the rains of life to our land, her gasps, the cooling breeze.'

Sindi eyed Dird's newly rising penis and Gano's quim, which continued to drip come.

'My servants,' said Artabaxa, 'are under instruction to maintain themselves in constant arousal. They will masturbate as they watch you caned, and for your humiliation Dird will spurt his sperm in your face; you shall lick and swallow every drop that falls on your lips, but not touch the sperm that splashes your breasts. Now, Sindi, stand with your buttocks raised and your belly on the chair back, with your hands grasping the arms of the chair. You may not move in any way without my permission.'

16

Artabaxa's House

Trembling, Sindi rose and bent over her chair, with her bottom raised, and thighs wide, allowing come to drip from her spread lips as the black girlslave flexed a springy brown cane. Inches before her face, the young ebony male stroked his erect penis. The medicine woman remained seated, her thighs still open, but her fingers now discreetly rubbing her swollen clito.

Vip!

'*Ah!*'

Sindi jumped, as the first cut from Gano's cane surprised her.

'No squealing,' said Artabaxa. 'I like to see a girl squirm silently.'

Vip!

The second stroke made Sindi gasp, and her bottom clenched tight, but she did not squeal.

'The rod of the baobab is one of the hardest instruments of discipline,' said the medicine woman, 'much harder than the fabled rattan, and much more adaptable. There are rods supple or hard to suit every caning purpose, as you shall see, at my home.'

Sindi's buttocks were squirming frantically as the cane seared her bare; before her, the male stroked the silky knob of his penis. Her mouth gasped towards it, as though to fellate him. Come trickled hot from her vulva

down her thighs and calves. Artabaxa had one fist fully
inside her own pouch and was twisting her huge extruded
clito with her other hand, the fingers twirling her nubbin
as the sharp nails pinched the swollen bud.

Vip!

'*Uhh . . .*'

A stroke to the left haunch made Sindi wriggle, and
tears misted her eyes. She moaned, her striped bottom
squirming and clenching and her knuckles white as they
clutched the chair. The last of her six cut straight across
mid-fesse. The black male's penis danced before her, the
peehole seeming to smile at her pain. Suddenly it
disappeared. She gaped as the silken penis stroked her
exposed anus bud. The medicine woman masturbated
vigorously; little gasps, twitches of her belly and blinking
eyes were all that indicated she had brought herself to
repeated orgasm. She had her buttocks raised and four
fingers inserted in her anus. The girlslave squatted at
Sindi's feet, frotting in tandem with her mistress, her
come mingling with Artabaxa's, which shone on her hard
thighs like dew on basalt.

'*Ahh . . . !*'

Sindi cried out, as the male's penis sank into her anus
and his peehole touched her root. He began to encule her,
slamming his penis so hard into her rectum that she
almost toppled over. His fingernails clawed the weals on
her buttocks, trapping the writhing globes in his embrace.
At the fifth stroke of his sex, Sindi's belly heaved and her
gasps became a moan, then she squealed.

'Oh, yes, do me! Oh, I'm coming! *Ohh . . . !*'

Having brought Sindi to orgasm, Dird withdrew from
her anus with a rapid plopping sound and resumed his
position in front of her face, frigging his now shiny ebony
penis. The crouching girlslave rose and took his whole
ball-sac in her mouth, as she inserted a finger into her
own anus and another into the male's. Her quim was
penetrated by Artabaxa's bare toes. Dird gasped and a

spray of spunk splashed on Sindi's lips and nose, followed by further ejaculate, falling thickly on her nipples until her whole bosom was glazed with his massive spurt of cream.

The medicine woman bounded from her chair and fastened her teeth on Sindi's left breast, biting the nipple as her tongue flickered on the flesh to lick all the male's sperm. She chewed Sindi's teats, licking them dry, and clutched her spread fesse-globes; her fingers traced and scratched the savage caneweals, then two digits found Sindi's anal opening and penetrated it, driving to the very root of her rectum. Her other hand was wedged inside her gushing slit, fisting hard. Her thumb pressed the clito and, as she fisted Sindi's anus, two fingers inside the wet pouch touched the skin on both sides of the pubic bone.

'*Ahh! Yes! Ahh . . .!*'

Sindi screamed and shuddered as further orgasm engulfed her. The medicine woman resumed her seated position, watching Sindi sit numbly down, while the two slaves departed silently. Artabaxa sniffed, then licked her fingers like a cat.

'Now, *Mademoiselle* Sindi,' she said, 'you are going to tell me your truth, why you are an addict of masturbation, buggery and the cane.'

Sindi obeyed. She told her whole life story.

'I was a slave, too,' mused Artabaxa, 'and still am – but before that I was a princess of my tribe. It is hard to be a mistress, then an abject slave, but it is a woman's lot. As it is to suffer the attentions of powerful males, in any of her holes. You shall come to luncheon at my house, beautiful Green-eyes, for further enlightenment.'

After a few days of hard military training, during which she had lost or been denied contact with Gunn and Fafni, Sindi returned to Artabaxa's house. She entered the large dining room, panelled with baobab wood, replete with sinister flogging-frames and instruments of chastisement and decorated with paintings, photographs and a single statue. The medicine woman sat at the head of a long wooden dining table, beneath a larger-than-life photograph, in stark black and white, showing herself in the nude against a jungle landscape. She held a snake and a cane. In a crevice on the facing wall stood an ebony statuette of a single nude female holding a similar cane.

The statuette's breasts swelled as though to bursting, yet jutted like young volcanoes, and the sweep of her back flowed perfectly into the largest, ripest buttocks Sindi had ever seen or could imagine. The hillock of the vulva swelled to match the croup, and both were framed by thighs whose every ripple was caught by the sculptor. Along one wall hung black and white photographs of nude Nilotic girls, all magnificently fessed and with painted bodies, arrayed on parade for auction; and paintings of the same, with the colours starkly restricted: just black body, brown rock and white sand under a luminescent azure sky. Four notable items of furniture adorned the room. One was an aquarium of live crustaceans, the others wooden and festooned with restraints: an upright flogging-frame, a caning-stool and a whipping-table, each beside a rack of corrective instruments.

'You admire my paintings,' said Artabaxa.

Save for her stockings and suspender belt, she was as nude as the statuette of her younger self.

'Yes,' Sindi gasped. 'And your photos, and . . . statue.'

The medicine woman laughed.

'The statuette is perhaps too flattering . . . somewhat exaggerated . . . by an enslaved sculptor from Zanzibar who wished to buy himself off a flogging. The photographs are by a woman, a schoolmistress. They show slaves awaiting auction on Socotra.'

'Not exaggerated!' blurted Sindi. 'I would give anything to be *your* slave.'

'Hm! Don't tell me you and Fafni haven't plotted desertion,' said Artabaxa, abruptly.

She gestured to the vast horizon beyond her window.

'Madagascar is a prison without bars,' she said. 'How I hate it! Desert at your pleasure, if you can change into a hedgehog, or a bird . . .'

She sprang to her feet and plunged her bare hand into the aquarium, selecting a lobster, which she extracted, wriggling. She slew it with a swift needle stroke to the neck, then gave it to Gano for boiling.

'I abhor cruelty,' she said.

Dird led in two girls, shackled together by wrists and ankles. Their naked bodies flowed with sweat. Sindi, instructed to kneel at the medicine woman's feet, gaped in astonishment.

Artabaxa intoned, 'We have two unsuccessful deserters, sent to me for mental evaluation, preceded, necessarily, by chastisement. One of them, as you see, is Fafni.'

Dird unchained the first prisoner, her face scarlet and sullen and her buttocks two large moons, bulging smooth and uncaned. It was Fafni.

'Fafni! How could you?' Sindi blurted.

'I knew you wouldn't go with me, and I didn't want to get you into trouble, and it was *her* idea, she frigged me till I consented, and . . . oh, I'm so confused,' stammered Fafni, and began to cry.

No sooner had Dird unshackled her than she was seized by the nape and forced down, to kneel over the high caning-stool with splayed legs, which thrust her buttocks high. Her wrists and ankles were padlocked to the legs of the stool, spreading her big buttocks and revealing her pink, hairless quim and anus bud. Dird's huge penis was stirring within his loinstring.

'You may crouch, slave Sindi,' Artabaxa said, 'and pick up whatever scraps I choose to throw you. That shall be your luncheon.' Sindi promptly obeyed.

A jug of wine and dishes of fried woodlice, cucumbers, mushrooms and whole hot peppers were daintily served by Gano, followed by the lobster. The medicine woman explained that she customarily dined in the nude, to avoid staining the exquisite fabric of her clothing. Cow-butter dribbled down her breasts and belly as she chewed her lobster, and she indicated that Sindi could lick up the hot droplets. Some of the melted butter splattered Artabaxa's pubis, and Sindi licked those drops with particular care, daring to flick the prominent clito with her tongue-tip.

The medicine woman made no sound, either of approval or disapproval, but her buttocks shifted and her thighs parted. Sindi's lips kissed her feet. Artabaxa smiled and her fingers crept to her clito, holding a lobster claw with hot flesh peeping from the broiled shell. Touching her nubbin with the lobster-meat, the black woman masturbated. She instructed Gano to use the hardest baobab rod from the rack; Gano curtsied and selected a gnarled but long and whippy cane. Fafni's chastisement began.

Gano caned her bare very hard; she slashed a vivid pink weal right across the central fesses, then another on top buttock, by the base of her spine, then one each to the haunches, which made a dry, slapping sound, and two more strokes to the soft underflesh of the thigh-tops. At the second stroke, the girl's cleft tightened. Soon she was clenching and unclenching her fesses, her brow knotted in pain. There were intervals of six seconds between each stroke. Fafni made no noise, except for a gasp in her throat at the sixth cut, between her thighs, where a bright rivulet of come seeped from her jerking lips.

Sindi shivered as her tongue licked butter from her mistress's pubic mound, but could not help watching, with mouth slack. Artabaxa dipped her lobster claw in her wet quim until it was coated with her come, then popped the morsel of sauced meat in her mouth, crunching it shell and all. Ripping another chunk of flesh from the lobster, she frigged her clito with it.

After a pause, a second set of six began, caning the same weals. Fafni did not cry or even moan, but her whole body trembled. Tears streamed in silence down her face, matching the come that trickled down her thigh-tops from the swollen lips of her slit. By the end of the second set, her fesses were striped with dark crimson bruises, deepening to welts. The other slave watched, cringing, as she awaited her beating. Sindi longed to masturbate, despite the ominous bulk of the whipping-table she was sure awaited her. Its surface was polished to a gleam, like the copper clamps at each corner for the victim's wrists and ankles, and it reflected the bottoms of girls about to be flogged as two trembling moons.

Fafni's body went limp. She had fainted. At once Dird doused her in cold water, reviving her speedily. He grinned, showing white teeth, and his penis stirred beneath his loinstring. Fafni's skin was mottled with puffy ridges, and she began to sob and whimper. Artabaxa decided that twelve cuts sufficed. Dird's penis rose to full height and burst from his loinstring. At a nod from the medicine woman, he straddled Fafni and pushed his swollen glans between her fesses.

She howled, then sobbed violently as he rammed his massive black shaft deep into her, grunting as his peehole struck her root. Enculing her hard, Dird reached round to tweak her stiff, throbbing clito. Fafni jerked and squealed in tearful protest, yet come oozed from her swollen quim. After two minutes, she squealed, 'Ah! Ah! *Do it harder!* Yes! *Ohh . . .!'* – in a shuddering orgasm, and Dird at once withdrew from her anus, unspermed. She was released and stood unsteadily, wiping the tears that streamed from her eyes. Her bottom globes were corrugated with welts and her anus bud was raw and red. Eyeing her friend's glowing fesses, Sindi could not help frotting herself.

The second deserter was a corporal of the guards; she seemed to accept punishment with placid resignation, though her rank made it more severe. Throughout it, Artabaxa rubbed her clito, which had swelled to full erection, using pieces of lobster meat or the shell itself, and always dipping the fragment into her quim juice before eating it. Meanwhile Sindi licked the come that glistened on her thighs, using it to sauce the scraps of mushrooms, cucumber and woodlice she was thrown. The medicine woman widened her thighs still further and clasped Sindi's head to her wet slit, so that she had to squint to see the girl chastised.

The corporal was strung upright into a vertical whipping-frame, gibbet-size, with clamps at each corner for ankles and wrists. In addition, a bar jutted at the centre of the frame, pushing on the victim's waist and forcing her buttocks to protrude as a target for the cane. Her feet balanced painfully on the tips of her toes. Gano first flogged her back with a whip of nine tongues. The girl's body was rocked by each lash, but her clamps restrained her from falling forward. Nine vicious welts appeared on her back at each stroke of the thongs. After ten strokes, her back was raw and etched with deep weals. Her spine and ribcage stood out stark beneath the whipped, puffy skin.

Leaving the corporal dangling, sobbing, in the frame, Gano began to cane her buttocks. This time, there was no pause between the sets of six strokes. Eighteen strokes were delivered at intervals of six seconds without a break. The girl's squirming became frantic. While she seemed to have taken her whipping quite calmly, the flogging of her buttocks maddened her and she gasped and whimpered. Her tiptoes danced, the soles of her feet clenching and wrinkling at each stroke of the cane, just like the livid whipped buttocks. At the seventeenth stroke she pissed herself. A jet of golden liquid steamed from her spread quim, flowing down her thighs and calves and puddling the floor. Seeing this, Artabaxa masturbated faster and more gleefully.

'Give the bitch an extra four strokes for foulness,' she murmured.

'You are crueller than any schoolmistress,' gasped Sindi.

'I certainly hope so,' said Artabaxa.

The corporal grimaced and gasped, as Gano continued the caning after the eighteenth stroke. At twenty she screamed, full from her throat. The medicine woman's finger was a blur as she masturbated, and come flowed from her swollen quim almost too fast for Sindi to lap and swallow the fluid, as she herself frigged, sopping herself with juice. The victim screwed her eyes and clenched her buttocks tight, her face a rictus of pain, until she had been caned her twenty-two. Then she took Dird's immediate buggery with enjoyment, or resignation, and parted her thighs as wide as she could for his masturbation of her clito. From her moans and wriggles, it would not be long before Dird brought her to a lusty orgasm.

Suddenly Sindi's tongue pushed Artabaxa's frigging finger out of the way and found the erect clito, big as a nut, in its fleshy den. She began to nibble, and the medicine woman moaned as the girl's mouth fastened upon her soaking quim. Artabaxa's belly heaved as Sindi tongued her to an orgasm which was utterly silent. Sindi then brought herself off and had to bite her lip to avoid crying out. Fafni frigged to orgasm at the same time and whimpered softly. The corporal was buggered strongly for three minutes, then frigged to a noisy pleasure-spasm by Dird – himself still not spurting – before being unstrung, clutching her wealed buttocks, her welts darker than her raw slit. Smiling, she exhaled loudly, as though she had been holding her breath all the time. Dird approached his mistress, his penis throbbing, and slick from the holes of the enculed miscreants.

Gano grasped his glans and rubbed it softly until, within moments, creamy spunk spurted in a powerful jet over Artabaxa's face, to drip down her bare breasts. Sindi licked the sperm where it flowed down the black woman's quivering bare belly and over her mound, and her sperm-creamed tongue again found her throbbing clito. Sindi swallowed the come that flowed uncontrollably from the quivering wet pouch and tugged at the quim-ring. At once the medicine woman orgasmed again, this time with loud wails.

'Congratulations, Fafni and Sindi,' she gasped. 'You have passed your tests.'

'Welcome to the guards,' said the corporal.

17

Zanzibar

The duties of a guard were scarcely less onerous than those of a slave, except that they were allowed to wear frilly skirtlets and to glory in sheer silk stockings with full garter apparatus. They formed a guard of honour, carrying their smartly polished cowhide whips, at all of Monsieur de Warebb's numerous ceremonies, including his wedding to Gunn, of whom he seemed much enamoured. She was not, of course, his only wife, but hand-to-hand combats with the others soon made her the supreme *odalisque*.

Their training did not stop: there were races, jumping, climbing trees, punishing route marches and swimming. Daily, they had to patrol the battlements of Warebb and take inventory of export shipments, dragged on massive sledges; nor were they exempt from a sound whipping of six or eight lashes on their bare bottoms, if they displeased Warebb in any way.

They were also responsible for supervising and attending to the constant demands of Giselle, Sylvie and the other greedy, petulant prostitutes of the Hôtel de Ville, which Sindi found a full-time job in itself. Frequent corporal punishments of slaves or surly prostitutes, was one of their duties. Sindi was especially fond of caning boyslaves, adding subtleties of her own to their anguish; for example, she would pin their nipples with painfully tight clamps, then pour hot wax on their fesses and, when it had hardened, whip it to shards, which fell off. Her diet improved, and she enjoyed oysters, crabs and other crustaceans as well as hedgehog, woodlice and sea cucumbers, along with succulent fruits.

One evening, six weeks into their guards-service, Sindi and Fafni were sitting at their dinner of wine, shrimp fritters, spider crabs in fish sauce, and steamed kelp, when Gunn came to visit them, or rather sneaked into the guards' mess, fearful of detection. She was sumptuously arrayed as Monsieur's wife, with the finest, sheerest white silk stockings. She sat with Sindi and Fafni and, after crunching a handful of crabs, washed down with a beaker of wine, lost no time coming to the point.

'We must escape,' she said. 'I have my business to run, for my customers in Madagascar will be getting anxious for their stockings – Warebb takes little interest in that – and I am sick of being treated as his plaything. His personal habits are quite disgusting. He insists on sucking the sweat from my stockinged toes! Neither is my bare bottom spared his lash. And he drools over his collection of lewd photographs, which he buys from Mr Patel in Madras, or else directly from Natalie the Schoolmistress. Ugh! I fear he will sell me quite soon. We have business, a consignment of stockings from Prince Loro, awaiting us on Zanzibar. Warebb will not dare look for us there. We shall steal a boat – tonight. A fine ketch I have had my eye on, Warebb's own, and poorly guarded. We shall be in Zanzibar in eight days. My contact will be waiting at the appointed place. He always does, for it is both his home and his warehouse. I am his best customer – he has some trade with Africa, but my people are not so appreciative of stockings as the vain Madagascarians.'

That night, while the others looted the Hôtel de Ville for copious stores of Monsieur's luxury foodstuffs and barrels of drinking water, Gunn eased the ketch from her moorings. In their guards' uniforms they went unchallenged, saying they were on a secret mission for their owner. Male helots, a rank above pure slaves, clad in loinstrings, even helped them load the craft, and at midnight they set sail. Gunn had been a sailboat hand on one of the ferries sailing the mighty Congo river, largest in the world, and though she enchanted the girls with her descriptions of sailing through piranha-infested waters with cargoes of fruit, dried fish and monkey heads – raw monkey brains being a delicacy in Congo, of which excess consumption drove men mad, trembling and incontinent and convulsed with manic laughter – they could not bring themselves to agree that a river might be so large, nor a land wide enough to accommodate it.

More fearsome than the laughing men of the Congo were the pirates of Comores, islands they must pass on the way to Zanzibar; it was said they dined on human brains, and exceeded the Congolese in madness. The girls were well accoutred with whips, catapults, staves, spears and harpoons, for catching swordfish and tuna fish on their week-long journey, and Gunn let them into a secret – that her stockings, undamaged by tree, pool or rock, were made of extra fine but extra tough rubber, stolen from the Rubberlord of Igfal, or traded with his vampire girls for live guinea-pigs and hedgehogs, with jars of a special sauce made from fermented lizards' livers.

When they were a safe distance from the port of Zanzibar, Sindi paused in her deckside labour to drink in the beauty of the sunrise over the calm blue sea, whose surface was broken only by the splashes of dolphins or flying fish. It was her first scent of liberty in what seemed ages of enslavement. Suddenly she saw on the horizon a small galley, powered by oars, speeding towards them. Fafni was at the wheel, and Sindi cursed, for she had let them veer too close to the dreaded Comores. Gunn ordered them to let the vessel come somewhat nearer, and to man their catapults. As the pirate vessel approached,

Sindi saw that the rowers were all pale, raven-haired vampire girls, their white bodies dripping with sweat as they pulled furiously on the oars, their bare backs frequently laced by a male overseer's whip.

At the bow stood a battery of catapults, and on the bridge presumably the captain, a hirsute man wearing rubber thigh-boots and a black rubber skirt. His chest was bare and tattooed with a human skull, and his head swirled with a jangling cap of mollusc shells, oysters, mussels and clams interwoven. He wore as a belt a coiled hide whip from which dangled small skulls. On his bloodcurdling whoop, the pirates answered with their own, and in a braying cacophony of screams the catapults twanged, sending smoking missiles cracking against Gunn's hull. The cannonballs were monkey skulls with smoke and flames belching from eyes, nose and mouth, and evidently designed to ignite enemy vessels.

Gunn contented herself with firing a few salvoes of rocks before picking up speed and rapidly eluding the marauder. She explained that if captured by the Comores they would be enslaved and likely transformed into vampires. Sometimes the Comores spared their victims, if they looted a ripe cargo, but since they were unladen, only the gloomiest fate would await them. Fafni was duly strapped to the mast and Sindi gave her six strokes of the cane on her bare bottom for her negligence.

The remaining days of their voyage were uneventful, and Sindi wondered if, after all this time, Gunn's arrangement still held good. But Gunn was irrepressibly confident.

'See!' she cried, as they nosed into a tiny deserted harbour a safe distance from the town of Zanzibar. Before them lay a huge palace, its windows twinkling with candle-light, and on the shingle beach stood two figures, a man and a girl, holding lit candles in welcome. Gunn waved.

'Hello, Matthias! Hello, Greta! I hope you have a fine cargo for me!' she cried but neither individual waved back. When they had docked, Gunn sprang from the boat and rushed to embrace the pair, although they had made no move to come and greet the girls. Gunn's jaw dropped.

'Oh . . .,' she exclaimed. 'Where are Matthias and Greta?'

'I am Peter and this is Pritzi,' drawled the man in a cold voice. 'There have been some changes since your last trip. Matthias and Greta are no longer with us. Pritzi and I are in occupation, as I am now head of the enterprise.'

'I hope we shall be privileged to be received by Prince Loro.'

'That will be difficult. As I said, there have been changes.'

He waved vaguely at the illumined palace, from which the noises of a workshop emanated.

'We have, as you would say, modernised the enterprise. The stockings are now woven here, at the point of despatch, and we use the girls of an ancient tribe who do not need sleep. Also, the prince's books are safely stored here, in an underground tunnel, at controlled temperature. Prince Loro cares more for social pleasures than taking care of books. All our storage is underground – your own capture by Mr Loleelo shows how easily one gains access to a fortress by trickery. Not so easy to penetrate my labyrinth.'

He was strangely dressed, in rubber stockings, a short hempen skirt and a headdress of little propellers like tiny windmills, which whirled in the breeze. By the candlelight Sindi saw that Pritzi was a vampire. Peter's bony, scarred face and bare, muscled torso were no less white than hers, and his hair was blond, and cropped to bristles – like a hedgehog, Sindi thought rather foolishly. He spoke French with a heavy, rather sibilant accent. He smiled thinly, wiping a trickle of moisture from his fleshy lips.

149

'You are wondering what tribe we belong to,' he said. 'Like Matthias, we are Germans.'

'I . . . I have never heard of that tribe,' Sindi said.

'We came from the far north, now the glowing black barren lands, but then lands of ice and snow. Some of our ancestors escaped the holocaust that destroyed half the world. We do not know exactly when the holocaust occurred, which is why I spend much time trying to decipher the old books, and construct a grammar and lexicon for all the baffling old languages . . . not just German, but Russian, Swedish and others.'

'Half the world!' cried Gunn. 'But this *is* the world.'

'The disaster, it seems, occurred almost beyond time itself.'

'Time?' said Fafni. 'What is time?'

Peter smiled.

'There is one theory, advanced by some scribes, that we Germans lived in Laurasia, before the great holocaust. Berlin, Hamburg, London, Paris, Frankfurt – these were cities before time, greater than you can imagine. I have renamed this palace Schloss Berlin. Some of us escaped over the sea of Tethys to Gondwanaland.'

'These are riddles to me,' said Sindi.

'Gondwanaland is where we are now, the old southern continent in the days when there were only two continents, which broke into many component parts. The schoolmistress Nathalie can explain further – she has many old books, books which I want to see – but she is arrogant and scornful. I have plans for her.'

He licked his lips with a nasty drooling smack.

'Ah . . . books, and the power residing therein . . .' he murmured.

'Well, I trust my shipment of stockings is ready,' said Gunn. 'We can load tomorrow, and set sail at dusk.'

'I am afraid that will not be possible,' Peter replied. 'There will be a delay, while we transfer the bulk of Prince Loro's inventory from his palace in Zanzibar to

Schloss Berlin. You see, Prince Loro was slipshod. He sold to too many customers in too many places, and did not appreciate the virtue of controlling the market.'

'I trust I am a favoured customer,' said Gunn suspiciously.

'Of course, my dear Gunn! A few days' delay, that is all. Meanwhile you may relax in the comforts of my modest home. Come, it is time for wine and dinner.'

The Schloss Berlin was cavernous and their footsteps echoed on the flagstones of the teak-panelled corridors, as Pritzi led them to an intimate dining room. They were served steaming platters of spiced fish and crustaceans by nude girls, some of them vampires (who had little taste for seafoods), and ate them with their fingers. Sindi recognised delicacies such as the little goby, which she had extracted from their home cavities in living sponges, and the tiny, gaudy clownfish, which lived in the fronds of sea anemones and was the only creature an anemone would not sting, for the clownfish ate butterfly fish, the anemone's principal enemy. Sindi was struck by the awesome symmetry of life: hunter and hunted, the eater and the eaten, predator and protector, slave and master.

Peter drank copious strong wine and bragged about the Germans of aeons past, with their gleaming swords and helmets, their fast raiding ships, their empire extending over half a continent. Fafni asked what a continent was. The high point of the feast was a heaped dish of deep-fried pygmy gobies, each no bigger than a fingernail. The minuscule fish melted in Sindi's mouth. Scrutinising one of the non-vampire servants, she detected a strong likeness to Hamm, the orderly in Monsieur de Warebb's guards. Wine emboldened her to say as much to Peter, and he laughed.

'Why, she is Hamm's sister. I bought her from Artabaxa. I have spies and agents everywhere, you know – Giselle is one, also. Warebb is a fop and a weakling, and though I am friendly with him, it is better to seduce females, the real powers behind the thrones. Except, that is, for Comores.'

Gunn recounted their adventure with the pirate galley.

'That would be Ogpan, chief of Comores. He sells me girls and Madagascar cloves, and in return I sell him salt, stockings, cucumbers and timber, which his islands lack.'

'Prince Loro must be very busy,' said Sindi.

'Not really,' said Peter with a shrug, and laughed again.

When they had drunk their fill of wine and the food was finished, all agreed that it was time for bed. Pritzi and Peter led them down a tunnel, off which branched several other, locked, tunnels, and showed them into a dark cell with three straw palliasses, blankets, jugs of water and a bucket for evacuation. There were of course no windows. Peter explained that, though primitive, their beds should be comfortable enough, and the underground accommodation was designed to keep out any hostile intruder.

'Tomorrow, we shall see about your shipment of stockings,' Peter said. 'Meanwhile, you are free to wander, dive and stroll, but there are certain installations it would be unwise for you to see. You must not, I am afraid, leave the compound. There are misshape creatures in these forests. Pritzi will organise a guard for you – for your own safety, of course.'

Thankyous and goodnights exchanged, the girls sank gratefully on their beds. Sindi felt a delicious wine-fuelled drowsiness creep over her and commenced a slow, luxurious frig. From the movements under Fafni's blanket, she guessed her friend was masturbating too. Her descent into cosy, relieved slumber was scarcely interrupted by Gunn, who rattled at the door handle, whispering that she wanted to go exploring. But the door was locked.

18

Misshape

The next morning, it seemed all Sindi's apprehensions
were groundless. She rose with the others; they drank and
washed themselves and found the door unlocked. Ventur-
ing out of the labyrinth of tunnels, they were greeted by
Pritzi, who invited them to breakfast al fresco. The sun
was already high in a cloudless blue sky, and the sea
tranquil; the view behind them was of Schloss Berlin and
then unbroken forest, with girl guards in skimpy rubber
uniforms prowling, whips and staves in hand. There were
boyslaves, too, in loinstrings, and blond and heavily
muscled. Pritzi said rather wistfully that once she too had
been blonde.

Like Gunn and Fafni, Sindi had donned a skirtlet of
palm leaves, but she soon found it easier to be nude, save
for her sumptuous silk stockings – lemon-yellow, with
matching frilly suspenders – as was Pritzi, her stockings
a vivid slash of scarlet against her alabaster skin. The
others likewise stripped, Gunn to green stockings and
Fafni to blue. A boyslave served them fruit, caviar,
onions, cucumber and bread, and Sindi amused herself by
staring fixedly at his groin, finding she could make his
extraordinarily large penis swell.

'Do you want him?' drawled Pritzi. 'He's called Adolf.'
Sindi blushed furiously.
'Well, I . . . he might be too big for me.'

'Only one way to find out. He's no misshape, as you can clearly see.'

'What is a misshape?'

'A cast-out slave who is less than perfect – who does not meet Peter's ideal of German beauty.'

Pritzi smiled, summoned the boyslave and whispered in his ear. He nodded gravely, without smiling, then continued to serve them. When Sindi asked what was to happen, Pritzi put her finger to her lips and said that surprise was part of the fun.

'But don't tell Peter.'

Peter joined them briefly, wearing an expensive papyrus robe in many colours. Papyrus clothing was normally the preserve of the uppermost *noblesse.* He said he must be away indefinitely on business, to see about Gunn's shipment of stockings, but that Pritzi would look after them. They should ignore any strange noises they heard in the night. It was only the complex structure of the tunnels expanding and contracting to adjust to the changing temperature. When he had gone, Pritzi seemed to relax. Sindi whispered to Gunn that it looked as if they might be staying longer than a few days.

'I don't mind, though. It's so beautiful! I'm longing for a dive.'

First, Pritzi took them on a tour of the estate, which Gunn said she had never seen before; in fact she had not been aware there was an estate, merely the old tumbledown warehouse which had been demolished and replaced by the towering Schloss Berlin. Escorted by muscled boyslaves, they walked around vast fields where slaves worked in lush plantations of pineapples, cucumber and bananas, and picked thyme, coriander and turmeric. There were pens of boars and chickens, and pools swimming with crustaceans.

At last, sweating heartily, although Pritzi said they had seen only a small fraction of the estate, they came to what Pritzi called the perimeter zone, the limit of the property, patrolled by armed girl guards, mostly vampires, in thick black rubber armour. Sindi observed that the vampire girls and the normal girls were divided into separate squads and did not mix. The actual border of the estate was a wide ditch, with a tall fence of sharpened staves clustered on either side. This was to keep out the misshapes, who made forays in order to steal food or slaves for their own use.

A sudden commotion signalled such an incident, which Pritzi said was rare in daytime. A group of misshapes had penetrated the fences, swum the ditch, and were screaming as the guards battered them with staves. Sindi gaped, for she had never seen such ugly or deformed creatures: naked, haggard and filthy, with obscene goitres and excrescences from their limbs; additional, withered breasts, fingers or hands; males with a shrunken extra penis beside their main, hideously deformed one; females with their bodies covered in fish scales, or crawling with skin-burrowing worms, or with two parallel vulvas; even a girl with two heads, the smaller growing from her neck, but with eyes wide open and sentient. One girl guard cracked the head of a scaly, fishlike girl with her stave, but instead of joining in the whoops of her colleagues she began to weep.

'Oh!' she sobbed. 'I didn't mean . . .'

'Back to work, ensign Molo, or I'll flog you on the gibbet!' barked Pritzi, and, snuffling, the girl obeyed.

This rabble of monsters was easily driven back by the staves, whips and boots of the guards, and they limped off, howling, into the forest.

'I expect you're ready for a swim,' said Pritzi.

Sindi asked how the misshapes could become so deformed.

'Oh, iodine deficiency,' said Pritzi, smiling sadly. 'It has always been a problem on this island. But Peter imagines himself too kind to put an end to their distress.'

'Surely you can get iodine from seaweed.'

'Can you? Well, misshapes are not allowed in the sea.'

Stockings removed, it was glorious to plunge at last into the ocean, and Sindi swam far out, then dived deep as if to try and escape the hideous vision of the iodine-starved misshapes. She led her friends through pink coral reefs, past shoals of shimmering, iridescent fishes, and down to the sandy sea bed, where they scooped armfuls of clams; only Sindi was brave, or trained, enough to capture lobsters and crabs. Fafni was sent to fetch a floating bucket, and when it was full of writhing sea-booty she towed it back to the shore, where the girls set about cleaning their catch.

While preparing a crab, Sindi noticed something unusual. The beast had apparently somehow swallowed or absorbed a sliver of papyrus. She turned her back to the others and read the message scrawled on it. It was incomplete, for the fabric was torn, but she read, *Help me . . . imprisoned in tunnel at Schloss Berlin . . . Peter . . . seize throne . . . fear I shall no longer be Prince Loro . . . reward for my rescue . . .* Sindi did not know what to make of this, then thought it must be a joke, as it seemed to make no sense. But her own sense told her to hide the scrap, and the only place, naked as she was, was in her vulva. Quickly she accomplished this, and not long afterwards the girls sat down to a huge luncheon with wine. Boyslaves anointed their heads with scented animal fat, which melted, and dripped down their nude bodies, perfuming them deliciously as they ate. Pritzi ate elsewhere, with the other vampires, of their own repulsive diet.

Adolf served her again, but did not acknowledge her, and she wondered if her conversation with Pritzi had been a daydream, brought on by the sun and heat. Afterwards they dozed in hammocks, then swam. Later they entertained themselves at a stocking swap party; Pritzi opened a locked chest and brought out a myriad beautiful silk stockings, in every hue of the rainbow. The girls squealed in delight as they paraded in their finery, although they might not keep them. The finest samples were too valuable to be touched, and Pritzi said they sold for a hundred thousand dinars and upwards to very favoured and discreet customers.

The days continued thus. Sindi had hidden her papyrus in the straw of her palliasse, and, as she lay awake at night, she thought she did indeed hear sounds that resembled human cries and sobs, although they could have been the creaking of the structure, as Peter had said. There was no word of his return date, and gradually all three girls forgot the urgency of their mission and Gunn's bales of stockings.

One day they were entertained to the grisly spectacle of a public flogging, administered by Pritzi. The victim was the guard Molo, who was dragged, screaming and weeping, to the wooden gibbet, to which her wrists and ankles were securely strapped by a punishment detail of guards. Her offence was taking pity on the howling misshapes and secretly (as she thought) bringing them baskets of food. Her sentence was fifteen lashes of the cane.

When the girl's nude body was stretched taut, her pinioned feet just touching the deck with her toes, Pritzi began her work, teeth bared in a fierce rictus of pleasure. The strokes were spaced at intervals of five seconds, for maximum agony, and Pritzi dealt five cuts each to buttocks, back and breasts. Molo shuddered and shrieked throughout her punishment, exciting the derision of her tormentors. When she was untied, Pritzi snapped, 'To the tunnel!' and the guards carried the sobbing girl away. Sindi was aghast, and determined to penetrate the mysteries of the tunnel without delay.

Their door was no longer locked, and that night Sindi waited until her companions slept, then sneaked out into the tunnel, which was almost lightless, save for a dim green glow far away. All around were groans and wails, and she decided these sounded too human to be the shifting of the earth. Her skin prickled with fear but she proceeded, ready to flee at the first hint of a patrolling guard. To her surprise, there was none; anyway, the lumpy, crevice-ridden rock wall of the rough-hewn tunnel afforded plenty of concealment. She passed a row of cells with barred windows. All seemed empty save the last, where she heard moaning and the rustle of an unquiet body. When she peered through the window bars, at once the inmate sprang up and her tear-streaked face looked at Sindi's. It was Molo.

'You must listen . . .,' she stammered. 'Warn . . .'

Almost incoherent, she babbled her tale, which enthralled Sindi, although she found it too strange to believe. Here there were only punishment cells, but at the end of the tunnel were the growing rooms where silkworms were bred.

'Silkworms?'

'You'll see, if you can stand it. *They shed their skins, and grow another.* But there are plenty of misshapes . . . hideous side effects. Sometimes Peter does it for amusement, or spite. The silkworms do not stay long in their cocoons, once they have established a pattern of growing and shedding, but are put to work in the stocking factory, where they remain hidden.'

Peter was in league with Monsieur de Warebb, Ogpan of Comores and the Rubberlord. Together they planned to invade Madagascar, using the captured Prince Loro as bait for Prince Een. Once rid of him, they would divide up Madagascar. Of course, in a world of shifting loyalties, it was not as simple as that. Peter had no intention of letting his accomplices enjoy the fruits of their treachery, but would eliminate them. In particular, he wanted to get his hands on Nathalie d'Ortolan's collection of valuable ancient books. Artabaxa, among many others, was his secret spy. This done, Zanzibar,

Comores and Madagascar would be his fiefdom, policed by his guards, his vampires and his 'enhanced' German boyslaves. With his books, Peter had learned *the secret of changing the human body*, and now he needed Nathalie's library to make his process perfect.

Suddenly Molo vanished and Sindi saw a swaying lantern approach. She had just time to flatten herself into a rock fissure before the guard paused briefly to look through Molo's cell door, then yawned and resumed her patrol. Molo did not reappear, and Sindi continued her solitary, trembling path.

She shivered in the near darkness, her bare breasts pimpled with cold, the nipples stiff, and she kept hoisting her only clothing, a sealskin skirtlet that billowed around her thighs but slipped, irritating her by exposing the top of her cleft. She let it slide down to her ankles, then stepped out of it and kicked it away. Nude and smutted, she prowled further along the tunnel until, rounding a corner, she found herself in a broad atrium. She halted and drew back into the rock wall. A cage hung from the cavern's roof, lit by giant slow-burning candles.

Within the cage, the nude figure of a girlslave hung by ropes binding her hair and her clamped nipples, the breasts wrenched upwards; her wrists were tied behind her back to her ankles, also bent behind her. A whip had striped the girl's bare buttocks to a patchwork of deep crimson welts. An unskinned tulipwood branch was thrust into her anus and a candle dripped hot wax on to the girl's exposed clitoris. Her slit was already fattened with hardened wax – or rather her slits: Sindi gasped to see that the girl possessed a double quim.

She plunged once more into darkness and shivered as a new glimmer lightened the tunnel. Her body was dripping with sweat, befouled by the mould and fungus that dampened the tunnel walls, and her sweat increased as an illumined chamber ahead seemed to radiate heat as well as light. Within the cage was the naked body of another girlslave, surrounded by books. She was cased entirely in hardened wax, apart from a breathing-hole at her mouth – a human candle. She hung, suspended by splayed, roped wrists, with her legs bent beneath her, heels held inside her quim and bum-cleft by twine binding her ankles and thighs. Her bare buttocks were dark with marks of recent thrashing. All of her, except for her face, was closed in the thick coating of wax.

The human candle burned with two wicks, the topmost being her tresses coiled in a rope and the second her luxuriant pube-hair, braided into spikes to extrude from her waxed body, sputtering like fireworks and scented with animal fat. Fragrant smoke, like temple incense, filled Sindi's nostrils; she panted, wiping sweat from her body. Her hand brushed her quim, which was soaked with sweat, then the lips below; they were swollen, and Sindi gasped aloud as she touched her fully stiffened clito. A seep of come trickled down her thighs, joining the rivulets of sweat. She squatted and pissed before the caged candle of the girlslave, touching her clito as she peed, shuddering at the shock of pleasure, then removing her probing hand but at once brushing it along her cleft, caressing her anus.

'*No! I mustn't . . .!*' she moaned, hurrying on.

Yet the next display of waxen torment was not far; nor the next, and the next. Cage after cage held slaves bound, gagged, branked, waxed and hogtied. The further Sindi went into the labyrinth, the more grotesque their deformities became: triple-breasted and double-quimmed girls, girls with two croup clefts, three buttocks or double anuses – the enticing anatomy of sex hideously exaggerated. These must be the misshapes. Her breasts heaved and her quim juiced at the raw spectacle of twisted, primordial sexuality.

Her fingers inexorably crept to her juicing pouch and in seconds she was masturbating hard. She squatted as though to stool and pinched her clito in her fingernails, tears springing from her eyes. Moaning, she thrust three fingers into her wet pouch, reaming the sides as she frotted her throbbing clito, until her belly began to heave; she gasped, then squealed. As she looked on the horribly voluptuous misshapes, with her own thighs and quim dripping and her clito pulsing, Sindi orgasmed. The cries of her climax ebbed, leaving the fetid air not silent, and she quivered in surprise. In the near distance, there was another woman's cry, and a male's grunt of triumphant pleasure. She stood, trembling, and ventured further into the maze: there was nowhere to go except forward, towards a woman screaming.

She had not far to go. The woman was imprisoned in a punishment harness of cowhide. Her limbs were bound with copper wire, casing her in a foetal position, her wrists and ankles cuffed beneath her thighs, teats and quim naked. A massive dildo impaled her pouch. It was roped to the cage's ceiling and carried most of her body's weight, along with a second rope around her belly, quivering at her haunches' motion: her hips held by the male who enculed her.

Her buttocks bore the weals of caning; her skull and eyes were enclosed in a sharkskin hood, while a copper ball between her teeth pressed down her tongue, gagging her, and fastened around her nape with a rubber thong. Her nipples were pierced and pinned, and likewise her top and bottom lip, each to a nipple, so that her screams wrenched the nipple flesh, and the bouncing of her breasts under buggery jerked her lips over her teeth. Her tresses flowed, waving like fronds beneath her. Numbed, Sindi gazed, while a black-robed German grunted, buggering the girl in leisurely fashion as if she was an aid to concentration.

'*Ach, Herr Doktor* . . .,' she mumbled through her gag, as she shook at the force of her enculement. '*Mm! Mm!*'

'*Schweigen, Greta!*' he hissed.

He glanced round but did not see Sindi, who was hidden in a fissure in the rock wall. Having finished with

161

the misshape girl – Sindi saw to her horror that she was double-anused – he grunted and withdrew without ejaculating, leaving her whimpering in the throes of orgasm, and returned to his study of his books. Could that be the Greta whom Gunn was expecting to see?

She passed on, following the dim green light at what seemed the end of the tunnel, and came within its unearthly glow. It emanated from a cell, not like a dungeon but more like a hospital room, where nude girls lay unconscious in a long row. Some were almost entirely encased in pink wax, and others were bare. The bare girls excited Sindi's curiosity, for they were sheathed from head to toe in deliciously fine and translucent white silk. Their torsos moved rhythmically as they breathed, sleeping, and Sindi saw to her horror that the silk did not sheath their skin: *it was* their skin.

These were the silkworms. Two of them were in the process of shedding their skins. Slumbering deeply, they lay half in, half out of human-shaped sacs of dazzling pure silk, which seemed to slide down their bodies with a life of their own. And underneath, the sleeping silkworms already boasted a coating of fine silk down. In the cell beside them lay stretched the unconscious figure of a naked male, the image of Prince Een, who, Sindi knew, must be his brother Prince Loro. He too had grown a thin down of silk for skin, but underneath it obtruded bony swellings, newly-grown fingers and toes and the shrivelled bud of a second penis. His front teeth had grown to fangs that overlapped his lower lip. Prince Loro, supreme fabricant and smuggler of stockings, was a silkworm – and a misshape.

19

Surprise

'Surprise, surprise! Been sleepwalking?' spat Pritzi.

Sindi jumped in fear. The girls' cell was brightly lit by candles; it was now more of a proper bedroom than a cell, with easy chairs, mirrors, brushes and combs, and a large armoire for skirts and stockings. There stood, in a ring, black-stockinged, booted Pritzi and three boyslaves clad in loinstrings. One of them was Adolf, his lips twisted in a sneer. Gunn and Fafni looked on curiously and not without anticipation. Sindi blushed, trembling.

'Perhaps ... I needed some air ... I can't have been gone long.'

Pritzi threw her abandoned skirtlet at her feet.

'Long enough to get *that* far,' she snarled. 'Well, I had brought Adolf to give to the pleasure you crave, and now it shall be more than pleasure. You will tell us what you saw.'

'I swear! I must have been delirious!'

'I'll make you delirious,' purred Adolf, in a surprisingly soft and melodic voice.

He was already massively erect under his loinstring, which he carelessly untied and let fall. Sindi was turned on her belly and her thighs pushed wide apart. She gazed at his monstrous organ and felt her insides melt; she was helpless to resist the power of his almost inhuman penis.

'Please,' she whimpered, 'Be gentle. I've never taken one so big.'

She shrieked, as Adolf's huge stiff tool entered her anus. 'No, please, it *hurts*,' she gasped.

The tool thrust into her rectum, slamming her root and thrusting to her colon.

'*Ooh!*' she groaned. 'Oh, stop, I beg you, stop . . .'

'It would help if you told us the truth,' drawled Pritzi.

The boyslave laughed as his buttocks pumped, driving his organ with an obscene sucking noise again and again into her rectum. She squirmed on the smelly straw palliasse, her buttocks slapped by his hips and balls and writhing under his fierce buggery. Sometimes, at a particularly hard thrust, her back arched, with her head thrown back and her lips drawn in a rictus, drool glazing her trembling chin. The boyslave's loins pummelled her tripes for over five minutes before spurting; then he gasped and Sindi felt a hot jet of cream at her colon, so copious that it dribbled from her penis-stretched anus, down her crack and into the lower quim lips, themselves leaking come from her juicing slit.

'Ahh . . . No! Not another! No more . . . you'll split me in half . . .,' she gasped, slumping on the palliasse, her legs still parted, with come oozing from her crevice.

She moaned softly, panting, as another male mounted her. Again a massive penis penetrated her open anus, driving hard to her rectum in a vigorous enculement. Sindi squirmed, impaled by the penis, her head shaking from side to side and her teeth biting the pillow. Her fesses moved in time with her buggery, the writhing globes thrusting upwards to slap the male's balls. Peering through tear-blurred eyes, she saw Pritzi watching her buggery and masturbating while sucking the third boy's penis, his balls at her lips and his glans bulging in her throat. When the second boyslave had spermed at Sindi's colon, after several minutes' hard buggery, Pritzi's mouth relinquished the tool she sucked, her hand grasped the buttocks of the third and, still masturbating with a lustful smile on her lips, she pressed him into Sindi's anus.

'Oh . . . ahh . . .,' Sindi gasped, as the third penis began to pound her colon. 'I'm bursting . . . oh, yes, do me hard . . .'

The boyslave penetrated her in a slow, hard swiving that lasted over seven minutes. Weeping, despite the electric thrill in her belly, she looked through her tears at her friends, for moral support at least, but Gunn and Fafni were smiling lustfully at her anguish and vigorously frigging each other. The penis buggered her for several minutes before washing her rectum with hot cream, which oozed into the slippery mess of come and sperm beneath her writhing quim hillock. To her shock, Sindi realised that she herself was masturbating as she was enculed. Now Pritzi was sucking Adolf to new erection.

'Feel like talking?' she said, pausing in her fellatio.

'I swear, I haven't done . . . *ooh!*' babbled Sindi.

Primed by the vampire's tongue, Adolf slipped once more into Sindi's anus, the moment it was vacated.

'Uhh . . . yes, do me,' she moaned, her fingers scrabbling at her juicing quim; she squeezed her throbbing clito and gasped aloud.

'Yes, bugger my hole, come inside me, I like you the best, Adolf . . . pour your hot sperm . . .!'

He enculed her as powerfully as before, while Sindi masturbated herself to orgasm, squealing and drooling, her impaled croup threshing on the palliasse. She spread her buttocks wide for the next penis to penetrate her and masturbated continuously, bringing herself to orgasm at each successive enculement.

'Oh, yes,' she gasped. 'Ooh! *Ah! Ah!* Do me hard, sperm in me . . . split me wide . . .!'

The boyslaves each spermed twice in her rectum, while the watching Gunn and Fafni masturbated each other twice to orgasm. Sindi knew her ordeal was over when Pritzi's arms encircled her quim basin and her lips kissed Sindi's hot bare bottom. A cool sponge rose, dripping, from the pail of water beside her palliasse, and Pritzi washed Sindi's raw anus.

'I'm most taken with you. I just *knew* you were made to be one of us . . . a vampire. I'll speak to Peter about it. Proper training, a good wholesome diet, and we'll be sisters.'

'No!' blurted Sindi, and began to cry.

Pritzi wrinkled her nose.

'Ugh!' she cried, with a grimace. 'You've wet the bed with quim juice, you filthy, ungrateful bitch. That means a session in the caning stocks, where you're bound to talk. The cane breaks the most obstinate will. Meanwhile, you'll be shut in a solitary cell, so you can't blab to your friends.'

The doors of the armoire swung open and Peter stepped out. He was nude, and Sindi's heart chilled when she saw that he had two penises, both huge and perfectly formed. They, like his balls and buttocks, were covered in a light down of silk.

'I'm disappointed in you, Sindi,' he purred, 'but you can still make amends.'

Sindi was hustled unceremoniously from her bedroom, as she had come to think of it, and thrust into a dank, lightless hole.

'Well, get a good night's sleep,' Pritzi said. 'You'll need it, before the caning stocks.'

'But . . . why?' Sindi blurted.

'First, for sneaking out and spying. Then, for the crime of wetting the bed, like some misshape. The punishment is caning, and there are no exceptions.'

'But I'm not a slave!' Sindi cried.

'Aren't you?' sneered Pritzi.

She locked Sindi in and returned to the bedroom to enjoy the spectacle of her master enculing both Gunn and Fafni at once, with their buttocks pressed tightly together, back to back, and their anal clefts presented fully open. The girls gasped and whimpered, giving every sign of ecstasy.

Sindi did manage to sleep, her bare body tossing and turning in the heat, to be awakened by a cut to her bare

166

buttocks from the duty guard, a vampire in rubber boots and panties with long raven tresses cascading like silk over her bare white breasts.

'Outside, at the double, bitch. To the caning stocks.'

She was obliged to trot, knees up and arms at her sides, out of the door and across the vast yard, past a brooding array of gibbets and flogging horses. She was halted at the stocks, a waist-high wooden frame of two parallel crossbars with holes for wrists and ankles, and between them a saddle with, rising from it, a cylinder of gnarled wood, polished and worn by use and gleaming in the bright morning sunlight. Sindi gasped, her face paling; it could only be a dildo. The guard slapped a handful of oil on to the wooden shaft.

'She'll slide up you like a tuna,' she said. 'What are you waiting for? Squat, bitch.'

'On that . . .?' she blurted.

'Of course. In the anus.'

Under the brandished cane, she straddled the greasy tube, parted her fesses and lowered herself on to the tip of the tube, until it poked an inch into her anus. Tears sprang to her eyes. Grimacing, and with a shudder that made her breasts bounce, she lowered herself in a rush on to the dildo, gasping loudly as she felt it penetrate her. The hinged top crossbar rose and meekly she placed her hands in the slots. The crossbar fell with a crunch, imprisoning her wrists. The guard fastened her ankles in the same way, leaving Sindi painfully bent over, breasts dangling and buttocks thrust outwards, with only minimal support from the narrow wooden saddle, and the massive dildo poking her colon.

'You've an hour's session,' said the guard, before striding away. 'Enjoy it, bitch.'

Sindi was alone under the sun, her wrenched body racked with groans of pain. Sweat dripped from her face and breasts to soak at once into the baked earth. Slaves passed across the yard, hauling carts or proceeding to other duties, but they averted their eyes from her.

Rather than shift her buttocks to try to maintain her balance on the ledge, it was tempting for her to let the massive anal shaft take her weight, despite the agony of the gnarled wood filling her belly. Yet, after several minutes, the pain in her rectum was such that she reverted to her precarious buttock-balance on the saddle's ledge. It was uncomfortable to keep her head high, and the rising sun made sweat blur her eyes, so she let her head droop over her breasts, despite the pain in her wrenched shoulder blades. After half an hour of constantly shifting position, her whole body was in agony. The guard came, placed a cup of water between her parched lips and let her drink it dry.

'Thank you,' she gasped. 'I can't imagine my crime of bedwetting merits such suffering.'

The guard laughed.

'You're supposed to make some confession, too,' she said. 'And if you're suffering now, just wait till I cane you. You've the juiciest croup I've seen in a long while, slave bitch, and I'll enjoy making it squirm.'

'You don't understand,' cried Sindi. 'I'm not a slave. This is all a dreadful misunderstanding.'

'Not to me it isn't. Every bitch is a slave.'

The minutes went agonisingly past, until the guard reappeared, carrying a rough, unpolished cane, which she swished in the air with relish before Sindi's frightened eyes. A small crowd gathered, including Gunn, Fafni and Pritzi, who clapped her hands together as the guard lifted her cane behind Sindi's upthrust bare. Vip!

'Ahh . . .,' Sindi groaned, as the wood sliced fire on her naked bottom.

Vip!

'Oh! No . . .'

Vip!

'Ah! Please, no!'

The caning continued, hard and rapid, despite Sindi's anguished squirming, her buttocks clenching madly on the dildo rammed in her rectum. At each stroke her bottom bounced up the dildo's shaft, which slid halfway from her anus, until Sindi's quivering, bruised fesses thumped down again, driving the dildo once more to her colon. Her body shuddered as the guard's cane wealed her bare; her stocks rattled, her hobbled wrists and ankles thudding against the wood at each stroke. New welts appeared on her heaving fesses, dark and shiny, over the fading bruises of the previous day, and reawakening those marks to puff up with new crimson lividity. The guard was careful to stripe her on every part of her spread buttocks, including the taut cleft, so that the whole expanse of bare glowed in a patchwork of puffy weals. Vip!

'Oh!' she moaned, sobbing in a long-drawn-out wail. 'I can't take any more. Oh, please stop.'

Yet her cooze, threshing on its platform, with the flaps slapping wetly against its wood, moistened her impaling dildo with come. Vip!

'*Ahh!*' she screamed, and a long jet of piss erupted from her slit, spraying the ground.

The slaves brayed with laughter as Sindi wept at her shame. Still the cane lashed her bare bottom, until the last drop of piss had fallen from her writhing quim and only her shiny come dripped from her lips. After fifteen strokes, the guard lowered her cane and wiped the sweat from her brow.

'Want to talk?' said Pritzi.

'I know nothing!' Sindi spat.

'Brave girl! You *are* one of us,' replied Pritzi, admiringly.

20

Vampire Master

It was so determined; Sindi had no choice, if she wished to avoid the fate of a silkworm or misshape: she was to be made into a vampire. Pritzi hurried her away to the vampire house, which lay some distance from the Schloss itself and was forbidden to all males except the master, Peter, or his guests. The vampire girls were the elite of the guards, sinister and merciless in their black rubber costumes. Their loyalty was exclusively for the vampire slavemaster.

They entered a large barnlike hall, spacious but very dark. There was an intricate system of beds hanging in mid-air, like the branches of a tree, all festooned with rubber boots, costumes and whips. Pritzi said vampires liked feeling at home above the earth, in a dark arbour. Pritzi's own bed hung at the very top. Rooms and corridors led off from the main hall, and by the walls stood punishment frames, from flogging-stools to racks, stocks and miniature gibbets. A group of naked vampire girls were lolling on their suspended beds, their chins dripping with blood from chunks of raw snake and lizard they were gnawing. Pritzi introduced Sindi as a new, if not entirely willing, recruit. The girls were to supervise her training and transformation.

'Can she take the whip?' sneered a big, muscular girl. Sindi tried to imagine her once as a blonde.

'That is why I selected her for the master's approval,' drawled Pritzi.

'Let's whip her, then,' chorused the other girls.

'Gisela, he will be here at any moment,' said Pritzi.

'Then he'll be pleased with our work.'

'She's just been caned.'

'Then he'll be doubly pleased.'

'Just ten, then, Gisela.'

Gisela sprang to the earthen floor and selected a vicious boar's pizzle, its thong stiff. Trembling, Sindi obeyed when ordered to bend naked over a flogging-stool, and took the first of Gisela's cruel lashes. The pain electrified her; though she did not cry out, she could not prevent her gorge rising at each stroke, nor her naked buttocks writhing as her eyes flowed with tears. At the tenth she prepared to rise, but Gisela continued the flogging to thirteen, the last three strokes delivered at lightning speed – Vip! Vip! Vip! – before she had a chance to react.

'I got carried away,' said Gisela, mock-sorry. 'It's such a luscious croup, and squirms so prettily.'

Sindi wiped the tears from her eyes and vowed revenge on the arrogant Gisela, just as Peter entered the chamber. The vampire girls greeted him with squeals and growls, both menacing.

'So, Sindi,' he said genially, 'you are ready to join the elite. I knew you would make amends.'

'What will happen to Gunn and Fafni?' she sobbed.

'Oh, they will enjoy themselves until I tire of enculing them, then I shall put them to work as field slaves.'

'And our shipment of stockings from Zanzibar town?'

Peter laughed.

'What shipment?' he said, and her heart turned chill.

From time to time, in the weeks that followed, Sindi dined with her slavemaster, sometimes wearing rubber, sometimes in ripped and stained panties or bra, sometimes nude. She crouched, roped to the table leg beneath Peter's chair, where she ate scraps of fat that he threw down to her and drank her wine from a saucer, like a dog. Sometimes her rope was fastened around her waist, wrists or ankles; sometimes it looped through pegs, painfully pinning her nipples or quim lips. At nights, Peter would summon her to bed, often with a young male or two, who would bugger her while Peter watched and smoked Kenyan cigars. She was always impaled in the anus, which never stopped throbbing.

Before every buggery, German boyslaves would frig her clito, then tongue the erect nubbin, bringing her to the brink of orgasm, until she was desperate to climax. All the other vampire girls took part, laughing, in these cruel caresses. Then she would orgasm after a few minutes of hard enculement, when she felt hot sperm spurt at her root. Neither did she cease to smart from daytime lashings in the fresh air, her buttocks sensitised by bucketfuls of salt water. When Peter planned a formal caning, trussed to one of his many flogging frames, he would give her a few hours' notice and lock her in solitary confinement, in the dark, with instructions to masturbate and fill a *vinaigrette* with her come, while she shuddered in dreadful anticipation.

She was beaten before every enculement, so that she could not help associating orgasm with the smarting of the rod on her fesses, shameful masturbation by the tongues and fingers of unabashed vampire tribadists, the taste of bloodied raw meat and the delicious agony of a hard penis ramming her anus. All those sensations merged into one, the most intense and most craved being the release of orgasm, anally, more powerful as the days passed. That pleasure seemed to obliterate her shame, pain and degradation – including near-starvation, for vampires were kept hungry – so that she came to love her humiliation. She could no longer imagine pleasure without restraint or orgasm without pain. Her skin whitened as her hair darkened, and her excreta assumed a mauve hue. She craved her daily bowl of animal blood.

Everything conspired to make her an animal. She had to piss or dung in full view of the other vampires, who laughed. Hygiene was a hosing with icy water by one of the slaves who had buggered her – she knew the males only by their size of penis, each equally painful. After her hosing and dunging, she was harnessed to a small, rapid chariot. Peter supervised her trussing with reins, bit, bridle and halter, and her feet were encumbered with heavy iron slabs.

She was not alone: any vampire erring beyond a simple bare-caning was sentenced to a day under bridle, which included any number of strokes from the riding-crop to her naked fesses, pumping, as she struggled to pull the chariot round the estate at the trot. Peter rode his chariot, standing close to the crupper of his steed, within range of his long whalebone riding crop, plaited with fragments of mussel shell. The slowest animal (as Peter called them) received a public thrashing.

There were usually two or three other girls – Gisela, Trudi and Eva were the most insolent offenders – who were sentenced to the bridle, which, for Sindi, was every day. Sneering, they conspired to lame or hobble her in some way, so that it was usually Sindi's bottom that received the public caning, as she was bent over her own chariot, with her companions in humiliation holding her down by wrists and ankles, to take her punishment from the master's cane. Sometimes he added to her shame by allowing the other girls to cane her. Palely naked like herself, they competed to see who could raise the deepest weals on her whitened bare.

During these cruel, maddeningly random chastisements she learned to stifle her squeals, as he rewarded weakness with further thrashing. Caning was rarely less than eight strokes. Vampires shunned mirrors, so she could not see how horribly her fesses were bruised, but, running her hands over her flogged skin, she shuddered at the deep welts and ridges, hardened to the consistency of ribbed leather.

She learned to fight, or rather to be shamefully defeated. Wearing bronze horseshoes, two naked girls would wrestle, no holds barred, in stinking sea mud. The combatants would gouge, claw or kick each other's quims and nipples, Sindi with squeamish reluctance, while Peter nonchalantly smoked a cigar. The ten-minute contests always ended in her defeat, but she still had to fight. She would be handicapped with iron weights suspended from quim flaps and nipples, or have her hands tied behind her back, or one ankle bent behind her and roped to one wrist, so that she was no more than a punchbag. In one contest, during her second week of training, Gisela ground her into the muck, walking up and down her spine and kicking her vulva between her spread, squirming cheeks, while Sindi burst into tears. No number of lashes from Pritzi's cane on her muck-sluiced bum could rouse her. She hated Gisela.

Peter would grind his cigar on her wet cleft and say she was free meat, whereupon the German boyslaves would set about enculing her in the sea-ooze. Adolf was usually the first to doff his loinstring, revealing an already stiff penis. He straddled Sindi and she whimpered and wriggled under his enculement for several minutes, before he spermed at her colon. No sooner was his cream frothing at her anal lips and drooling down her thighs than another – Fritz, Hans? – took his place, and Sindi's sobs did not cease, nor her impaled buttocks stop writhing, until several Germans had enculed her.

As she lay motionless and whimpering, Peter would decree a further whipping for insolence. Four girls stood on her ankles and wrists while Adolf wielded the riding crop, lashing her wet buttocks and drawing howls from Sindi, whose every shudder slimed her further with sea-ooze. After ten or so strokes on the wet bare, Fritz hauled her up and, with a sneer, held her quim open for all to see, with rivulets shining on her thighs. Hans applied his thumb to her clito and, after a few jabs to the

174

distended nubbin, she cried out again in belly-fluttering orgasm.

The second week dragged into the third, and Sindi was no more than a whipped and buggered animal: an ever more perfect vampire, pale and raven-haired, yet a female animal, brought to orgasm several times each day by cruel males, her senses honed to crave any shame and pain as long as they led to the ecstasy of climax. Peter himself never took her. His ministrations were limited to the whip or cane on bare, never to penetrating her bruised flesh. Sindi endured penetration from the boyslaves alone.

The whips left no inch of her body unbruised; even the soles of her feet writhed under the canestrokes of one male while Sindi, bound by cords, was restrained by another, sitting bare-fesse on her face, and making her lick his balls. During suspension from the gibbet they would weight her nipples and quim flaps with stones, the attaching strings clamped or pinned to her membranes. Her breasts would be stretched upwards, with clamps wrenching her nipples, baring the flesh for caning; or weighted down, so that the upper teat was stretched for strokes. Her nipples would be tightened in a clamp, swelling them to bursting, and a special breast-quirt applied to the popping teat plums. For the slightest relief or kindness she was grateful; she wanted to show her gratitude to her slavemaster by giving herself to him.

One evening, when she was crouching beneath Peter's dining-table, she sneaked beneath the linen drapes and got her head to his crotch. He did not respond as she clawed open his robe, releasing his naked penises. With a few flicks of her tongue, the two penises swelled to frightening hugeness.

'Why do you never encule me, master?' she whispered, her tongue playing around one peehole and the corona of the glans, after she had pulled his foreskin down, stretching the membrane fully. 'I've such a tight hole for you, and it's thirsty for your cream. I know you give it to Gunn and Fafni, and Gisela and Trudi and Eva, as well as Pritzi.'

'Insolent bitch,' drawled Peter, and began to slap her face, while still allowing her to fellate him.

Her mouth played on the glans of one, then the other penis, swooping to engorge the stiff helmets while her fingertips stroked the tight, massive ball sac. Eventually, her lips nuzzling the balls, she sucked and squeezed on his huge shafts, both plunged to the back of her throat. As she fellated Peter, her hands were at her quim, masturbating, her fingers slopped with eager wet come.

'I'm having to frig,' she whispered, lips brushing his stiff balls. 'I'd much rather have you inside my hole, then I'd come without frigging when I felt your cream.'

Peter's response was sudden. Without a word, he flung aside the tablecloth, revealing Sindi with her lips at his balls and his penises deep in her throat. The other girls gasped in pretend shock.

'This one is impudent,' Peter hissed, slapping Sindi several times more across the cheeks, until she withdrew from her fellatio, rubbing her stinging face. 'She is addicted to vile pleasures, the filthy jungle whore.'

He doffed his robe and stood before her, his bare penises monstrously erect. Lifting his whip, he began to lash her buttocks. She screamed as her skin flamed in red weals under rapid, vigorous thrashing, but after a few strokes her screams turned to gurgling shrieks of ecstasy, as her belly fluttered and her quim gushed in the intensity of her climax. Her beating did not stop; Peter flogged her until, after twelve lashes, she had climaxed twice more. He parted her buttocks and, with a grunt, plunged his first penis into her anus bud, thrust hard for several seconds, then joined it with the second, slamming both organs to her root. Sindi uttered a piercing wail as the giant tools seemed to burst her rectum.

I, a princess . . . a queen! Whipped, filled by two organs at once! Oh, by the sun, why do I crave it?

176

Her wail grew to a scream as Peter filled her greased rectum with both his organs, obscenely stretching her anus bud to the girth of a pomegranate. Her body jerked as the lash flailed her bare breasts, now streaked with pretty red bruises. Pritzi held a short rubber breast-quirt and flicked it hard against Sindi's extruded clito, the tips of the quirt slapping her swollen quim lips, while he penetrated her anus from behind. She howled at the impalement she craved.

'No . . . no . . .,' she moaned.

Yet her body writhed to the rhythm of her torment, quim thrusting forward to meet the whipping tongues, buttocks opening to welcome Peter. Her fesses clenched around his tools, squeezing and caressing; each withdrawal made a sucking sound as Peter bared his organs right to the corona of the glans before slamming them back inside her rectum. The quim-whipping grew fiercer; Sindi's white breasts were striped dark with welts; the vampires masturbated as they watched. Sindi gasped and panted, wriggling and drooling, her lips tightened in a rictus of agony.

A deep gurgling sound issued from her throat as she felt the droplets of hot cream seep from both Peter's peeholes; her anus tightened, trapping the organs at her root, and then her sphincter began to squeeze powerfully, milking him of sperm as he creamed copiously at her colon. The vap! vap! of the whip on her teats and the quirt on her bruised quim flaps grew louder in her ears, as she shuddered in her most intense orgasm ever. When Sindi was released, she sank to the floor and began to lick his feet.

'Vampire master,' she whinnied, 'thank you for your cream. My hole is yours. I promise I shall be a good vampire.'

'You've almost proven yourself and earned your cane, Sindi,' he said. 'So you may rise. Your next tests will be in disciplinary police work – misshapes, lazy girlslaves, stocking thieves and the like. I have in mind a couple of cheeky new girls, whose bottoms need a taste of your lash.'

21

Yoked

Sindi enjoyed her work as an elite vampire guard, and even enjoyed being that strange thing, a vampire. She lost her lifelong appetite for the fruits of the sea and wondered how she had ever enjoyed eating those spiny, slimy things when there was succulent raw meat, wet with blood, to devour. She relished the strangeness of her taut new body, pale and muscled, and would masturbate while caressing it all over, feeling her silky skin and lustrous black hair, her ruby lips, spanking her buttocks and pinching her nipples for a frisson of pain to go with the voluptuous pleasure of a frig, often with a finger inserted into her anus. Frequently that act was enough on its own to make her climax, during her erotic daydreams of Antarctique and Kerguelen, and boys miraculously endowed with two organs. But as for those fishy places where she had lived, she shuddered to remember them. Better to live on a diet of raw meat and cucumbers. Sometimes she was disturbed by dreams of the tunnel, the hideous silkworms, Molo and the stocking-lord Loro, but a good frig put paid to such morbid recollections, which seemed to belong to a distant time.

She was aware that she was not yet totally accepted by the others, for there were still wisps of blonde in her hair and her skin was not quite alabaster white – which Gisela mocked – so she strove to excel in the daily disciplinary duties, the reward often being an enculement by Peter's double penises. Just being penetrated and filled by those two massive cylinders at her colon had her gasping for breath, as orgasm succeeded orgasm. Her whip grew worn and shiny with constant use, often on the stunted or grotesque bodies of intruding misshapes, but Eva assured her that misshapes had a much lower sensitivity to pain, because their senses were dulled, and so they needed to be whipped longer and harder. Her training as one of Monsieur de Warebb's guards stood her in good stead, and even Gisela had to admit grudgingly that she wielded a cunning lash. Sometimes they patrolled on foot, sometimes mounted bareback on boars, which were easy to ride, and Sindi even relished the erotic chafing of the boar's bristles on her naked quim.

Lazy girlslaves, too, were punished harshly. One day she espied Gunn and Fafni, not lolling with wine but naked, filthy and chained, stooped in a cucumber field. Peter had made them slaves. A blonde guard was screaming insults at them: they worked too slowly, and half their crop, which had to be picked when green and young, had ripened and yellowed and was unfit to eat. A number of intact green fruits lay on the earth, gleaming with fluid, while others were drained husks, and the guard reported that she had found the girls using the cucumbers to masturbate and to slake their thirsts afterwards. Sindi had the uneasy feeling that this scene had been arranged for her benefit – had Peter not promised something of the sort?

Gunn and Fafni shrieked as the vampire girls grabbed them in fierce arm locks, lifted them to shoulder height and carried them, kicking and screaming, to the vampires' lair, then through their labyrinth to a teak door, its hinges red with rust. The door creaked open. It was a cell with two wooden ox yokes dangling by chains from the ceiling. The shrieking girls were hung naked with the yokes pressing their napes, arms bent back and roped to

179

the wooden beams, which held them painfully suspended, backs and buttocks temptingly bare for their beatings. Eva wound their chains, raising them until their toes just touched the dirt floor. Gisela and Trudi each took an ankle and pulled, spreading the legs. They roped the girls' twitching ankles to the yokes, so that their weight was taken by the shoulders.

When this was done, Peter entered, wreathed in fragrant cigar smoke, and accepted Pritzi's proffered chair behind the trussed victims so that he could view Sindi's whip lashing them. He allowed his papyrus robe to fall open, revealing his two massive sex organs, at which his victims gaped in fear and desire. Pritzi wound their manes into knots and tied them to slender chains which Sindi lowered from the ceiling. The chains were then wound up, wrenching their hair by the roots and plucking their heads high.

'Oh . . . oh . . .,' Gunn sobbed. 'Oh, you filthy bitches.'

'It's agony. Please don't,' whimpered Fafni. 'Sindi – if this horror is really you – how *could* you?'

'How could you two frig, while watching me buggered?' Sindi snarled. 'As for horror – the master is kind enough to find me quite pretty.'

Peter smiled and nodded; Pritzi's eyes flashed ominously, but he ignored her.

Sindi cracked her whip and her bound friends shuddered as she promised them deep stripes. The more the helpless girls whimpered, the greater the watchers' merriment, especially when Fafni pissed herself, letting a torrent of smoky golden fluid pool beneath her. A slatted bone corset was fastened around her belly, with pointed studs on the inside, and the corset tightened till she squealed. The quirt handle of a boar's pizzle was inserted into Gunn's anus and the whipthongs allowed to dangle, licking against her legs.

Trudi pressed her fingers between Fafni's moist quim lips – she said the bitch was begging for a good thrashing

– while Gisela and Eva sucked Peter's penises to erection. He patted their heads like pet dogs as they worked. The vampire girls took turns at fellating their master and frigging the yoked victims. They masturbated vigorously as they gamahuched. Gisela fastened come pots beneath the victims' gashes and there was a plinking sound as come dripped into the tortoiseshell *vinaigrettes.*

'Are you really going to beat us, Sindi?' Gunn gasped.

'Why, yes,' said Sindi. 'I am a vampire now. Don't you find me pretty?'

'No! you're a monster!'

'A very pretty monster,' murmured the master, drawing another black look from Pritzi.

'After we bring you bitches off,' Gisela said, 'beating you is Sindi's privilege.'

The pitiless masturbation continued for an age, during which Gunn and Fafni were brought to the brink of orgasm but left gasping and trembling, unfulfilled. A vampire would slop at her quim flaps, then spring away, leaving the clito distended and the belly fluttering, as the victim begged for more to bring her off. Drool dribbled from the corners of Fafni's slack mouth.

'Please,' she moaned. 'Tongue me harder . . . I so need to get off.'

'If you won't frig me to climax, then thrash my fesses. Please! Please!' Gunn sobbed.

Trudi would respond by flicking her clito, making Fafni squirm and her quim drip come into her pot, while one of the others would jab the coarse pizzle into Gunn's colon, making her squeal. The vampires, lips glazed with the girl-come they had swallowed, would swap quims, licking and chewing powerfully, but in their mocking game refusing to take the weeping, yoked slaves to spasm. Fafni pleaded and wriggled as they teased her wracked body, throbbing with the need to climax. Sindi knelt and began to gamahuche both her friends, sucking and chewing quite harshly, while frigging herself as she relished their whimpers.

'You are vile, Sindi,' laughed Peter. 'Addicted to beating and frigging and coming. You'll soon be a true vampire.'

Pritzi, who had been fellating Peter, obediently relinquished her master's penises, for he did not always wish to ejaculate. According to an ancient doctrine he had learned from the old books, a long stimulation to the balls caused energy to flow up the spine, rather than dissipate itself in sperm – and enrich the brain. Pritzi lifted the *vinaigrettes* and swirled them, making a sloshing noise, all the time sneering in the girls' tear-soaked faces. She upended the pots over their naked fesses and the vampires rubbed it into the skin until their bottoms shone, glistening wet.

'Whipping on the wet,' said Peter, 'Exquisitely painful. Do your worst, Sindi.'

'With pleasure, master.'

She licked her lips and took position behind the two wet bottoms. She lifted her snakeskin whip and laid a first, sizzling stroke across Gunn's ebony globes. Gunn grunted and her body jerked, but she did not cry out. With Fafni it was the same; only after the fourth lash did the girls' breath become harsh and rasping, and little whimpers bubbled from their risen gorges. The two nude bodies jerked and squirmed as the whiptongue rose and fell, and after the tenth stroke Fafni cried '*Ahh!*' as the tongue took her between the stretched buttocks, striking squarely on her anus. Gunn took the same lash with a whimper and rapid panting.

Sindi took them both to twenty, then stopped, for her heart was no longer in the work; she felt a twinge of sympathy for her two friends – they were still her only real friends, and, like Fafni, she was still technically Gunn's slave, after all – and nostalgia for their adventures together. Wiping her brow, she realised that her whip had created a delightful crosswork pattern on each pair of still-twitching fesses. The master applauded.

'Beautiful work, Sindi,' he said. 'Come . . .'

It was not long before Sindi was writhing on Peter's lap, both his engorged organs filling her rectum as she bounced up and down, gasping, while Pritzi, Gisela and the others gazed in jealous scorn. After minutes of this passive enculement, the master permitted himself to orgasm, filling Sindi's anal cavity with his hot-flowing cream, which bubbled from the lips of her anus, down her buttock cleft and over her thighs. He signalled to her to rise and she released herself from his fleshy prongs with a sucking squelch, accompanied by a seep of sperm mixed with her come. Pritzi's eyes glowed with jealousy.

'You have admirably passed your tests, Sindi, and I pronounce you now a fully fledged member of my vampire pack,' he intoned, 'in commemoration of which . . .'

He snapped his fingers and one of the less aggressive vampires brought a set of heavy silver rings on a wooden tray. Two fitted her pierced nipples and two her quim lips. Accoutred with these, Sindi pranced in joy, while the others looked on with undisguised loathing, exchanging sinister smiles. When the master had departed, after releasing Gunn and Fafni and sending them back to their cucumber patch, the door had scarcely closed before Gisela and Pritzi fell on Sindi, toppling her and pinioning her to the ground.

'You evil, arrogant bitch,' hissed Pritzi. 'How dare you seduce my master? *Mine,*' she added for emphasis, slapping Sindi's beringed nipples several times.

She squealed in pain and protest but was helpless under the crushing weight of the girls' bodies. It was agreed that she would be strung for a whipping, the like of which she had never experienced, for her cords were to suspend her by the rings at nipples and quim.

'No! no!' Sindi screamed, 'you'll tear me apart!'

'That had occurred to me,' smirked Pritzi. 'Peter will find it highly amusing. He is eclectic, as you know. You'll probably end up a silkworm, for vampire silk is the finest kind, and work in the stocking factory until the end of your days. I was quite efficient in getting rid of Hildegard, his big ugly slut of a German whore, in this way. A princess, indeed! Hah! You impudent bitch.'

They hoisted her to her feet, ready for binding. Sindi saw her one chance and took it. Her leg stiffened rigid and in a brutal kick her foot struck Pritzi between the thighs. Howling, Pritzi let go of her, and when Gisela received the same treatment, right to her crotch, Sindi was free to leap over their writhing bodies and make for the door. Since the room was a punishment cell, the door bolted from the outside. Sindi slammed the bolt shut and began to run, past astonished girlslaves and guard patrols alike, to the only place her whirling brain could think of: the entrance to the tunnel.

22

In the Jungle

Sindi made rapid progress through the tunnel, with memories of her first hideous visit only too clear. There were the punishment cells, empty; she tried to ignore the misshapes groaning in various degrees of bondage or agony, and focused ahead on the ghastly green light of the silkworms' prison. She crept past the figure of the black-robed doctor, mumbling over his arcane medical texts while probing the body of a misshape silkworm, covered in a fine sheen of silken skin, and she reflected that books could be for ill as well as good purpose. The green glow was nearer; she averted her gaze from the chill room of silkworms, and saw that Prince Loro was no longer in his cell. What dreadful fate had overtaken him? She determined that she must get to the city of Zanzibar and warn – whom? His palace staff? His guards? Any of them might be in on the plot. Nevertheless, she felt it her duty to try and, she hoped, to rescue Gunn and Fafni from cruel servitude.

Now there were no more horrors, and, as the tunnel sloped upward, the green glow receded and a dim white light began to glimmer. It grew brighter and she saw that she was nearing the far end of the tunnel. She cursed her luck; she had not escaped from Peter's compound. Or had she? Poking her nose around the jagged, muddy rock opening, scarcely big enough to wriggle through, she took a deep breath of damp arboreal air, full of an acrid scent of moss, trees, flowers and decaying vegetation. She crawled through the opening, wincing every time a piece of rock scraped her wealed buttocks, and, caked with mud and grass, hoisted herself into a dim glade. She *was* outside the Berlin estate – but in the forest, home to the misshapes. She looked helplessly for a way out of the jungle. Suddenly there was a rustling in the undergrowth and a grotesquely deformed misshape girl was by her side. She carried a basket full of vile-looking nuts and berries.

'Molo!' Sindi cried.

'Ssh! I am on food duty ... how lucky I have found you. I must find a place for you to hide, before our leader Hildegard and the others get here!'

'Hide? I want to escape, and get to Zanzibar.'

As Sindi blurted her story, there was a rustling, a slithering, the squelch of moss and a crunch of broken branches. Suddenly they were surrounded by a troop of misshapes, mostly girls but with a few males.

'Well, what have we here?' cried a statuesque blonde girl, evidently Hildegard, the misshape leader. 'An intruder, to be flogged!'

Her deformities, hinted by the lumps and bulges under her tunic of leaves, which left only her magnificent breasts bare, were grotesque: her face was bisected by a small parasite nose growing out of her real one, and her lips were stretched obscenely into a thin slit, almost covering her lower visage, right to her jawbone. She carried a long, springy cane, apparently of the rattan trees which grew all around, but none of the other misshapes was armed. Sindi tried to blurt her story again, but Hildegard spat and told her to be silent.

'No! She is good, Hildegard!' cried Molo.

'How can a vampire be good?' sneered the German girl.

Sindi had forgotten she was a vampire.

'I hate them for what they did to me in the silkworm chamber and for my torments in the stocking factory. Take her to the flogging stump and bind her well. I shall beat her raw.'

Despite her and Molo's protests, and the livid welts on her fesses, Sindi was dragged through the rotting undergrowth by the howling misshapes until they came to a clearing ringed by shacks of leaves and mud, with smoke trickling through holes in the roof; in the centre was a massive tree stump, about waist high, in the shade of an overhanging tree. Quickly she was bound to it by wires and thick tendrils, some alive with ants and other insects. Her breasts were secured by wires passed through her nipple piercings. Her back was arched, since her hair was twisted into a rope and fastened to a branch, stretching her trussed teats and straining the nipples to slivers of pale flesh. Her feet, bound in wire, wriggled above the ground; her hands were roped at the small of her back, and a whittled branch was embedded in her anus, stretching the anal pucker to several times its normal girth.

'Matthias!' barked Hildegard, and another misshape hobbled towards them, wiping drool from a harelip, ungainly on the three extra toes which disfigured each foot. He lacked big toes, however, which are essential for straightforward walking motion, and thus had to shamble from side to side, like an ape. Like the other misshapes, save Hildegard, he was nude and filthy, with a monstrously huge penis and balls, bigger even than Peter's.

'Matthias is one of my sperm slaves,' rapped Hildegard to Sindi. 'While I whip you, contemplating your fate, you will suck his penis and take his sperm into your mouth, but not swallow, for you must then transfer it to my own quim. So hideous is my body that no male, even those few who are capable, can get an erection for me. It has been so long since I enjoyed a true caress . . . but enough. On with the taming of this intruder.'

187

'You are not hideous, commander!' cried a small misshape with three bulbous breasts. 'You are the most beautiful ... Ahh!'

She screamed as Hildegard's cane lashed her thighs.

'Do not lie, worm,' snarled Hildegard, then raised her cane over Sindi's helpless bare body.

Vip!

'*Ahh!* Oh, that *hurt!*'

Sindi's squeal of pain was real, as the cane sliced her bare croup. She strained against the tree stump, her lips and tongue straining to engorge the penis of her sperm slave. Was this Matthias, Gunn's former business partner? She supposed it must be.

'It is supposed to hurt, slave,' murmured Hildegard, shaking her golden tresses over the massive gleaming cones of her breasts.

Her leaf dress was damp with sweat and seeping come, after Sindi's squirming bare had taken only a few stripes from her rattan.

Vip!

'*Ahh ...!*'

'Your cries are pleasing, as if you are in real pain. I shall enjoy my frig as I watch you writhe, getting me my sperm.'

Sindi's bare buttocks wriggled, clenching at each lash. The heavy cane was trimmed to tiny sharp nuggets along its length, and the tip splayed in a snake's tongue. Each stroke etched a welt deep in colour.

Vip!

'Ahh ... *ahh* ... no more!'

Sindi's eyes blurred with tears and her sobs erupted in a long, choking wail. It had never been this bad ... such agony!

The cane cracked squarely on mid-fesse, then top buttock, then the thigh tops; at every third stroke the caner stood away, so that the splayed tip took Sindi on the tender haunch skin. Her haunches were already wealed a sullen purple, darker than the crimson that blotched the whole expanse of her croup, and the weals made more lurid by the paleness of her vampire's skin. Two cavities in the overhanging tree cupped lighted candles, slanted to hang over Sindi's teats so that scalding wax dripped steadily on to the buds of her nipples. Each canestroke jarred her breasts as well as the crimson croup-globes, shaking crusts of hardened wax from her teats, to be replaced by new wax as fast as they fell from her. At each shudder of her caned buttocks she howled, as the impaling branch reamed her anal elastic. Her feet, seeking balance in the wet moss, disturbed an anthill, whose inhabitants climbed her legs, invaded her quim and horribly stung her. Her buttocks writhed in a frantic rhythm, slamming her quim against the gnarled tree stump, yet she did not cease fellating Matthias's giant penis, which filled her mouth and throat, it seemed to bursting.

'Ah! *Ooh . . .!*'

'Hurry! Make him sperm for your new owner. Do your duty, unless your thighs and cooze want an upside-down whipping.'

Vip!

'Uhh . . .'

The sun was high and hot and the sweating Sindi's quim juiced heavily, as her bottom squirmed under the caning and her mouth drooled over the sperm slave's huge, rock-hard erection. Her tongue flickered on his peehole, with frequent interruptions as her head dived and she took the entire shaft of his penis to the back of her throat. By tightening her uvula, she could frig the glans with her gorge, but a length of penis-meat protruded from her lips; Sindi could not fit the whole shaft into her. Tears streamed down her cheeks as the cane stung her bare buttocks; even the ants and the scalding wax seemed insignificant compared to such stinging agony.

'Hurt, vampire?' said Hildegard.

'Mm . . . mm . . .!' she mumbled.

Vip!

'*Ahh!*'

An upender, flicked vertically, slapped Sindi hard on the anus bud and quim, the cane's tip expertly striking her exposed throbbing clito. Come dribbled on to the chocolate mud beneath her spread and straining bare thighs.

'You're juicing,' observed Hildegard. 'You vampire slut.'

Sindi was slammed forward by three strokes across her bare back, across the spine at the bottom of her shoulder blades, and her mouth engorged the whole shaft of the male's penis. No flesh was left visible above his balls, as the glans sank into her throat. Her body shuddered as choking gasps bubbled from her lips; she felt Hildegard's hand clamp the back of her head, holding her in position.

'Make him spurt, slave!' she hissed. 'I'm thirsty for cream.'

Gasping for air, her bare croup writhing under a flurry of strokes, Sindi bobbed her head up and down; she exerted no pressure on the penis, for it filled her to bursting, and her mouth and throat strained to take its bulk. Vip!

'*Mm!*'

Hildegard's cane began to lash her breasts, and she bit the male's penis just above his balls. He grunted, and her quim gushed more copiously as she felt the first hot droplet of sperm from the peehole plunged in her throat. Her fellatio grew more vigorous as the penis began to buck, filling her mouth to the brim with spurts of hot cream, which distended her cheeks as she pressed her lips together, struggling to hold in her precious cargo. At the last jet of seemingly inexhaustible sperm her belly heaved, and she began to moan in the onset of orgasm.

A single stroke sliced her extruded throbbing nubbin and Sindi pissed herself, just before her quim exploded in an orgasm so intense that her knees buckled and the hot piss mingled with her quim juice in a steaming lake. She was dimly aware that Hildegard was masturbating, under her leaf dress. After a final stroke – she must have taken nearly twenty – Sindi was released and ordered to kneel before Hildegard, who lifted her dress so that no one else could see. Sindi felt nausea at the ugliness of the girl's deformities: scars, blotches, warts and nodules surrounding a quim so distended and misshapen, like a rotten turnip, that it was scarcely recognisable as such, with an obscenely large purple clito poking from the discoloured folds.

She prised the thighs open, with no resistance from Hildegard's writhing wet loins. Sindi's mouth fastened on a forest of foul-tasting pubic tendrils. Having spat her entire mouthful of sperm deep into the girl's slit – 'Ah! Yes! At last!' Hildegard gasped – she licked her clito, sucking the distended nubbin. She got the quim lips inside her mouth and began to suck, chew then bite.

'Oh . . . yes, slave!' Hildegard moaned, writhing under Sindi's expert gamahuche.

Sindi plunged her tongue into Hildegard's soaking cooze, and began to tongue the sperm-filled pouch, while her nose rammed the erect clito. Hildegard's come flowed faster and faster into Sindi's mouth, filling it almost faster than she could swallow the hot juice.

Hildegard's haunches wriggled, then stiffened, clamping Sindi's head between her thighs, as her body shuddered and she cried out in staccato yelps of orgasm. Then Sindi gurgled as a jet of hot golden pee erupted from the girl's slit, overflowing her mouth, soaking her stiff bare nipples and her breasts and obliging her to swallow in frantic gulps, in order to get all the mingled fluids down her throat.

'Ah! Ah! *Ahh . . .*'

Hildegard screamed, slamming and bucking her quim against Sindi's face and lathering her in come, as she shuddered in new orgasm. Sindi continued her caress until a third climax made Hildegard howl and sob with pleasure.

Later Sindi managed to blurt her story: how she was an unwilling vampire, tormented by Peter and Pritzi, and herself a fugitive from their cruelty. She must get to Zanzibar and raise a force to liberate slaves and mis-shapes alike.

Hildegard stroked her hair.

'No one has done that to me for such a long time,' she murmured.

'I try to please,' said Sindi, kneeling to cover her grimed feet in kisses and lick her toes. 'And if I succeed in Zanzibar, I promise to come back and free you all . . . and to caress you as you wish, Hildegard.'

'Very well,' Hildegard said with a sigh. 'Wash the girl, clothe her and let her go.'

23

The Bookbinder

It took Sindi three days to walk to the city of Zanzibar, although she could have made it in one. She had to avoid roads and creep through the forests – *like some misshape!* – at night, or shaded by deep jungle from the sun that hurt her eyes. She caught mice, lemurs and lizards and ate them raw, stole cucumbers, ate coconuts, sucked the nectar from wild fuchsia, and drank from streams, before sleeping under the stars. She took a small amusement in peeing in streams, to stain their water mauve. Dressed in a skirt of leaves, she supposed she looked like an ordinary farm girl, but when she approached the few people she encountered carrying baskets of food and asked for some they started in terror and gave her the whole basketful before fleeing from her, babbling some sort of incantation. She remembered she was a vampire, although not wearing any uniform, and supposed she looked as if she were on some undercover mission. This insight gave her a new plan.

She could scarcely approach the royal palace dressed as a poor girl, so on her next encounter with a farm girl, who was presentably if not lavishly dressed, she demanded her boots, a surprisingly fine pair in black rubber; from the next, her skirt; from the next, her shirt. Her haughty princess's demeanour had returned to her, and all obeyed before running away in terror. Then she came upon a tree-climbing girl, collecting fruits, leaves and twigs; she was wearing white rubber stockings, like Gunn's back in the rain forest. Imperiously Sindi summoned her and she scrambled down, promptly unrolled her stockings and handed them over, thankful that was all that was required. Sindi washed them, with her new boots and clothing, in a stream and just before she reached the outskirts of the city she changed into her new attire and was once more a guard girl.

The town was still asleep when she arrived just after dawn, and she had time to find her way round. There was the clink of breakfast dishes and smells of baking bread and hot chocolate, as traders with their tame boars and monkeys began to fill up the streets, which were constructed of honey-coloured stone in an unfamiliar antique design. The traders sold food, tools, clothing and especially stockings, great piles of hose in delicious pastel colours. Sindi saw through Peter's excuses for not delivering Gunn's shipment, for there seemed to be a glut of stockings. On impulse, she went into a bread shop and ordered hot rolls and chocolate, and the frightened shopkeeper served her abjectly, not demanding payment. Refreshed, she strutted to the royal palace. She snapped at the barefoot guard that she had an urgent message for – for whom? Prince Loro? some usurper? – and adroitly said, 'for the ruler'.

'The Bookbinder himself?' he drooled.

'Of course the Bookbinder, you fool!' she drawled, disguising her surprise at this strange title.

Thus she secured her entrance, whereupon she repeated her demand to several other guards, requiring that she be taken forthwith to the Bookbinder. There were bales of stockings everywhere and much scurrying of draymen – the palace seemed to serve as warehouse as well as royal residence. There was also the tangy scent of fine leather and paper, and she saw crates filled with newly printed bound books, more closely guarded and more reverently

194

handled than the bales of hose. After ascending a grand staircase, she was led down a corridor carpeted in rush matting, where a few boars prowled. They stopped before elaborate doors painted blue and gold, where a larger boar snarled at her while the guard knocked on the door with his fingertips. Eventually it was opened by a statuesque black girl wearing nothing but white silk stockings with frilly tops and white frilly suspender apparatus. Sindi had to fight her astonishment at recognising Artabaxa, who did not, however, give any sign of recognising Sindi.

Artabaxa, whose lips were pursed in evident distaste for vampire girls, led her to an anteroom, twittering with caged birds, where she waited for seeming ages. At last she returned with a pinched smile to summon Sindi into a vast room, like a banqueting chamber, with a large ornate rosewood table, high blue and gilt ceiling and a balcony open to the square below. There were books everywhere, and the chamber seemed to serve as an office, for some girlslaves were sitting at a long desk, writing on various documents of papyrus. They were supervised, whip in hand, by another vampire, whom Sindi recognised as Pan.

At the head of the table, concealed behind a pile of books, sat the Bookbinder, and beside him a nude blonde girl, cane at her belt. Sindi recognised her all too well. She was turning the pages of a large book of photographs, and Sindi could see some of herself, blonde and golden, her naked body enculed by the Rubberlord and his henchmen. Looking at her old self, she began to wish she were no longer a vampire. She thought nothing else could surprise her, until the Bookbinder moved a pile of books and scrutinised her with a kindly though triumphant smile. There was a carillon of silver bells from the headband of his black and yellow silk tricorn hat.

'Why, I have looked everywhere for you,' he said, 'here and in Madagascar. I never like to let an escaped slave get away, and you are quite an escaper, I hear. But various business opportunities presented themselves, and one must never neglect business. You know my associates Nathalie D'Ortolan, the schoolmistress, of course' – Nathalie, beside him, looked up, peered and her eyebrows rose – and Artabaxa too. How strange you should turn up transformed – a very handsome vampire.'

'Oh, sir, I don't want to be a vampire ... I mean, I didn't ... I mean, I want to stop being one and change back to normal.'

'That can easily be arranged, with the correct therapy.'

'And what must I do, sir?'

'Obey me, of course.'

'Anything!'

'Excellent! There is an important task for you in my strategy. In due course, you shall learn of my plans to dispose of certain business rivals and, ah, dominate the islands. The key is not just the trade in stockings but in books, where great money is to be made. So I am the Bookbinder, as well as the lord of stockings.'

He rubbed his hands in glee, and Sindi would have recognised him by his hands alone, which had touched her so many times. It was Monsieur Loleelo, the slave-snatcher.

She was bewildered but pleased at being treated as an honoured guest. She was given sumptuous lodging, slaves to wait on her and a mouthwatering array of silk stockings, finer than she had ever seen. Zanzibarian suspender apparatus, however, was slightly different from the kinds that were exported, and she needed Nathalie's help in fastening them, which Nathalie gladly gave, using the opportunity to stroke Sindi's naked pubis and discreetly masturbate both Sindi and herself, while each pretended nothing untoward was happening.

Initially she must dine apart with Pan on raw meat, but Monsieur Loleelo promised that she would soon feel the effects of the rather noxious herbal solutions Artabaxa made her drink, and the stinking ointments she rubbed into her skin, and be able to look in the glass, as her hair and body returned to normal. Sure enough, she saw that a few blonde hairs peeped in her mane, increasing rapidly every day; that her skin no longer feared the sun, and was ripening to gold; that her pee, too, was becoming clear and colourless. Pan scrutinised her silently, in mingled envy and scorn.

'Too good to be a vampire, eh?' she sneered, but Sindi was too happy to respond, save to make a face and say that raw meat was really quite horrible and she was sick of it.

She was proud to be invited to dine at Monsieur Loleelo's table, and gorged herself on the seafoods recently distasteful to her. Monsieur Loleelo was eager to hear every detail of Peter, Pritzi and the Schloss Berlin, Warebb's Hotel de Ville and what she remembered of her former master Prince Een. These sessions took long days, as Monsieur Loleelo drew maps and plans on sheets of papyrus, and she began to realise the vast extent of her captor's, or protector's, ambition.

'You have returned to normal, but perhaps you have forgotten some of your slave's training, Sindi,' he said one day. 'A period as an army slave will do you no harm, while hastening your body's recovery. Say two weeks. For our plans, you must be prepared to play any role required of you.'

'Must I, sir?'

'Obedience will get you more of *this*,' said Monsieur Loleelo.

He opened his robe to her and she was soon wriggling joyously on his lap with his tool plunged in her anus. Lifting her by her nipples, then squeezing her whole teats in his hands, he bounced her on his huge shaft, drawing her up until his glans was exposed, then slamming her down until her buttocks slapped his balls.

'Oh, yes . . .,' she gasped. 'I need it so.'

This enculement resulted in a spurt of Monsieur Loleelo's sperm, so copious that it splattered from the lips of her anus and mingled with the come that her vigorous frig elicited from her swollen wet quim. Pressing a palmful of his sperm to her mouth as she frigged herself, she masturbated herself to orgasm, just as his ebbed.

He led her naked outside the palace, to the forbidding door of the guards' barracks and slave quarters. It was opened by a full-breasted blonde, clad in boots and skin-tight pink rubber. The three other trainees cowered in the dirt.

'Good!' he said. 'I leave you now to the tender mercies of Corporal Hoon.'

Hoon banged the door shut after them. Under her were three other guards in her 'pink' squad. Around her waist was a mussel-shell lanyard, from which dangled a whip and a cane. Her breasts and buttocks rippled slightly as she leered at her new charges, then she laughed and, raising her whip, lashed all four across the nipples. She did this twice, until tears glistened in all their eyes.

'Welcome to servitude,' she said.

The new slaves joined those already captive in an unbending routine of obedience to strict rules, changed at whim. Any breaking of the day's rules resulted in a bare-bottom caning or full body-whipping, in addition to those already prescribed by routine.

All girlslaves lived nude, save when wearing punishment dress. An apple was strapped inside the miscreant's vulva, and she was released from the rubber suit or hair shirt only when the fruit had completely rotted in her quim juice and pee. Worse, her quim or anus, or both, might be filled with live sand-worms or sea cucumbers and taped shut.

They slept in a coop, chained by the ankles, the four newcomers occupying adjacent palliasses. The walls and ceiling of the coop were lined with mirrors, so that girls could practise grooming and watch themselves and each other masturbate, which was obligatory; each slave had a tin *vinaigrette* to fill before sleep. Hoon measured the come and emptied the cups into labelled flagons, with canings for those juicing insufficiently. The come, mixed with wine, refreshed Monsieur Loleelo's guests and buyers, and popular girls had to masturbate incessantly to top up their flagons. Most in demand was Sindi's.

Outside the coop, overlooked by the far end of the Bookbinder's palace, was the slave yard and the auction platform, known as the punishment zone. It was here that full-body whippings were administered, on one of two gibbets, to 'civilian' girlslaves. The yard was enclosed by unclimbable outer fences, but the public gleefully flocked to peer through the wire at girls' striped bare bodies, twitching and squirming as they dangled from tight ropes. They had to be broken, for total obedience. Then they would be auctioned as slaves to the guests, perverts who came from as far away as Zuid-Afrika or India. Flagellation and sexual humiliation were the normal expressions of power, and slaves must accept any degradation, however foul, with theatrical signs of distress.

Army slaves had to learn the arts of disguise and maquillage and grow their hair untrimmed, sculpting it in various styles. Every day the girls' hillocks were shaven clean or, if Hoon felt cheerful, the hairs dry-plucked, one by one. Rising at dawn, each slave touched toes by her bed, to receive a bare-caning of four strokes from the duty sergeant, and only then was she allowed to bathe in the fountain beside the punishment zone. Meals were simply piles of scraps, thrown at whim on the dirt. There was always water to drink from the fountain, but the girls might spend a whole day with only a few morsels of slop to fight over. This was to break any sentiments of comradeship. Now that she was no longer a vampire, Sindi longed for crabs and lobsters and oysters and giant clams.

One performance demanded was the ritual caning of young male slaves, whom Monsieur Loleelo used as loaders of freight. Chained, the boyslaves would shuffle to a flogging-stool and bend over, exposing their buttocks for six or eight canestrokes on the bare. His most perverted buyers of books and stockings were submissives and wanted female slaves to beat and humiliate them, often with pissing and dunging involved. The girlslaves must learn to masturbate themselves and their owners, and would stand opposite the young males, pressed to the wire, to practise the art. Otherwise, no touching between the sexes was allowed.

The days passed with drill, punishments, no-rules wrestling, endless toughening runs round the wire, close-combat fighting with staves and clubs, military formation and other exercises, before training in dress, perfume, maquillage and stocking appreciation. Often, sipping wine and cracking lobsters, Monsieur Loleelo, Nathalie and Artabaxa would watch from their balcony.

Bare-canings were given for imperfections like a loose strand of hair or smudged make-up. Every other day, each girl automatically received a ten-stroke full bare-body whipping with a cow-whip while suspended from a gibbet. Girls were flogged in twos, with the second of the pair, just flogged or about to be, lying with mouth open beneath the whipped girl's open quim. If the victim pissed herself, the supine girl had to drink every drop of her pee, on pain of double whipping. The gibbets were furnished with rubber belts, to squeeze the waist agonisingly tight, as well as wrist and ankle ropes, hair clamps and nipple clamps. After every beating, girls were rubbed with cooling balms and permitted to soak for thirty minutes in a hot bath of bubbling sea-mud. Darkness had its own rituals, as Sindi learnt on her first night.

She had just stretched, exhausted, on her palliasse, when a bare, scented body straddled hers. It was Hoon, carrying a giant rubber penis. Her slit was wet and warm, pressing against Sindi's, which Hoon began to masturbate with rough fingers.

'What . . .? Mm!' Sindi squealed, in sleepy protest, to be rewarded with a slap on the bare breasts, with Hoon raking sharpened fingernails across her nipples.

She began to sob. Soon her sobs turned to panting moans, as her come flowed under the crude but passionate frigging of Hoon, who frotted her bare breasts and nipples against Sindi's own. Hard fingers manipulated her clito until her quim was sopping with come. Hoon clasped her croup, pressing the rubber tool into her wet slit, then, when the implement was slick from the vigorous tupping, into her anus.

'Yes . . .,' Sindi moaned, 'in my hole, yes, yes . . .'

Hoon directed Sindi's fingers both to her clito and to Sindi's own, and, as she was enculed, Sindi frigged them both to orgasm, twisting and squeezing their throbbing naked clitos. Come gushed from her swollen slit lips, under the pounding of the belly against her quim-hillock. She saw the pumping croups of other slaves kneeling with spread buttocks and dripping quims, their fingers frigging anus and slit, as though beseeching Hoon to attend to them, but she shook her head.

'I like *your* fesses the best, Sindi,' said Hoon.

In the morning, Sindi smarted under her ritual caning of four, not expecting such a small number would hurt so much. But they were from Hoon. The other slaves shrieked, clenching their caned bums as other guards attended to them, and their croups squirmed at each whistling smack of the rod on skin. Many girls, however, frigged into their pots. Sindi bit her lip, awaiting the scorch of the cane on her own bared nates, but she too masturbated as she watched the squirming fesses of the girls caned before her. Vip! Her gorge rose and she stifled a scream, as a fierce stroke lashed her tender top buttock.

Vip!

'*Nnnh* . . .!' she gasped, her only sound of distress throughout the vicious wealing.

The caning was cruel and slow. Her fingers found her throbbing clito and she frotted hard as the cane whistled towards her squirming bare fesses. Come dripped into her *vinaigrette* and overflowed; her buttocks squirmed so violently that some drops of hot quim juice splattered her bare feet. Her fingers were a blur, pounding the clito that throbbed amid the wet, writhing folds of her swollen quim. Vip!

'Ohh! Ohh! *Ahh* . . .!' she gasped as her belly spasmed.

'Good girl,' grunted Hoon.

On the first morning of new, if temporary, slavery, Sindi was told she must learn to handle carrier pigeons, an order she thought odd but knew better than to question. She took to the work, as the pigeons seemed to like her and always found her promptly on returning from a flight. They even seemed to understand her commands and would pick up small objects, especially shiny ones, in their beaks and bring them to her. There were only a few other girls in what Hoon called the 'Signals Corps'.

By the end of her training, Sindi's body was golden – though well striped with pink weals – and hard with muscle, her hair a dazzling blonde and her eyes green. The dark days of vampirehood at Schloss Berlin were only a distant memory.

24

Good Luck Present

Sindi had never dreamed she could be so happy. Though trained for two weeks as an army slave and suitably obedient, she was treated almost as an equal by the Bookbinder, who allowed her to inspect certain areas of his personal library, as well as the books for export. How she loved the smell of leather and papyrus! She loved, too, the stockings she was liberally issued, which she was able to change for each meal, otherwise remaining nude. More and more, she was instructed about events which would shortly come to pass. One day she wondered aloud what had happened to Prince Loro, and Monsieur Loleelo smiled one of his tantalising, superior smiles.

While searching for Sindi, he had heard that there was a plot at the Rubberlord's to unseat and exile him, Sindi's escape with Fafni being deemed somehow his fault. Haroon, the master of excise, having already disposed of Abatt the treasurer, would seize his wealth. Alerted to this by Nathalie the schoolmistress – with whom, he charmingly admitted, he himself had been intriguing to overthrow the Rubberlord – he did not return to Igfal but continued his search for Sindi in Warebb, where he made his own plot with the decadent and corrupt Monsieur de Warebb.

Artabaxa, for a long time also his secret agent, gladly joined him. Having securely concealed his house-on-wheels, they headed for Zanzibar. During a brief landfall in Comores, he took into his plans the greedy and disgusting Ogpan, always eager for plunder. He knew well that these 'allies' would betray him as soon as they could, so he intended to betray them first. This included Peter, most dangerous of all, with whom he had formed a pact, and whose confidence he had gained, once he, or rather Artabaxa, had disposed of the feeble pretender Peter had installed as his puppet in Loro's place.

'Vanity, more than greed, is the worst failing of shortskulls,' he said. 'I admired Peter's, ah, bodily enhancements, and he began to trust me, especially as I agreed to supply him with stockings at a generous discount. He readily fell in with my plans as my ally, scarcely disguising his lust to take the prize for himself, though that is not to be. He is a fool, with his confounded silkworms, and wanting to breed a master race to rule the world. I shall dispose of him easily enough. Only business rules the world.'

The Bookbinder was fond of the useful phrase 'dispose of', which he pronounced with an ironical curl of his lips.

On one of his diplomatic journeys to Schloss Berlin, Pan and a squad of girlslave soldiers had liberated Prince Loro – of course blaming the misshapes – and carried him off. Although Sindi could not see him, he was happy and, under Artabaxa's care, rapidly reverting to normality. Loro was the key to the prize, Prince Een's palace in Toleara, and with it empire over all Madagascar and Zanzibar, after which Ogpan would easily be . . . disposed of. Entering Toleara, they would explain to Prince Een that they had brought his hated twin as a hostage, in tribute; he must come to inspect the captive in the Forest of Sacred Rocks. There, while Monsieur Loleelo's disguised army of slave soldiers overpowered the indolent guards of Toleara and occupied key points of the city, Prince Een would be captured and whisked away on boarback to a secret hiding place. At the same time,

Nathalie would lead a force to overpower Peter and seize his books, having mobilised the slaves – already she had spies amongst them whispering of liberation. After Monsieur Loleelo's triumphal entry and disposal of anyone he thought suitable, Toleara would be his; he would be ruler of all the islands.

'Of course, I shall need a queen,' he mused, crunching on a crab leg.

Sindi's heart leapt. Could he mean *her*? Or would she too be disposed of, once her usefulness was over?

'It is a wonderful plan, worthy of your greatness, master,' she said. 'What is my role?'

Sindi was to sail all the way to Toleara with a wardrobe of the finest stockings and present herself as a great queen from beyond the seas: say, Madras or Mokka. She would communicate with Monsieur Loleelo, and he with her, by carrier pigeons. She was to let it be known that she possessed a treasure, at a price, for Prince Een, namely the person of his brother. She was to make contact with her former owner, Lady Tamrod Gazee, and her circle, who would be eager to secure the prize for themselves. She would take Loro's ring, which bore his personal seal, to prove her ownership of him, and a sturdy crew of soldier girlslaves would both crew her ship and protect her in Toleara.

In this way would dissent be sown in Prince Een's capital, perhaps even a civil war, to make the Bookbinder's annexation all the easier. In case of upset plans, Sindi must be ready to adopt any disguise – slave, farmer, soldier – to keep her precious person and her mission intact. She related her promise to free the misshapes and Loleelo airily assured her that all would be done – in fact, they sounded like ideal recruits for his invasion force.

Artabaxa and Nathalie, nude but for stockings, entered the chamber, smiling pleasantly at Sindi, who had a premonition that something was amiss. The Bookbinder explained that they would help her with her kit, check her physical condition and give her any last-minute instructions.

'But first,' he purred, 'since I shan't see you for a while ...'

Artabaxa and Nathalie seized Sindi and stripped her to her stockings, which were of powder blue silk. With Nathalie's in lemon and Artabaxa's in pink, they made a pretty rainbow, which at any other time would have gladdened Sindi ... but Nathalie carried a giant dildo, studded with tiny cockle shells. Sindi gulped.

'Let her approach,' said Monsieur Loleelo, throwing off his robe and revealing his huge, stiff penis.

'Oh ... please ... no ...,' Sindi whimpered.

He smiled and shook his head. With her quim squelching at each trembling step, she approached him, hypnotised by his massively erect organ. He grasped her nipples, pinching them hard, and pulling her nipple and quim rings so that she squealed; then spun her and seated her atop his glans. He pulled the nipples sharply down, ramming her buttock cleft on to the tip of his penis, the glans slightly penetrating her anus. She winced, her face wrinkling in pain.

'Ohh ... sir, please, not so fast. You'll split my hole, sir. *Ahh!*'

He tugged firmly on her nipples, stretching her teats white, and forced his organ fully inside her anus. Sindi's buttocks wriggled on the impaling tool, as she gasped, clenching her cheeks and trying to open her rectum.

'Oh! Ooh!' she panted. '*Yes ...*'

Pulling her body towards him, with a single thrust of his hips he sank his penis right to the balls. He began to tease her erect nipples, tweeking them up and down like puppet strings, so that her anus was obliged to rise and fall on his penis. The master gave a little buck, plunging his glans right to her colon, then pumping hard, while slamming her thighs hard on his. Sindi shrieked.

'It hurts! Ooh! I've never been done so hard, master.'

Her impaled croup threshed on his balls; she extended her hand to her split quim lips and began to rub her clito.

'Oh, yes! Fill me up, sir . . . it's so good . . .'

She began to bounce up and down, slapping her buttocks on the master's balls, which were being licked by the masturbating Nathalie. Sindi's hand clasped her swollen, lumpy belly.

'I love your penis inside me, ramming my belly,' she panted. 'Yes, do me harder, do me . . .'

Her buttocks jerked and wriggled, squeezing the giant penis, as it thrust to her root. Come dripped from her frigged quim on to the bare back of the crouching Nathalie, whose lips also pressed against Sindi's writhing buttock flesh. The Bookbinder clawed Sindi's stiff nipples, scratching the teats raw and pinching the squeezed buds, while slapping the naked teats together like apples, with a wet cracking noise. He used her teats to steer her, rolling her buttocks round and round in a grinding motion as the tip of his penis reamed her colon.

'Oh!' she gurgled, frotting vigorously. 'I'm going to come . . . oh, yes, *yes*!'

She yelped as her belly fluttered in orgasm.

'You . . . you didn't sperm in me?' she whimpered, rubbing her sweat-blurred eyes.

The Bookbinder lifted her from his penis, which slid from her anus with a loud sucking plop.

'Rather impudent, Sindi,' he murmured, as Nathalie licked his balls and penis.

'Is that all the business I'm getting?' she pouted.

'Vulgarity upon impudence! Artabaxa! Nathalie! Secure her.'

The girls dragged Sindi by her hair, pinioning her on the floor, and Nathalie began a vigorous penetration of her quim with the giant striated dildo, causing her to overflow with wetness. Nathalie thrust the dildo into Sindi's mouth and commanded her to suck it dry of her come. Trembling, she obeyed, swallowing her own fluid, though some dribbled on to her breasts, bruised by the Bookbinder's mauling. Parting her quim flaps, Artabaxa squatted over Sindi's face, ebony-stockinged thighs well apart, to reveal her naked croup and glistening pink quim flesh, her musky perfume filling Sindi's nose.

She lowered her buttocks to crush Sindi's face. Writhing on her squashed mouth, she masturbated by rubbing her clito on Sindi's flickering tongue. Meanwhile, masturbating her own clito quite vigorously, Nathalie worked the dildo in and out of Sindi's squelching rectum. Sindi took the black girl's quim fully between her lips, sucking her come, until Artabaxa's ripe bare fesses shuddered and she gasped in a heavy, spurting orgasm. With both hands she clamped Sindi's jaw open and pressed it to her quim, crushing her with the full weight of her buttocks. Sindi writhed, gurgling, as a jet of piss spurted straight into her throat. Artabaxa did not release her until she had pissed fully and Sindi had swallowed it all, while the ebony medicine woman masturbated herself to orgasm, glazing Sindi's face with come mingled with golden acrid droplets.

'Oh! How *could* you?' spluttered Sindi, sobbing, her buttocks still writhing under Nathalie's savage enculement, which continued until Nathalie had frigged herself to groaning climax.

'I give you good medicine, joyous medicine,' hissed Artabaxa.

'Oh!' Sindi gasped. 'Oh! *Ahh!*' as she exploded in her own spasm. The pink fleshy orchid of her slit glistened with come that trickled down her croup cleft into her anal pucker.

'Excellent,' purred Monsieur Loleelo, as Artabaxa commenced a fervent sucking of his penis until it was newly erect, and Nathalie knelt beside her to lick his balls. Each girl frotted the other's clito until come streamed down their quivering thighs and wet their stocking tops. Sindi could not help masturbating as she watched, her tongue flicking her drooling lips. The Bookbinder touched the two fellating girls gently, and they relinquished his engorged penis, shiny with their saliva.

'A good luck present for our new friend,' he said, taking Sindi by the hair and thrusting her head down on his organ.

She took the penis to the back of her throat, her lips almost reaching his balls, which she cupped and tickled with her palm, while her tonguetip flicked on his peehole and her lips pressed firmly on his shaft, drawing the foreskin back and forth in firm, sucking strokes. She felt the tongues of Nathalie and Artabaxa licking her quim and nipples, with spine-tingling caresses to her throbbing clito.

'Yes . . .' murmured Monsieur Loleelo. 'Yes . . .'

At length, Sindi felt a hot droplet of sperm at the peehole, and sucked as hard as she could. The giant penis bucked, spurting copious hot cream. She gulped it until only a glaze on her mouth and chin remained. As she felt the fluid warm her stomach, and two tonguetips expertly pleasuring her clito, her belly heaved in another electric climax.

'Well done, Sindi,' said the Bookbinder. 'You are ready for anything. You leave tonight.'

25

Fortunate Isles

The sea was balmy and azure, the sky cloudless, and Sindi passed the days basking nude under her parasol, sipping cold fruit juice. An enticing variety of seafood was served at the captain's table – for she was nominally the captain, although the first officer controlled the ship – and at mealtimes she took the opportunity of showing off her stockings, being the only girl permitted to wear such luxuries. Her attire alone won her respect – that and Prince Loro's seal and the hoard of coins with which the Bookbinder had entrusted her. Her only work was when it was time to administer corporal punishment to a lazy crewgirl, strapped naked and horizontal to a wooden pole, or else bound to the mast. In either case, the girl took fifteen hard lashes on the full bare from one of the captain's chilling array of flogging tools. Sometimes, Sindi would invite a tasty crewgirl to her bed for a night of gamahuching, which was especially passionate if she had whipped the girl earlier.

She was excited by her mission, not least for the opportunity to avenge the humiliation Een had heaped on her as his slave-consort. She thought with satisfaction of Peter's ruin, and hoped that would fulfil her promise to liberate the misshapes. She fully intended to become that queen of Monsieur Loleelo's, and on the serene ocean everything seemed so delightfully easy. Would

Prince Een recognise her? It scarcely mattered if he did, for she was now a *grande dame* and attired in finery and stockings far superior to any in Toleara, with its primitive stocking manufacture. They even passed Comores without incident, until, one dark night, disaster struck.

There were grey clouds in the sky, forming themselves into a wall in front of them. The only warning they had was the departure of Sindi's homing pigeons. A storm blew up, which shook the ship like a child's rattle, drenching the deck in water, until she began to founder. Boats were launched, bobbing like corks, in a struggle of oars. Several crewgirls were washed overboard and rescued by the boats, and as Sindi prepared to board the last one, a falling spar struck her in the back, knocking her into the foaming ocean. She waved at the boats but, beaten away from her, they could not see her. She spluttered, as the water engulfed her, then lapsed into black unconsciousness.

She awoke, coughed, spluttering a little, and found that her lungs were clear. She lay nude on a palliasse of hemp leaves, in a dank cell lit only by a stinking tallow candle. Her left ankle was cuffed to the stone floor by a heavy rusted chain. The walls and her palliasse were crawling with insects and tiny lizards. She wailed – gone was her money, her fine clothing, Prince Loro's seal. She was a naked, helpless captive. Above her towered a man's shadow.

'Welcome to the Fortunate Isles. You may know them as Comores. What a pretty bounty the ocean has given us! We watched as your ship went down – such merriment! – and eventually captured all your crew in their leaking boats. I am Ogpan, your new owner. I shall call my doctor, to see if you are well enough to be transferred from the hospital to a prison cell.'

Sindi had never seen such an ugly man. He was squat and muscled, but stooped and bow-legged, with a nose squashed like a marrow; his hair was straggling and filthy, and his skin vilely pock-marked. He was like a misshape. She closed her eyes and started to cry, unwilling to believe her new nightmare. But her tears dried and she gasped in stupefaction, as a tall lady entered the fetid cell in a jingle of crustaceans. She was dressed in a skin-tight black rubber skirtlet, boots and pink stockings, with the frilly garter apparatus also pink and clearly visible beneath the thigh-hugging skirt. From her bare breasts hung nipple rings fashioned from shark's jaws. Her hair was piled in a massive beehive, from which dangled polished pink or brown seashells. She carried a cane at her waist. Accompanied by three muscular, naked girlslaves, wearing caps of coral, and three slave males in tight rubber slips, she stood beside Ogpan, staring at Sindi. It was her former owner in Madagascar, Lady Tamrod Gazee. She smiled, recognising her former slave.

'I knew fate and the sun would bring us together again, miscreant,' she purred. 'But that body, those muscles, are too pretty for my lord Ogpan to waste. You are fit for labour, so my nurses will take you to your cell. But first, right of ownership must be established . . .'

Tamrod watched with approval, and her nurses impassively, as Ogpan stripped, then lifted Sindi to his waist, turned her round and, holding her to his foul torso, penetrated her anus with his massive penis. There followed a brief enculement, while Ogpan bounced her on his penis, until quite soon a flood of sperm filled her rectum; yet she had not come, despite frotting her clito as he enculed her. Perhaps it was fear of these new surroundings of ill omen? Ogpan frowned.

'No spasm?' he said.

'Do all Comorans have such big organs?' she cried, half in jest.

'We tend to be large. You, *mademoiselle*, have a deliciously elastic anus: you make me nostalgic for the girls of Madagascar, with their magnificent croups and tight holes. Like my lady Tamrod's. Mademoiselle Tamrod wants to be pure but she too begs for my penis in her hole. And *she* comes in torrents.'

Ogpan snapped his fingers and barked orders at the three male slaves, who stripped off their loinwear – a naval uniform of some kind, she later learned – and revealed organs already throbbing in erection. Crouching, she was serially buggered by the three men, while Ogpan watched and Tamrod masturbated him. They took her brutally and silently, as though she were no more than an animal. She gasped, and her quim moistened as each male penetrated her and enculed her to his own spurt. Yet she did not climax, and she sighed in frustration.

They, however, ejaculated quickly, excited by her fervent frotting of her clito and the way her impaled buttocks squirmed at their ruthless penetration. Ogpan spurted into Tamrod's palm and she brought Sindi his sperm to drink, as the last young male orgasmed at her colon. Degraded, submissive, swallowing Ogpan's fluid, she masturbated frantically. Her rectum and colon ached after the savage enculements, yet she had not achieved orgasm. As Ogpan cursed her for a slut, she began to sob.

'You are to be broken, slut,' he said. 'You *will come*.'

Tamrod followed the nurses as they dragged Sindi up into the open air, which she gulped thankfully.

'My lady Tamrod . . .,' she stammered, 'how . . .?'

'I too was a captive, a sacrifice of the sea, rescued, enslaved and placed in the navy of Comores, as you shall be. But by wiles I rose to be Ogpan's chief concubine. It is the turning wheel of fortune, like the revolution of the sun around us. One day you are Een's consort, the next a common girlslave, kidnapped by the treacherous Loleelo.'

'He's not what you think!'

'Don't think I haven't had *his* tool up my rectum,' Tamrod said with a sniff. 'But soon, when Ogpan launches his attack, Loleelo will be *my* slave.'

213

'I've heard that the Comores eat their captives,' blurted Sindi, and Tamrod frowned.

'In the good old days,' she sighed.

'One day I shall be queen of all Madagascar, and Comores too!' spat Sindi, as a jailer clanked her keys and she was hurled into a larger cell in a block beside several others.

It was occupied by two creole girlslaves, nude and begrimed like herself. The bars allowed a view of a bleak dirt yard festooned with devices of punishment and patrolled at lazy intervals by guards. The cell was reasonably clean, even homely, with a variety of slaves' military costumes and canes hanging from the ceiling. Her new companions, Ak and Enfin, lost no time in pawing and caressing her filthy body. Sindi did not resist the rough caresses, and in fact responded to them, for her brief enculements had left her unsatisfied and hungry for orgasm. Enfin produced from under her palliasse a huge striated dildo, carved from the shoulder blade of a whale. She crouched, parting her buttocks. The dildo had a waistband and at Enfin's request Sindi strapped it on, embedding one end in her own rapidly juicing quim before penetrating the submissive girl.

She straddled Enfin's croup and thrust the tool against her anal pucker. The girl squealed, her globes clenching, and Sindi slammed her hips against the wriggling buttocks, pushing the shaft further into the anus until, with a final gasping thrust, she had the huge tool fully inside the girl's rectum. She slapped her belly against the squirming globes, slamming the dildo in and out of the anus and pushing it right to the colon. Her fesses jerked and waggled in the air, until Ak lifted a cane and sliced it across Sindi's bare. Vip! Vip!

'Ooh,' Sindi cried, as her buggery of the squirming girl was driven faster by the cuts. 'Don't, Ak . . .'

Vip! Vip! New livid weals striped Sindi's pumping buttocks, and she gasped in agony as she drove the bony tool into Enfin's anus.

'Ah! Yes! It hurts so,' the impaled girl squealed.

'Do her harder,' snarled Ak to Sindi.

Sindi's quim dripped come over her victim's fesses as she enculed the girl. Enfin was held tight and, despite her wriggling and threshing, was powerless to escape Sindi's buggery. She groaned, as the tool slammed her colon, but her quim was soaking wet. She pressed it to the floor and churned, rubbing her clito in the dirt. Her wails softened to sobs and moans as she juiced more and more copiously, and her croup sprang upwards at each jab to meet Sindi's thrusts. Both Ak and Sindi frigged their quims, moistening Enfin with their come. Masturbating, Ak laughed, as Sindi jerked under the caning. Vip! Vip!

'Ahh ...,' Sindi and Enfin whimpered in unison, as Sindi's bare darkened with puffy blotched weals and Enfin's buggered anus squirmed. Enfin's wails grew shriller.

'Yes ... yes ... do me,' she panted. 'I'm nearly there. Split my hole, burst me, I need it, oh, yes ... *ahh* ...!'

After a dozen more thrusts, Sindi sank down to straddle Enfin's back, the dildo now filling her own pouch. Ak continued to lash her bottom, and Ak and Enfin both masturbated hard. Sindi's fingers were in her quim, rubbing her clit against Enfin's buttock cleft, and she masturbated vigorously until her come bathed the girl's buttocks, and she panted long and loud in her own climax. It seemed like a small victory over Ogpan. The others brought themselves off with firm strokes to the clito, and Sindi continued to frig her quim with the dildo until she orgasmed a second time. Ak's cane stilled. She seized the dildo, ripping it from Sindi's quim, thrust it into her own slit and frigged herself to another climax.

'Ahh ...' gasped Sindi. 'I needed that so!'

Darkness fell, and the three slaves slept.

Like the others, Sindi began every day with a bare-caning. Ak and Enfin cheerfully donned their rubber seagirl's costumes after bending over for their wake-up four strokes on the bare. However, Sindi's routine was different. Tamrod awoke her, hobbled her in bilboes and clamped a leash to her nipples. Helpless to resist the pinching clamps, she followed Tamrod to her private bathroom, where she was obliged to bend over a primitive commode and lick it clean, with Tamrod's hand twisting her hair while Sindi's naked buttocks received four strokes of a springy cane, under the eyes of Ogpan.

Her food was taken in the filthy slaves' canteen, where she crouched like a dog, ordered to hold her hands behind her back. She ate scraps and drank rainwater. Sometimes Tamrod took her for a walk on all fours and, leading her by her teat-leash, ordered her to bathe in one of the ornamental pools, which were stocked with man-eating fish. She was forbidden to shave her body or comb her hair. If she felt cold in the evening, she could wear a single garment, a coarse sharkskin tunic, many sizes too small, that swathed her tightly from neck to ankle. It itched abominably, the itching made worse by the sprouting of new pubic growth on Sindi's previously shorn quim-mound.

After her miserable breakfast she was given her morning task, designed to be as humiliating, arduous and useless as possible. She had to pick up pebbles and crabs from the beach with her quim, fill her slit, hold them inside her and run on the spot until Tamrod decreed halt. She had to polish floors with her quim while frotting herself. Failure to comply meant strokes of a rubber quirt on buttocks or breasts, or else a full formal whipping, which required Ogpan's presence. She was tied to a flogging-post with her wrists cuffed and her arms wrenched, dangling from a peg that only just permitted her toes to brush the ground, and her back and buttocks received twelve stripes each. She might also be flogged while shackled to a moving cart.

Ogpan was for preference nude in Sindi's company. If his penis rose, Tamrod fellated him, then let him spurt

216

into Sindi's face, whence his copious sperm would drip on to her nipples, down her breasts and belly and into her growing quim-bush. Tamrod frigged herself to orgasm during such operations, and liked to smear Sindi's nipples with her own come, or put her fingers in Sindi's mouth and make her lick them clean.

There was a tariff of rules, and punishments for breaking them, which Sindi was not allowed to inspect. At the end of each day Tamrod computed her tariff, reading from a scroll: insolence, three strokes of the quirt on the breasts and three on the buttocks; laziness, a caning of six on the bare fesses; sluttish or non-naval demeanour, a whipping of six strokes on the back and twelve on the buttocks. Sindi would be informed of her evening punishment, which could amount to twenty-four strokes, in combinations of whip, quirt or cane. She was suspended in a flogging-frame in the yard, with a tin come pot beneath her quim. Her body was stretched, as Tamrod administered her flogging. Ogpan usually observed but was sometimes absent. On these occasions, Tamrod masturbated as she whipped the crying girl's bare fesses and back.

On her first evening whipping, Sindi cried out at the searing agony of the quirt on her buttocks. For two days thereafter she was gagged in a rusty iron brank with a tongue depressor, and could only gurgle as she was flogged. But she came as avidly as before, and often the cuts of the cane on her croup would bring her to orgasm. In her cell, she would rub the weals on her ridged and puffy bottom and frot her quim to two or three more orgasms, until the tingling of her smarting bottom was assuaged, then sink into an uneasy sleep. She sensed that Tamrod needed her, not least to show off her varied wardrobe of clinging stockings and rubber costumes, and underthings which she deliberately soiled, often pissing in her panties before stuffing them in Sindi's throat to gag her under lash.

217

One day Tamrod obliged her to don her own soiled panties, then blindfolded her with another pair. The jailers dragged her a short distance into the bush and Sindi had her arms cuffed around a tree branch, raising her on tiptoe. She was caned twelve times on the buttocks, which were left almost bare by the skimpy thong. Fired by her flogging, she rubbed her quim against the rough tree-bark and brought herself to come. All night she hung there, shivering and masturbating, sobbing in her joy of humiliation. In the morning, she heard the cruel laughter of girls as Tamrod released her.

'Slowly, I am achieving purity,' said Tamrod, 'and my addiction to frigging and the lash is purged by having that sweet firm croup of yours to stripe. You will be happier here than in Madagascar, sea-slave. These are indeed the Fortunate Isles.'

After these nostalgic longings, Tamrod, as if in a dream, would brutally frot her to come after come, tweaking and pinching Sindi's swollen throbbing clito and masturbating herself as she whipped. Sometimes, Sindi received a whipping while wrapped in rubber, which Tamrod ripped to shreds, to fall from Sindi's body like a sloughed skin.

After testing days of shame, she was proud to receive her first naval uniform and better rations. The uniform rubber skirt clung to her mound and buttocks, and her legs were graced with itchy grey goat-hair stockings – but at least they *were* stockings. Her waist was squeezed in a horrible blue rubber corset with whalebone stays. Soon she began her naval training proper and toiled with Ak and Enfin at sails and nets, oars and masts, in the exhilarating fresh sea air and salt spray, at first under the command of male sea-dogs, then alone, supervised by Ak or Enfin, practising close combat with whips and staves. They caught fish and picked crustaceans and seaweed for their suppers, being supplied with pepper and fermented clam sauce, or even a fresh cucumber, over which they wrestled. Often, in sport, they ate live crustaceans from each other's quims or cupped teats. None of the girls escaped enculement but, as the days passed, Ogpan would say they were nearly ready to go a-pirating. Little use telling the others that she had been *captain* of a vessel

. . .

26

Ice Girl

The days on the water helped Sindi forget her plight, and she submitted to constant beatings and enculements by the male cadets, by lesbian guards armed with enormous bone dildos, or by Ogpan himself. She was growing curiously fond of the squat, ugly 'misshape', and knew that her growing desire to submit to him and oust Tamrod – who, she sensed, was increasingly jealous – would bring her no good. Already her punishments of Sindi were growing more and more arbitrary and vicious; more lustfully inventive, as well.

There was an ice room for Ogpan's personal enjoyment – like most Comorans, he was frequently drunk, favouring a fiery spirit called rum, chilled with ice, looted from Antarctique ships – and Tamrod often used it as a punishment room. One day, Sindi had been sentenced by Tamrod to a flogging, then one hour 'on the ice', squatting until her quim and buttocks were almost frozen. The punishment was for 'pilfering land food', specifically roots and grubs, which Sindi would cook on the beach, along with a potful of sea cucumber, crabs and periwinkles. Seagirls were forbidden to take anything from land, and must content themselves with the sea's offerings.

Sindi did not protest her innocence, or the punishment, for though she was indeed grubbing for sand spiders and tasty roots, she had found something apparently much more precious. Buried deep in the sand – beyond the beach, and thus technically 'inland' – she found a small, mouldering metal box. She quickly reburied it when Tamrod approached and arrested her, but later returned to the spot and managed to pry the box open. Inside was a book, its leather binding and pages as crisp and scented as if they were new, and only the obvious age of the box suggesting otherwise. The book was cool and dry, clean, tingling and soft to the touch, as if some device had preserved it through centuries, or millennia.

On the front was embossed in gold: LES SIÈCLES À VENIR DE NOTREDAME DE CAYENNE/NEW CENTURIES BY NOTRE-DAME OF CAYENNE. She did not know what this meant, but sensed the book was of great value. Who or what was Cayenne? Quickly she scanned the pages, scarcely under-standing a word. It was a mixture of poems and prose, written half in a form of bizarre antique English and half in equally bizarre antique French. She took the box back to her cell and hid it under her palliasse; when Ak and Enfin were out, she dug a hole in the dirt and buried it.

In the ice room stood a huge block of ice, with Vava, the nude Congolese ice slave – strangely resembling Gunn, though more petite – chipping at it to make shards for her lord's refreshment. The girl shivered at this task, and her firm black teat-skin and buttocks were pimpled with gooseflesh, but her shivers turned to cruel laughter as Sindi was hoisted astride the ice block and her wrists and ankles bound so that the whole weight of her body pressed her quim and nipples to the ice. Tamrod, her nudity swathed in a fine down blanket, sat down to enjoy Sindi's distress. Leering at her grimaces, she spread her thighs, touched her clito and began a slow and leisurely frig. The girlslave Vava watched, smiling, and began her own masturbation, her tongue flicking between her dazzling white teeth.

When their quims were glistening wet and their clitos engorged, Vava suddenly ripped off Tamrod's blanket, with no protest, and climbed on to her naked body, with her torso between the thighs pressing the quim, and began to rub her breasts up and down Tamrod's beringed teats, belly and pubis. Tamrod, making a *moue* of pretend anger, kneaded the girl's fesses, then began to spank her lightly on the bare. The black girl's fesses were beautifully large, firm and pear-shaped, almost unnaturally so, as though subject to some hormone treatment or age-old refinement of breeding.

'*Mm! Oui!!*' she trilled, excited by the spanking and rolling her cheeks, welcoming bare-skin chastisement. Sindi shivered in agony, but could not prevent her quim from juicing; the come froze on the ice block.

Suddenly, Tamrod was holding Vava upside down, plunging her face between her thighs to suck the ebony quim lips. She forced the girl's thighs apart, revealing a long, wet slit and an extruded stiff clito amid a lush pubic jungle. She fastened her teeth on the nubbin and began to chew, causing the Congolese to wriggle in helpless pleasure; her head bobbed back and forth, in a thigh vice, and her tongue flickered on Tamrod's clito, while Tamrod began to spank the girl's quim, her hardest slaps on the engorged pink nubbin. They gamahuched each other to shuddering climaxes.

Ogpan entered, to scold the Congolese slave for tardiness with his ice (he was holding a drinking party), and roared with laughter at Sindi, whose skin was mauve with cold.

'I'll give you something to shriek about, Vava, you slut,' she said. 'My beauteous Sindi is frozen enough. Release her!'

He snatched Vava's quivering body from Tamrod's embrace and sat. He raised his short cane, pinioned Vava's thighs on his own and began to lash her bare buttocks. His erection was apparent beneath his thin robe, and Vava pulled the robe open so that the huge stiff penis sprang up. By twisting her spine, she presented her bare for the cane, while clamping the whole penis between her thighs. Ogpan quivered in delight, swiving her intercrurally.

Vava's bottom, already mauve from spanking, now purpled with weals under strokes of the springy wood. Panting, Tamrod released Sindi from bondage and forced her to her knees to gamahuche her. She pushed the shivering girl's head to her quim, so that her nose was squashed into the wet fleshy channel, and squirts of come invaded her nostrils and throat. Sindi sobbed that clito-sucking and come-drinking were surely *instead of* punishment, not *as well as*. Tamrod chuckled, and Sindi put herself to her gamahuching work with new enthusiasm, sensing this was a way of finding favour. The Congolese girl giggled with pleasure, masturbating as Ogpan flogged her bare fesses.

After a good dozen strokes to Vava's wriggling bare, Ogpan withdrew from her thighs and slid his sex into Tamrod's cleft. No words were spoken; Tamrod sighed with pleasure and spread her cheeks, bending over and parting her legs so that her master could fully penetrate her rectum. His swollen glans nuzzled her anal pucker for a moment, sliding in and out, until he suddenly entered her anus right up to his balls. The three girls made themselves busy, lips on quims, nipple caressing nipple, fingers in rectums. Ogpan continued to thrash the pert Congolese, who wriggled her taut young buttocks to entice harder lashes.

Suddenly Tamrod cried out in dismay as her lord's tool plopped from her anus, and he rasped that his sex must taste Sindi's hole.

'It will warm you up, Sindi!' he bellowed, grabbing her to begin a vigorous enculement.

Vava sat, frigging and panting, with her slit and buttocks crushing Tamrod's face and her fist in Tamrod's juicing quim, frotting the stiff clito. Sindi masturbated until Ogpan's jet of cream at her anal root made her buckle giddily in gasping orgasm. He grunted as he spurted. Vava and Tamrod shrieked with ecstasy as they came.

'An excellent tight hole,' said Ogpan, licking his lips and slapping Sindi's buttocks. 'Certainly tighter than yours, Tamrod. Your hole's slacker each visit. Maybe it's your *quim* I should visit next time, though I don't normally like that soppy stuff.'

Tamrod shot Sindi a look of hatred and scorn, and Sindi knew her caresses had been in vain. It was hopeless to expect mercy or aid from Tamrod or anyone else here. Unforgotten was her neglected mission to Toleara, recalled in the intervals of bodily exertion, torment and frigged ecstasy, and she felt guilty at letting down Monsieur Loleelo, knowing she must make up for lost time. Tamrod could so easily arrange for her to have an accident at sea ... She *knew* she must escape from Comores.

The engine of her escape was, by happy chance, her favourite carrier pigeon from her army training in Zanzibar. It was dusk, one evening. The jailer lay snoring and drunk on rum outside the cell, and Ak and Enfin had not yet returned from their naval duties. There were rumours that a big expedition was being prepared, an invasion force, but whither, and for what, no one knew. Sindi was awakened from a doze by a merry warbling, and at once recognised her avian friend, which fluttered up to perch on her wrist. Secured to its leg was a scroll wrapped in oilskin. She opened this and found it was a letter from the Bookbinder. Briefly, he related how his army had easily overrun the Schloss Berlin and freed the misshapes, most of whom were now proud wearers of his uniform. Peter and Pritzi and other unsuitable individuals had been disposed of. He wanted a progress report from her.

She found a piece of burnt stick and scratched on the papyrus, 'All is well. Beware of Ogpan, who is preparing to invade. Cannot be more precise at this time.' That done, she replaced the scroll on the pigeon's leg, the bird fluttering in alarm at a drunken snore from the sleeping jailer. That gave Sindi her idea. Fallen from the jailer's paw, a bright shiny key lay in the dirt; it was the one which she used to open the cell door. Sindi stroked the pigeon – her pet pigeon – and directed its attention to the shiny key. The bird hopped from her wrist, fluttered down, deftly picked up the key in its beak, then brought it back to Sindi. She kissed the pigeon and lost no time in reaching through the bars to unlock the cell. Suddenly she remembered her hidden book and quickly unearthed it, pressing it to her like a talisman.

Dusk was rapidly giving way to dark. With a pat she sent the pigeon fluttering skywards and clanged the cell door shut, locking it and replacing the key by the jailer's fingers, though she knew the deception would fool no one for long. No use, and too much risk, feeling in the jailer's pockets for money, for slaves were allowed none. She walked as rapidly as she could through the least crowded parts of Ogpan's compound until she found herself once more naked on the beach. She started at a footfall. It was Vava, the ice girl. She greeted Sindi, who told her to keep silent. She was ready for anything, desperate, prepared to overpower the slender Congolese beauty if she threatened trouble, so instead, gambling on the truth, she blurted out her deeds and intentions. Vava smiled, her teeth as radiant as the stars that were just appearing.

'I'm coming too!' she hissed.

Sindi nodded happy assent. A row of small fishing-boats, with oars, were drawn up for the night; sweating, the pair propelled one into the sea, waded after it, jumped in and grasped the oars. Taking bearings from the stars, they began to row south towards Madagascar.

The boat was well appointed. There was a little stove and a barrel of rainwater, easily replenished by the brief morning downpours. The girls took turns at rowing, and in her leisure time, when she had caught and cooked fish, or dived for armfuls of seaweed, oysters and mussels, Sindi studied her book. Gradually she began to make sense of it: it was a book both of history, the world since its beginning, and of prophecies for the world's future. In small print on the first page, she read, in archaic French, 'Written in the sun-year 1,509,873 after the nuclear winter.' It meant nothing to her; she could not imagine the world being so old, when the priests insisted that both it and the moon had been created by the sun a few centuries ago.

Most of the verse prophecies, even those she could decipher, seemed obscure and deliberately ambiguous, but in one section of the book she found that many of them could be applied to her current situation in Madagascar: 'Borne by boars, the armies of the lord of books shall vanquish the lords of rubber and silk, and the fair girl from the southern seas shall wear the sacred stockings and be queen,' and the like. It also said ominously that 'all who touch this book are part of it, and must suffer all consequences.' She did not have much time for study, however, between periods of fishing, cooking, sleeping and gruelling work at the oars. Vava seemed quite content and whistled mysterious African tunes as she worked. Occasionally they gamahuched, when sleep would not come, but mostly they were too tired, although Sindi enjoyed sucking Vava's succulent quim as she rowed, gasping in pleasure.

They passed the city of Warebb but, seeing smoke billowing, did not pause; Sindi feared the Bookbinder was disposing of things that displeased him. One night, Vava offered to creep ashore and speak to the peasant women. She returned with news that a Zanzibar army of girls in rubber and fearsome naked misshapes, led by a lord in a smoking, clanking house on wheels, had vanquished Comores, then Monsieur de Warebb, and was pressing on to the domain of the Rubberlord. Sindi guessed that

Monsieur Loleelo would be occupied there for a while, before his assault on Prince Een in Toleara; still, though they were taking the shorter route down the west coast, and the Bookbinder would certainly have to subdue Een's highland capital of Rivo before proceeding across the island to Toleara, she urged all possible speed.

27

Toleara

Vava made several more clandestine trips and, as they progressed down the coast, they heard that the Bookbinder had subdued the Rubberlord, had overthrown the governor of Rivo and occupied the city, and was marching across difficult country towards Toleara, a march which would occupy several days. He carried with him a most important captive – surely Prince Loro. The capital was a day's journey away, and Sindi reflected that she had arrived just in time. At dawn, she and Vava concealed their boat in a deserted cove just below the Forest of Sacred Rocks and found leaves to fashion into skirts, leaving their breasts bare and thus signifying their status as free girls, but not of superior class.

Deciding against burying her book among the rocks, Sindi fashioned a pouch for it, which fitted snugly round her waist and tickled her quim, now a luxuriant forest, longing to be shaven – though Vava seemed to revel in her own lush pubic jungle. They made their way on foot into the city, uncertain of their next move. Emboldened by the eerie stillness, Sindi toyed with the idea of seeking Tamrod's palace, a place she knew, guessing that she would find Qimon in occupation. Caution was unnecessary, since the streets were almost deserted save for a few guards, mostly drunk on wine, and a few scurrying girlslaves and free women. Some dwellings had obviously been deserted in such a hurry that the fleeing occupants had not fastened the doors, and the girls crept into one opulent house. It had already been ransacked by looters, but they found some women's apparel – boots, skirts, robes and even a pair of shoddy stockings with a large hole in them.

Sindi took those, having repaired the hole and positioned it so that it would not show under the hem of her new, crimson, knee-length skirt, which had a roomy pouch to accommodate her book. Soon she and Vava were proceeding as a middle-rank lady and her girlslave, for which Vava agreed it was better that she should be naked. Sindi also equipped herself with a strong, supple cane, which she belted to her waist. Reaching the central square, they saw the harbour bereft of ships, and only priests at the windows of Prince Een's palace and the government buildings. There was an air of abandonment, impending doom and manic, despairing gaiety, as the guards quaffed their wine.

Sindi looked at the scenes of her unhappiness, her kidnap by Monsieur Loleelo, her whippings, and felt a sudden rush of vengeful anger. She was once more the noble girl, bearing a whip, in Kerguelen or Antarctique: she would take vengeance on *anyone*! She spoke to a frightened woman, who blurted that Prince Een had gone out with every fit man and woman to do battle with the invaders, fanged sea monsters from the north.

'But he will surely lose,' she wailed. 'And then the monsters will tear us in pieces and eat us.'

Sindi felt somewhat at a loss; there seemed to be no one here as targets for her mission, so, hungry and thirsty, they pressed on to Tamrod's dwelling, a small, trim palace not far away with forested lawns and overlooking the sea. They concealed themselves behind a tree and observed the haughty Qimon, who, as Sindi had expected, was lounging beneath a parasol on the lawn, in the nude apart from an amber lizard brooch at her neck.

She slurped wine and feasted on crustaceans dripping with fermented fish and pepper sauce, whose stink wafted through the baking air. Dark girlslaves served her crabs, clams and live eels from their shaven slits, and Qimon devoured in a leisurely fashion, laughing at the girls' evident discomfort.

A dozen robed priests, in the sacred headdress of whirling wooden suns and jingling bells, squatted in the shade, reading from books as they dined simply on wine, bread and octopus, indifferent to the display of naked female flesh. Often Qimon let her lips dally on a girl's slit as she sucked both her luncheon and an erect clito. The sauce ran down her body, flowing to the earth in rivulets, giving her the appearance of some strange striped animal of the jungle.

They left their cover and boldly approached, Sindi introducing herself, in French, as a traveller from the north and giving a false name.

'Not a spy, I hope,' said Qimon, laughing. 'I fear that there is nothing left here to spy on. But make yourself comfortable, my esteemed guest. *Salut!* Strip off and eat ... sea cucumber, baby lobster, there is everything for our delectation, including juicy girl-slit. *Bon appetit!* Soon we shall be doomed to eat whatever our conquerors decide. Do not mind the priests, for they are soon to be my servants, when I am princess of Toleara – I am the only lady beautiful enough to greet our conqueror and new overlord, the Bookbinder. Prince Een is too vain and weak to vanquish him. Lol! Naz! Okka! Bring food and wine for our guest.'

Vava placed herself behind her naked 'mistress', who was lolling in a hammock. Sindi joined Qimon in her feast and the handsome creole lady scrutinised her.

'I feel I have seen you before.'

'Possibly,' drawled Sindi, spitting out a crab claw for Vava to scoop. 'I have visited here. In fact, I was expecting to see my friend, lady Tamrod Gazee.'

'*That* bitch!' cried Qimon. 'She is long departed, and I'm well rid of her. Enslaved, or more likely a traitor to our enemies. I may tell you in confidence that I, Qimon, intend to seize power and welcome the monster lord of Zanzibar, the Bookbinder, when he marches victorious into Toleara. I have been talking to my priests, who mind the palace, and they have agreed that I may take occupancy, to greet the Bookbinder as his ally and – who knows? – his consort. The priests are cowards and do not wish to face a conqueror but to be left alone with their books and mumbo-jumbo and swindles. I shall be the new prince's consort, but not a slave or a plaything of the augurs, like that dreadful blonde slut Sindi, with whom Prince Een was besotted, and who fled with an agent of the Rubberlord. I'd like to give *her* a good whipping.'

Sindi's eyes blazed.

'Oh, would you? Well, *I am Sindi*. You've already seen me whipped, *Mademoiselle* Qimon, and now you're going to receive a taste of your own medicine.'

She seized Qimon and got her in a lock grip, but the girl's slippery body managed to wriggle free. She called to her slaves to overpower the intruder, and the priests joined in the tussle. Sindi and Vava fought valiantly, kicking, punching and gouging with abandon, until the girlslaves were clutching their teats and groins, but superior numbers overpowered them.

'String them both up for immediate whipping,' hissed Qimon. 'I recall that the last time we met, you took a mere thirty lashes. Well, there shall be none of that feeble stuff *now*. I shall whip you raw – and with your own cane, slut.'

She rose and kicked Sindi's discarded robe to free the belted cane. In doing so she dislodged the book by Notredame de Cayenne. The priests pointed and, falling to the earth, began to gibber.

'*She is the one . . . she has the sacred book . . . she is the one . . .*'

231

On their knees, they shuffled towards Sindi, each kissing her hand and crying, '*Notre Princesse*', before pinioning their erstwhile mistress Qimon.

'So! The tables are turned,' Sindi sneered. She retrieved her book, as none of the priests dared touch it. Then she ripped Qimon's lizard brooch from her neck and placed it around her own.

'That is *mine*,' she declared.

'You bitch! You shall pay for this!' spat Qimon, as she and her slaves were bound tightly.

'No, you shall pay, with naked weals,' Sindi retorted. 'My good priests! Take me to my palace.'

Soon Sindi had settled once again into the palace of Toleara, where she shared her bed, and her caresses, in the royal chamber with Vava. She led the easy life of an absolute ruler, treating herself to the most sumptuous food and stockings and the biggest nipple and quim rings. From her balcony she displayed the sacred book to a sparse crowd, which fell to its knees in awe.

One day, in the pink light of late afternoon, a quartet of robed priests led the whimpering Qimon to the gibbet in the central square before Sindi's palace. The still defiant Qimon's hands were bound in front of her, on a pole knotted to her hobble bar, causing her to stumble. Her face was wet with tears.

'I warned you, Qimon,' Sindi repeated. 'I am *an agent* of the Bookbinder.'

'Liar! But . . . be merciful, I beg you,' Qimon pleaded.

'Were you merciful, when you had me whipped?

Sindi wore white moleskin boots and a pair of the finest lemon yellow silk stockings and suspenders, which she had found in her palace. Her royal crown was a garland of tiny whirring windmills, interspersed with silver crabs, which jingled in suspension on her brow. A small crowd watched, standing in rows below the platform of chastisement, while the priests gathered around the gibbet. A pink sun illumined the cross beam, festooned with pulleys and restraining straps, and the frame fitted with cuffs for the wrists and ankles of a victim. Of the choices of restraint, Sindi and the priests opted for full suspension from the cross beam. Qimon burst into frenzied sobbing.

'Oh, no!' she wailed. 'Please whip me at the crouch or bind me to a pole!'

'Strip her and hang her,' Sindi rapped.

The priests tore off Qimon's cape then contemptuously ripped off her undergarments. She was released in the nude from her ropes and hobble, only to have Vava and two helpmates pinion her wrists behind her back, while two more crushed her feet with their tuna hide boots. Her breasts bounced and trembled with her choked sobbing, and drool trickled from her mouth.

'I pronounce the traitor fit to receive punishment,' Sindi intoned. 'She is a sacrifice to the sun, who has gone long unappeased.'

The priests replaced Qimon's wrist binding with a long rope, stouter than the cords before. It was looped through the pulley on the cross beam and Qimon was hoisted, wriggling and sobbing, until her feet were a few inches above the platform. Her legs were stretched wide apart, and each ankle tied by a rope to the edge of the platform. Her back faced the assembly and her buttocks were splayed to the full, her slit clearly visible between her quivering bare thighs. Her wrenched back muscles rippled as she writhed, her whole weight suspended from her straining arms. One priest seized her torn panties and hooded her with them, obliging her to breathe through her soiled crotch gusset. The fabric heaved in and out with Qimon's frenzied gasps and moistened rapidly from her tears. Sindi took position before the girl's buttocks and lifted a well-pickled boar's pizzle.

'Thirty strokes to the bare buttocks,' she said.

'No . . . no . . .' Qimon wailed. '*Please!*'

The sun glowed pink on the victim's breasts and glistened on her sweating pubis and fesses. Sindi flexed the whippy pizzle and swished it in the air, with a loud whistle. The suspended girl whimpered under her hood, and her ankles shook her tethering ropes. Vip! The cane slashed the air, falling across Qimon's ripe mid-fesses and striping the buttock skin with a vivid pink weal. She gurgled and shook, her bare melons clenching. Vip! A second stroke took her slightly above the first. The flogged girl began to moan. Vip!

'Ah . . .,' she whimpered, as the third stroke lashed the tender skin of her top buttocks.

Sindi, breasts and nipple rings bouncing, continued to cane Qimon's bare in hard, rhythmic strokes, at intervals of three seconds. She worked on the upper thighs, beating the stretched flesh halfway down to the knees, and on the haunches, which darkened the fastest, while at every fourth stroke she returned to the darkly wealing central globes. The caning rocked Qimon's body back and forth, her back muscles rippling and her legs rigid under her clenching fesses. Vip!

'Ohh . . .'

Vip!

'*Ohh!*'

Qimon's naked teats bounced, as her whole body shook, dripping with sweat, and a trickle of come appeared on her thighs. Sindi's quim was also moistening, and her lips slick. The girlslaves watched with bright eyes and darting tongues, holding their hands behind their backs while wriggling to press their thighs together. Vip!

'Ah . . . no, please stop . . .'

Vip!

'*Ahh!*'

A gush of piss erupted from Qimon's quim, splashing Sindi's feet.

'You bitch,' Sindi hissed.

234

'*Ahh!*' screamed the pissing girl, as three hard cuts landed on a single welt, mid-fesse, deepening it to an angry crimson trench.

Three more lashes fell on the same spot, and her buttocks jerked, clenching and squirming, as her whole body shook, straining against her ropes. Then her wriggling grew more frantic, and staccato cries bubbled from her lips. Vip!

'Ah! Yes . . . yes . . . *Ahh!*'

Qimon writhed in orgasm.

Sindi continued the beating to thirty strokes, by which time Qimon's head hung low over her breasts. A final stroke sliced hard between her thighs, the cane slapping her anus and dripping quim. The flogged slave sobbed helplessly, still shuddering in her suspension, a trickle of pee dribbling from her quim, caneweals crusting into hard ridges all over her buttocks. Sindi turned to the priests.

'Seen enough?' she cried.

'It is in order. The sun and the sacred book have been satisfied. We may yet hope for deliverance from the Bookbinder and his army of monsters.'

Qimon, cut down, knelt and licked Sindi's boots.

'Oh!' she stammered. 'Mistress, majesty, please accept my loyalty.'

At that moment, in the distance, trumpets sounded, and there was the roar of girls' voices baying in anger, the clattering of boars' hooves, the rumble of giant wheels and the crack of whips.

'We must flee!' cried Qimon.

'I think not,' said Sindi. 'We shall await them here peacefully.'

It was not long before the Bookbinder's house-on-wheels rolled into the square, accompanied by a host of girls – misshapes and Germans from Schloss Berlin, and creole girls from Zanzibar. Even Ak and Enfin were there, proud to be in Monsieur Loleelo's marines. Sindi cried out as she recognised Gunn and Fafni amid the army.

'Gunn!' echoed Vava, and Gunn waved.

'She was your owner once?' Sindi asked.

'She is my sister,' said Vava with a pout.

Monsieur Loleelo emerged from his vehicle, accompanied by Nathalie, Artabaxa and Prince Loro, seeming fully fit and dressed in a simple papyrus robe. He smiled, seeing Sindi and her royal adornments. The Bookbinder knelt and kissed her hand.

'Mission accomplished, I take it, Princess Sindi? I have disposed of Een, so he shall cause no further trouble.'

Sindi glowed with pride.

'I knew you would find the book,' he drawled, 'when I left it in the sand on Comores. It is prophesied in the book itself, on page 119, quatrain 432: "And she who will rule the empire of islands shall find me here in the sand, and wear the sacred stockings from the dawn before time." The page and verse numbers refer to the precise map coordinates where the book was to be hidden. The book, you see, dictates its own fate, and is a character in its own text – as are we all, in the end. You are fated to become my quee–'

He stopped, a quizzical smile on his lips, as Sindi frowned.

'I am already a queen,' she declared. 'It is you, sir, who shall become my consort.'

He put his fingertips together and pursed his lips, his eyes twinkling with laughter.

'That, too, seems fated, according to the book.'

'You have your army and your books. I take it you have captured the libraries of the Rubberlord and Schloss Berlin?'

'Of course. I am followed by a boar train carrying every book on these islands. Enough to fill a palace.'

'Then you shall rule as you see fit, while I remain here as Bookmistress, with Vava and Nathalie to assist me. Gunn shall be my chef and Fafni my valet, with Ak and Enfin my bodyguards. Prince Loro being of no further use as a hostage, I shall make him my stocking master. I wish to retire from public life and devote myself in my library to study of books. As for the trading of books, according to my needs, that is your domain.'

He nodded.

'There is one further thing, again from the sacred book,' he said. 'For me to accept the role of your consort, you must prove yourself . . . *the one*. That is, the girl for whom the sacred stockings are a perfect fit. Pan was avid to try them, but I would not permit it.'

'You talk in riddles, sir.'

Prince Loro fetched a gleaming metal box and handed it to Monsieur Loleelo, who opened it. Inside lay a pair of stockings, shimmering and translucent like their box, with matching suspender belt. They were the most beautiful that Sindi had ever seen.

'This box is an alloy of iridium and osmium, the hardest and densest metals, proof against all corrosion and practically indestructible. It has lain in the earth of Zanzibar for eons – perhaps millions of years. These stockings are as fresh as when they were woven, in the dawn of time, by my people, the longskulls. It remains to see if they fit you.'

Sindi ordered Qimon to take off her boots and unroll her stockings. She slid the new stockings up her calves, slowly, relishing every skin-prickling touch of the unbelievably ancient silk, which seemed to change colour as it advanced towards her gleaming, shaven hillock. The touch of the stockings was a caress, and her fingers were trembling as she attached the suspenders and garter straps. Already come was trickling down her inner thighs towards the priceless hose, and her clito was throbbing. She could not help it; as she stood for Monsieur Loleelo's inspection, she began to masturbate, groaning and gasping in unearthly pleasure, as the pink sun illumined her quim. Monsieur Loleelo clapped his hands.

'A perfect fit!' he cried. '*Empress* Sindi, you are *the one*.'

237

Sindi frigged faster, feeling her belly flutter, and begin to shudder at the sweet electric pulse in her quim.

'Sir – master – consort,' she blurted, 'something still troubles me. What about Pan and her troop of vampire girlslaves?'

'They have been disposed of,' he purred, as Sindi exploded in orgasm.

nexus

The leading publisher of fetish and adult fiction

TELL US WHAT YOU THINK!

Readers' ideas and opinions matter to us so please take a few
minutes to fill in the questionnaire below.

1. Sex: Are you male ☐ female ☐ a couple ☐?

2. Age: Under 21 ☐ 21–30 ☐ 31–40 ☐ 41–50 ☐ 51–60 ☐ over 60 ☐

3. Where do you buy your Nexus books from?

☐ A chain book shop. If so, which one(s)?

_____

☐ An independent book shop. If so, which one(s)?

_____

☐ A used book shop/charity shop
☐ Online book store. If so, which one(s)?

_____

4. How did you find out about Nexus books?

☐ Browsing in a book shop
☐ A review in a magazine
☐ Online
☐ Recommendation
☐ Other _____

5. In terms of settings, which do you prefer? (Tick as many as you like.)

☐ Down to earth and as realistic as possible
☐ Historical settings. If so, which period do you prefer?

_____

☐ Fantasy settings – barbarian worlds
☐ Completely escapist/surreal fantasy
☐ Institutional or secret academy

☐ Futuristic/sci fi
☐ Escapist but still believable
☐ Any settings you dislike?

_____

☐ Where would you like to see an adult novel set?

_____

6. In terms of storylines, would you prefer:

☐ Simple stories that concentrate on adult interests?
☐ More plot and character-driven stories with less explicit adult activity?
☐ We value your ideas, so give us your opinion of this book:

_____

_____

_____

7. In terms of your adult interests, what do you like to read about? (Tick as many as you like.)

☐ Traditional corporal punishment (CP)
☐ Modern corporal punishment
☐ Spanking
☐ Restraint/bondage
☐ Rope bondage
☐ Latex/rubber
☐ Leather
☐ Female domination and male submission
☐ Female domination and female submission
☐ Male domination and female submission
☐ Willing captivity
☐ Uniforms
☐ Lingerie/underwear/hosiery/footwear (boots and high heels)
☐ Sex rituals
☐ Vanilla sex
☐ Swinging
☐ Cross-dressing/TV
☐ Enforced feminisation

☐ Others – tell us what you don't see enough of in adult fiction:

_____

_____

_____

8. Would you prefer books with a more specialised approach to your interests, i.e. a novel specifically about uniforms? If so, which subject(s) would you like to read a Nexus novel about?

_____

_____

_____

9. Would you like to read true stories in Nexus books? For instance, the true story of a submissive woman, or a male slave? Tell us which true revelations you would most like to read about:

_____

_____

_____

10. What do you like best about Nexus books?

_____

_____

11. What do you like least about Nexus books?

_____

_____

12. Which are your favourite titles?

_____

_____

13. Who are your favourite authors?

_____

_____

14. Which covers do you prefer? Those featuring:
(Tick as many as you like.)

- ☐ Fetish outfits
- ☐ More nudity
- ☐ Two models
- ☐ Unusual models or settings
- ☐ Classic erotic photography
- ☐ More contemporary images and poses
- ☐ A blank/non-erotic cover
- ☐ What would your ideal cover look like?

_____

15. Describe your ideal Nexus novel in the space provided:

_____

_____

_____

_____

16. Which celebrity would feature in one of your Nexus-style fantasies? We'll post the best suggestions on our website – anonymously!

_____

THANKS FOR YOUR TIME

Now simply write the title of this book in the space below and cut out the questionnaire pages. Post to: Nexus, Marketing Dept., Thames Wharf Studios, Rainville Rd, London W6 9HA

Book title: _____

NEXUS NEW BOOKS

To be published in May 2007

LOVE SONG OF A DOMINATRIX
Cat Scarlett

Dinah is a tough-talking bisexual dominatrix with a weakness for redheads. So when she meets Grace, a beautiful hotel receptionist looking for excitement, she can't resist converting her to a life of lesbian submission. But Grace is forced to overcome her timidity and take up the whip herself when ex-boyfriend Aidan finds out about their relationship and decides to teach Mistress Dinah a lesson.

£6.99   ISBN 978 0 352 34106 8

BLUSHING AT BOTH ENDS
Philip Kemp

Funny, full of surprises and always arousing, this is a brilliant collection of stories about innocent young women who find themselves faced with the delicious, scary, sensual prospect of a sound bare-bottom spanking. Half against her will, each of them is inexorably drawn towards the moment when, bent over lap, desk or chair, she tremblingly awaits that punishment for which her rearward curves were so perfectly designed.

£6.99   ISBN 978 0 352 34107 5

ENTHRALLED
Lance Porter

Matthew Crawley has always dreamed of sleeping with a beautiful woman and when the stunning Jasmine Del Ray suddenly walks into his life he believes his prayers have finally been answered. But Ms Del Ray proves to be no ordinary girlfriend. Rich, successful and supremely confident, she expects complete obedience from her men and knows exactly how to get her way. An expert in teasing and denial, she soon has the hopelessly infatuated Matthew Crawley jumping to her every command and begging on his knees for her slightest indulgence. Skilfully brought to heel, he is ready to commence the next stage of his training in which liberal applications of the cane and a variety of cruel and unusual punishments will play an essential part. But how much suffering and humiliation can a man endure to win the favour of a superior young woman – and what will be his reward?

£6.99   ISBN 978 0 352 34108 2

If you would like more information about Nexus titles, please visit our website at www.nexus-books.co.uk, or send a large stamped addressed envelope to:
  Nexus, Thames Wharf Studios,
  Rainville Road, London W6 9HA

NEXUS BOOKLIST

Information is correct at time of printing. To avoid disappointment, check availability before ordering. Go to www.nexus-books.co.uk.

All books are priced at £6.99 unless another price is given.

NEXUS

☐ ABANDONED ALICE	Adriana Arden	ISBN 978 0 352 33969 0
☐ ALICE IN CHAINS	Adriana Arden	ISBN 978 0 352 33908 9
☐ AQUA DOMINATION	William Doughty	ISBN 978 0 352 34020 7
☐ THE ART OF CORRECTION	Tara Black	ISBN 978 0 352 33895 2
☐ THE ART OF SURRENDER	Madeline Bastinado	ISBN 978 0 352 34013 9
☐ BEASTLY BEHAVIOUR	Aishling Morgan	ISBN 978 0 352 34095 5
☐ BELINDA BARES UP	Yolanda Celbridge	ISBN 978 0 352 33926 3
☐ BENCH-MARKS	Tara Black	ISBN 978 0 352 33797 9
☐ BIDDING TO SIN	Rosita Varón	ISBN 978 0 352 34063 4
☐ BINDING PROMISES	G.C. Scott	ISBN 978 0 352 34014 6
☐ THE BOOK OF PUNISHMENT	Cat Scarlett	ISBN 978 0 352 33975 1
☐ BRUSH STROKES	Penny Birch	ISBN 978 0 352 34072 6
☐ CALLED TO THE WILD	Angel Blake	ISBN 978 0 352 34067 2
☐ CAPTIVES OF CHEYNER CLOSE	Adriana Arden	ISBN 978 0 352 34028 3
☐ CARNAL POSSESSION	Yvonne Strickland	ISBN 978 0 352 34062 7
☐ CITY MAID	Amelia Evangeline	ISBN 978 0 352 34096 2
☐ COLLEGE GIRLS	Cat Scarlett	ISBN 978 0 352 33942 3
☐ COMPANY OF SLAVES	Christina Shelly	ISBN 978 0 352 33887 7
☐ CONCEIT AND CONSEQUENCE	Aishling Morgan	ISBN 978 0 352 33965 2